Hexagon Dilemma

Regarding Hayworth

Book II

L. P. Suzanne Atkinson

lpsabooks
http://lpsabooks.wix.com/lpsabooks#

Copyright © 2016 by L. P. Suzanne Atkinson
First Edition — May, 2016

This is a work of fiction. Names, characters, and incidents either are the product of the author's imagination or are used fictitiously.

Cover Design by Adam Murray
Cover Photography by David Weintraub
Editing by Lesley Carson

ISBN
978-0-9949-5902-7 (Paperback)
978-0-9949-5901-0 (eBook)

1. Fiction, Contemporary Women
2. Fiction, Psychological Suspense

Distributed to the trade by the Ingram Book Company
Printed in the USA

Table of Contents

Ethics is knowing the difference between
what you have a right to do and what is right to do.
—Potter Stewart

There are only two types of people in this world;
those who have a conscience and those who do not.
—P. A. Speers

For David

Thank you to Pauline, Wyneth, Kat, Marguerite, Barb,
and my editor, Lesley Carson.

Chapter 1

Don't discuss the situation with anyone

November 10, 1981

The investigator is wedged behind an aged government surplus mahogany veneered desk. His back is to the wall. His elbows look elevated. He is a diminutive man. The desk seems to envelope him. Perhaps the office chair could be raised into a more optimum position. She does not suggest this. His feet probably wouldn't touch the floor. He possesses the look of a rodent with glasses—a balding ferret peeking out at her from behind the desk, and from behind black readers that serve to bisect his pointy, moustached face. She speaks only when spoken to. It has been a gruelling morning.

Edgar Novakovic works for the Canadian Counselling Alliance, of which Gaby Ridgway has been a member in good standing for the last eighteen years. There is the distinct possibility her status will change when the ferret completes his report.

"Miss Ridgway." He looks up from the sheaf of papers askew on the desk—bereft of accoutrements, except for a telephone and a lamp.

She propels herself back from her drift to safety. "Sir?"

"Our *Code of Ethics* clearly states, and I quote: 'Information from counselling sessions must be kept confidential unless the counsellor is made aware of a situation that obviously puts the client or another party into immediate danger'. Are you telling me you believe you have fulfilled this requirement in our *Code of Ethics*?"

Gaby forces herself not to wipe her sweaty palms on her stove-pipe wool slacks purchased especially for this interview. Under normal circumstances, she would be in soft, baggy linen, and certainly more comfortable. In most meetings, she brings her knitting. It helps her to focus; helps her to think. "Mr. Novakovic, I feel I did not perform unethically, regardless of the letter from my former client. She is a ruthless person. She will be held accountable for her behaviour. That is her doing, not mine. I merely tried, when asked, to assist in the protection of a third party. I'm happy to continue to answer all your questions. I did not betray her confidence!" She worries she might sound whiny, or even desperate.

Her ass is sore. The chair she was offered at the commencement of this meeting is a straight-backed, armless wooden one. Her slacks are itchy and her bum is even more annoyed with this experience than her brain. She has been trapped in the sterile, ownerless office for almost an hour, and he continues to grill her with the same questions.

"Do you mind if I stand up for a bit, sir?"

He looks quizzical but not annoyed. "Back problems?"

"I like to stretch now and then," she explains as she unfolds her lean frame into a vertical position. She can't force herself to sit on that chair, in these pants, for a moment longer. Besides, perhaps if the ferret is forced to look up at her while he asks his questions, he might be a wee bit intimidated. Maybe that's not a good idea. She'll sit again soon.

"Let's review your education history, Miss Ridgway. Tell me where you went to school, university. Paint me a picture." He looks up. His face is blank. She tries not to let this absence of expression unnerve her.

Gaby returns to the wooden chair. She attempts, with limited success, to smooth her curly, yet wispy hair, and sighs as she begins. "I grew up in a little farming community called Clair, about an hour outside Kingston, Ontario. I loved our counsellor in high school. I wanted to be exactly like her." She sighs again. She feels, with sudden realization, that sharing her personal story may be a fruitless attempt to improve her sinking status. It will, in all likelihood, make no difference.

Edgar Novakovic nods when she pauses. This simple gesture gives her the right amount of encouragement, enabling her to continue.

"When I graduated from high school, I went to Kingston Community College. I would have preferred university—like Waterloo or Toronto—but going to KCC enabled me to live at home. We didn't have a lot of money. I obtained my counselling certificate and landed a position at the Middle School in Clair, as their guidance counsellor. I was with them from 1963 until four years ago, the summer of 1977, when I accepted a position in the Counselling Division here at Provincial Government Services in Hayworth." She leans her back against the hard chair, satisfied with her answer.

"May I ask you why you left your guidance counselling position five years ago?"

Gaby smiles—a sad smile—and responds. "I wasn't investigated for an ethical issue, if that's your question, Mr. Novakovic. My husband died of cancer two years after we were married. He was a math teacher. I stuck around for a while, but was in desperate need of a change, so here I am." No more details, she hopes. "You can check with the school administrator, sir. You have all the contact information in your file. They will confirm my tale of woe." The words have a tenor of resignation about them. She doesn't care. "I signed a waiver so you may discuss the situation with them."

"I already have," is his immediate reply.

Gaby's mind starts to wander again. She wishes she could talk to Joe. He has been such a good friend, a rock, throughout this mess. He doesn't ask questions he realizes she can't answer. It helps. Office colleagues are as supportive as they can be considering she can't discuss her circumstances. Right now she feels abandoned, regardless. She fights to muffle another sigh.

Her attention is drawn to the narrow window in the corner. Mere slivers of natural November light snake into the shadowed office. She thinks she can see snowflakes whirling around outside. Snowing already. White is here to stay for sure, and it's only the day before Remembrance Day. Gaby still has a bit of trouble coping with the long, dark, and oftentimes decidedly cold northern winters.

Edgar Novakovic switches on the desk light. It only serves to make the room appear shadowed as the gloom increases. Gaby misses her mid-morning coffee break. She tries a hostess approach. "Mr. Novakovic, would you like a cup of coffee or tea? I can slip out to the staff room and get you whatever you might prefer. It would only take a moment."

He looks up from his file folder, startled, as if he's surprised she's still there. "That would be very kind, Miss Ridgway. Coffee, please, with a little cream and one sugar. I appreciate the offer."

She jumps to her feet, turns, and reaches for the door knob before he can reconsider. "Coming right up! Back in a flash!" She sprints down the hall, feeling temporarily free of her jailer. The staff room is shared by all the divisions—Addictions, Child Protection, Mental Health, Adoption, Income Security, and her own group, Counselling. Staff members mill in. There are four coffee pots full and waiting. Gaby is thankful someone has put the coffee on already. One of the biggest complaints in the office is that people will drain the last of the coffee and leave the empty pots on the counter as if they're too good to grab a filter, empty in a packet of coffee, and add water. The process isn't rocket science.

She fetches her own mug from the cupboard and finds a guest mug upturned on the sideboard. As she's filling both, co-workers appear in the doorway. There are looks full of unasked questions and grunts of acknowledgement. Everyone knows the investigator is here today, but there won't be a soul with the balls to ask her how she feels—at least not for now. Everyone is skittish. They have supported her all along as she's tried to navigate the unpredictable behaviour of a sociopath, but now that there's an official inquiry, people keep their distance. She doesn't blame them. Mimi, their secretary, is the exception as she openly expresses her outrage at the Canadian Counselling Alliance for even considering Gaby as the subject of their questions.

As she leaves the staff room and starts down the hall toward the central reception area and through to the counselling wing, she passes Cheryl Nadler from Adoption Services. She never goes for coffee. She must be in reception to meet a client. Cheryl walks by, looks Gaby in the eye, nods, and pats her gently on the arm. "It'll be fine," she whispers. "Don't worry." She continues on her way. Gaby is thankful for the support, but how the hell would Cheryl know if it will be okay or not? She may have to explore the possibility of bussing tables at the Hayworth Diner before this ordeal is over, and here she is with a mortgage barely two years old!

She quietly slips back into the interrogation room—office—occupied by Edgar Novakovic. She places his coffee on the desk, and responds to his nod of appreciation with one of her own. She returns her bum to the hard wooden chair, and holds her coffee in one hand while she smoothes her sweater with the other. She loves this sweater. It is cotton, pale yellow, and her own creation. She thinks of it as her lucky sweater; her "you-can-get-through-whatever-happens" sweater. She knit it when she took a leave of absence from her job to care for Grant as he died from testicular cancer. She rubs her hand across the ribbing one more time. It gives her comfort.

Edgar Novakovic looks up. "Miss Ridgway, we are almost done for now. I have to meet with the complainant to get her side of the story. To be frank, I would rather hear that before I get more details from you. I have her letter. I will meet with her to fill in any blanks I have resulting from the letter. Then I will contact you for a second interview. Please don't discuss this situation with anyone. I expect that's difficult, but circumstances are better served if you keep the details to yourself until the inquiry is resolved. I hope you understand."

Gaby's mind snaps back to the night in October when, in desperation, she called her sister and told her every detail. Her sister is back east. That discussion shouldn't count. "Fine with me, sir. Honestly, an investigation by one's professional association is not a topic of conversation in which I'm anxious to engage. Do you have any idea how long before you would like to see me again?"

"No later than a couple of weeks. Let's set a date for November 25th, early in the morning. Would you be kind enough to book this spare office once again?"

Gaby nods. Another two weeks to stew. Well, tomorrow is a stat holiday, so getting away from the office for the day will be a blessing she can count.

"Enjoy your day off tomorrow, Miss Ridgway." He stands and offers his hand across the desk. "I will finish my coffee while I sort out my notes. You may go back to your own work now."

She is summarily dismissed.

A couple of minutes later, she's seated in her own cozy office with the door firmly shut. She gazes out her window at the snow now starting to drift. It will be a challenge at the cenotaph tomorrow.

She thinks about all the wonderful people she's met in Hayworth since she came here five years ago—intriguing clients and fabulous people in the community. Initially, it was hard to make friends outside of work but that has changed over time. She feels accepted, and now this. It is no secret who wrote the letter of complaint to the Canadian Counselling Alliance. Her former client has no credibility in the office, but the CCA may look at the issue from a different perspective. They will follow the rule book to the letter. She hopes she won't have to leave Hayworth, her house, her friends, or Joe.

Chapter 2

This won't be easy

1977

Nina's chaotic kitchen is bathed in soft late July afternoon sunshine. The white on white colour scheme is accented with Victorian majolica pottery— green leaf platters and jugs shaped like tree trunks with exotic birds for handles. The stuff is the epitome of ugly meets beautiful. It once belonged to their mother. Gaby told Nina she could have it all and has never regretted the decision, regardless of what some people said about value and collectability.

Gaby has come to Kingston for lunch and the afternoon. Her task is to tell her younger sister about what has been a heart-wrenching decision to move away. She watches Nina make sandwiches and carry on what seems like three conversations at once while she lays out bread, assembles ingredients from the fridge, and periodically looks at Freddie. The baby is busy pounding the tray table of his high chair with a green plastic car. The older Nina gets, the more she reminds Gaby of their mother. She wonders what it would be like to see them side by side now.

"Lunch will be ready in a minute, Elly. You can take your brothers out on the deck to eat. How's that? Craig. Josh. Go wash your hands. Lunch is almost ready. You can eat outside with Elly." She looks over at Gaby with amusement. "Can you make sure they get washed up? I'm almost organized, and then we can have a proper visit." She pushes a strand of soft brown hair off her forehead while she puts the finishing touches on the sandwiches.

Gaby rounds up the children and settles them outside at their table-set on the deck. She delivers sandwiches and juice in colourful plastic cups. They're all excited that Aunt Gaby's come for the afternoon. They're good kids; rowdy but good. Nina encourages them to explore and ask questions. She insists they play together without fighting. She does a good job with them. Gaby returns to the kitchen and beams down at Freddie, named after his grandfather. She hopes Freddie grows up to resemble his namesake, a kind and generous man who loved his family and worked hard every day. Fred Ridgway and Eleanor, their mother, were killed in a head-on crash with a tractor trailer while on their way to Nina's to celebrate Nina and her husband's first Christmas together. It was a horrible time. Gaby has since struggled with the celebratory aspect of the holiday. She wonders what it might be like to spend Christmas without Nina's children to salve the wound that reopens every year.

This won't be easy. Once the children are settled, Nina brings the coffee pot and two sandwiches to the round glass table in the eating alcove. "You look so sad, Gaby. Are you okay? You'll be back at school in no time." She's smiling, but there's anxiety around the edges.

"I've accepted a job as a counsellor in Hayworth, Alberta, Nina. It starts right after Labour Day. The house sale is finalized. I've notified the school board, and the Alberta government will move me in a couple of weeks." She manages to get it all out in one breath.

Nina's lips purse in thoughtful surprise. She absentmindedly occupies one hand on Freddie's tray while not taking her eyes off her sister. Tears start to well up as Gaby blunders forward.

She drags her eyes away from the loose thread on the pocket of her pale blue sun dress and forces them to meet her sister's gaze. The rest of the words come out in a rush. "I have to make a change, Nina. I can't stay here. I feel like I'm trapped in a dark room. Everyone looks at me like I'm the poor young woman who has no children and whose husband died from cancer. They're right, but it doesn't help."

Nina finally regains her composure. "Gaby, why didn't you talk to me? All the details seem to be settled. You sold your house, landed a new job, and never said a word to me!" Her voice is brittle somehow. Gaby doesn't want her to be angry. She needs her support.

"I was afraid you'd talk me out of it."

"Where the hell is Hayworth, Alberta, anyway?"

The pressure in Gaby's chest is relieved like magic. Nina will be okay, eventually. She knows her sister. She'll come around. She just needs information. "Hayworth, if we look on a map, which I have done a dozen times already, is about a six hour drive north of Edmonton. It isn't very big—a few thousand people—but it has a hospital and a couple of schools. People farm, I guess. There are churches and a grocery store. There's a Ford dealership. The supervisor for the Counselling Division has found a house for me to rent within walking distance of the office. The people who owned it moved to Edmonton but decided to keep their house. I sold my car, too. I thought I'd keep Grant's truck and drive it to Hayworth. It seems more appropriate to own a truck since I'll be well into cowboy country."

She's aware that people have often wondered out loud why she never parted with Grant's 1973 Mazda Rotary pick-up. She says it comes in handy and is easy to drive because of its size, but the truth is that she loved the little black truck from the moment he bought it. She loved how happy he was in it. She knew, at the time, he wouldn't get many opportunities behind the wheel. When they chose it together, he had already started to go downhill. It was important to him that she like the truck, and the reason why floated rudderless between them.

Nina gets up and starts to tidy the kitchen. The older kids are still outside. Freddie looks like he needs a snooze. With her back to Gaby, Nina asks, "How did you manage to find a job to apply for way out there?"

Nina isn't quite on board yet. Gaby can tell. Her sister asks questions to fill in the space as she makes an attempt to rationalize. She wants to avoid the inevitable—there won't be a lot of afternoons like this in their future. "I went to the Ontario Teachers' Union office and read about guidance counsellor competitions in the north. Alberta Department of Health and Welfare had an open competition for counsellors and I applied. They did telephone interviews and offered me a position in either Hayworth or a place called Bear Creek near the Territories border. I opted for Hayworth." She grins at her sister's back. "Bear Creek has an ominous sound—bears and all that. Besides, the location is about five hours north of Hayworth again."

Nina turns to look at Gaby. "You sold your house and I didn't even know you put it on the market! God, Gaby! I thought we were friends! I thought we could tell one another all our secrets! I feel betrayed by you. I don't want to feel this way. Talk to me."

Gaby shakes her head and runs her fingers through her hair, fine like Nina's but a lighter shade and annoying with natural curls that never behave themselves. "I made up my mind I would not be talked out of this, Nina." Her voice is firm. "The last two years have been hateful. You know that. You know every detail. You told me I needed to see a therapist, for God's sake!" Her voice softens a little. Nina has returned to the table, reached for a drowsy Freddie, and has started to cradle the little boy in her arms. "If I told you what I was up to, you would have tried to change my mind, and I would have let you. It breaks my heart to leave you, Craig, and these little mutts." She points at Freddie and sweeps her outstretched arm toward the backyard. "I have to do this, Nina, for myself." She looks straight at her sister with what she hopes is an expression of resolve.

"How did you manage to sell your house without me knowing about it, Gaby?" There's a hint of forgiveness on Nina's face now.

"Do you remember the teacher who came up to me at Grant's funeral and asked about my house? You remember the big guy with the sloppy suit and the worse manners?"

Nina nods.

"Well, I went to him after I accepted the position out west and told him he could have the house if he still wanted it. I told him ninety thousand and we would each have our own lawyer. He took the deal and possession is in two weeks. Once the movers get here, the place is all his. At least I'll have a few extra bucks since the mortgage was insured, plus Grant and I paid less than sixty when we bought it. I think he might have handed over a hundred but I didn't want to push my luck." She giggles. "I never could stand the guy!"

"Well, I feel better now that I know you'll have money in the bank. What about your pension?"

"The union says they can roll it over to the Alberta government, so there's no problem. It will all work out, Nina."

At that moment, their attention is diverted as Elly and Craig Junior roar through the back door. Josh has fallen and is on the deck screaming. Nina hands Freddie to Gaby and follows her two older children back outside. Gaby can hear her coo away to Josh as she promises him a Band-aid and some lemonade.

****

After a three day drive from Clair, Gaby puts Kenora, Ontario behind her. She settles in on the Manitoba section of the Trans-Canada Highway, finally able to permit herself recollections of her goodbyes to Nina and her family without puddling up.

The whole troupe made the eighty kilometre drive from Kingston to Clair to say goodbye—no small feat with all four kids. When they turned up, the moving van was long gone. Gaby was sitting on the front steps waiting for the lawyer to come and fetch the keys. The money would be deposited in her bank account that day. She gazed out at the tree-lined street. The air was heavy in the late morning August heat. She started to doubt her decision. She talked to Nina and everyone on the phone last night. She was missing them already, when she saw their station wagon round the corner. It was a complete and total surprise.

By the time the lawyer arrived, they were all hugging and crying. They were a mess. Yes, she would call. Yes, she would call collect until she arrived in Hayworth and had her phone installed. No, she wouldn't pick anybody up on the way. Yes, all her reservations were made ahead of time. Yes, she had enough money, and no, they couldn't talk her out of it. By the time they returned to their respective vehicles and the kids were safely tucked in, they had caused a neighbourhood stir.

As the granite-trimmed landscape that surrounds Lake Superior begins to merge into fields of wheat and pastures of cattle, Gaby actually grins as she thinks about the elderly couple next door, who came out on their step to see if there had been an accident—after all, everyone was crying.

Upon her arrival on the outskirts of Edmonton, Gaby calls the moving company, and sure enough, they will be in Hayworth in three days. She will have enough time to drive to her new home and get the lay of the land. She's excited. The remainder of the trip won't be complicated. She was told the key to her house would be tucked under a flower pot at the side by the water tap. *Note to self: ask the owner if she can replace the locks.* She will have a couple of nights without a bed, but prepared by packing an air mattress and a sleeping bag in the truck. With a week before her job starts, she'll have lots of time to get organized. Gaby is anxious with anticipation as she lets herself in to what will be her last motel room before her arrival in Hayworth. She'll call Nina and tell her the trip has proceeded along exactly as expected.

****

After a six hour drive almost due north from Edmonton, on roads often desolate and in disrepair, Gaby rolls into Hayworth. She looks straight through town from one end to the other. The community is designed like a bowling alley for heaven's sake! Through the insect graveyard that is her truck windshield, she sees the Hayworth Diner to the right. Main Street appears to run through town until it becomes bereft of buildings on either side and disappears on the horizon, like it goes off to infinity. There are a couple of streets that run parallel to Main Street. There aren't a lot of trees, although it appears some residents on the streets have made a feeble attempt at shrubs and flowers. She drives slowly up and down the streets, noting the little hospital, the two schools—one obviously the elementary and the other the high school—the Creek Tavern, the churches that look more like warehouses with signs and crosses that identify them as churches, and the Hayworth Regional Provincial Building—six-sided and presenting itself like an odd brick misfit in this town of western, 1950s architecture. The whole place appears more like a movie set assembled in the middle of nowhere. The address of her rental is 15 Poplar Street. The letter from her new boss says the house is one street east of the diner as she enters town. The little house is not hard to find.

Gaby pulls the truck into the side yard. It isn't a driveway per se, more worn down grass with tire tracks that extend to the open gate in the wooden privacy fence. She can see the flower pot at the back corner, retrieves the key, and makes her way up the front steps to the tiny porch—perhaps big enough to hold a wicker chair and a small table, if she happened to have them. She turns around and looks across the street at another house almost the mirror image of hers, and through its backyard to the rear entrance of a building on Main Street.

She has spent most of the last week excited and afraid at the same time. Her heart pounds as she turns the key in the lock while she props the screen door open with her hip. The design looks like what someone from the east might call post-war housing. She enters straight into a living room which takes up most of the front of the house. There's another small room to the left that she isn't sure what its purpose would be—perhaps a den. That room has stairs that Gaby knows lead to an upstairs attic. The rental letter said it hasn't been used in years. She walks through the front room, her footsteps hollow on the bare wood floors. Her eyes dart around before they come to rest on a small watercolour that hangs on the wall to the left of the kitchen entry. She moves closer and peers at it through the subdued light. The illustration is of 15 Poplar Street, this very house, but from the look of it, painted years ago before there was a fence or other residences nearby. Her landlords must have left it behind.

The whole place smells dusty and closed up. She wants to fling open the windows. The back half of the house is comprised of the kitchen and bedroom, with a small bathroom off the bedroom, nestled in behind the den-like space in the front. The house is not even half the size of her bungalow in Clair. *Look on the bright side. It won't be hard to heat.*

Gaby returns to her truck and begins to unload. She has brought some cleaning supplies as she wasn't sure what the condition of the place would be. She hauls in bedding and a few groceries. She thinks she'll go back to the diner for supper tonight, and spend tomorrow getting settled. As long as the power and water are both on, which they are, she'll manage.

****

The Hayworth Diner looks straight out of a scene from *Happy Days* on television. She slides into a red leatherette booth along the front where she has a good view out the windows, and accepts a menu from the waitress whose name tag indicates she is Nancy.

"Can I get you a drink?"

Gaby nods politely up at the woman who looks down at her with practised patience. "Tea, please."

"Ontario plates," observes the waitress as she looks out the window and motions with her order pad toward the Mazda. "Visiting?"

Gaby is happy for the conversation. For the past week, she has heard little except for references to her reservations and what she wants to eat. She discussed the weather one day with a grocery clerk in a place called Indian River somewhere in Saskatchewan. "No. No. I just took a job as a counsellor over at the provincial building. I start after the long weekend. Drove in today." *Too much information? Too needy?* Gaby titters self-consciously. "I'm really looking forward to getting to know the community. The place is beautiful."

"If you like being stuck in the 1950s." Nancy's remark is said with no malice; like she's merely pointing out the facts. "Want an old-fashioned chicken dinner? I still have some left from the special. People eat pretty early here, so the supper crowd has almost all cleared out, but Danny and I can scare you up a dinner, even at 7:30 PM."

"Thanks. That sounds wonderful."

"I'll be right back with your tea." Nancy takes off and Gaby can hear the saloon-style swinging doors flap as she barks out her request to the cook. The few other people in the diner include an older couple at a booth in the back, and two young men sitting at the counter. The latter are drinking sodas and not saying much.

Nancy returns with the tea. "Have you found a place to live? There aren't many rentals in town."

"In fact, my new boss managed to get a place for me. The house is little, but it will do for now."

"All by yourself, then?" Nancy busses the table beside the booth where Gaby is sitting.

"Yeah. Time for a fresh start." Nervous about getting too deeply entrenched in her own history, she flips the conversation toward the waitress. "You a local girl?"

"Me? Oh, yeah. Born here. I guess I don't know any better. Been waiting tables here at the diner for almost fifteen years. Started full-time the minute I graduated from high school. Pathetic, eh?"

"Not if you're happy."

Nancy looks up when a big guy in the kitchen slams his paw down on a bell positioned on the pass-through counter. "Order's up."

Nancy springs into action and settles a beautiful meal down on the urethaned table. "Enjoy, my dear. I'll be back. We have Saskatoon pie!" She grins down at Gaby who has no idea what that even means.

Chapter 3

Where to, Miss?

After two nights of less than adequate sleep on an air mattress in the corner of her new bedroom, the moving van finally arrives. Although exactly on schedule, to Gaby it has taken forever. Two burly gentlemen hump her worldly possessions up the few steps to the little front porch and into the living room. "Where to, Miss?" becomes the phrase of the day.

The heavy oak dining room table and six chairs are almost too big for the eat-in kitchen. She makes a quick decision and delegates the ornate matching sideboard to the living room. It will serve double duty as a console for her tiny television. Her mattress and box spring get dragged unceremoniously through to the bedroom. She brought both bureaus, but one will have to go in the little den at the front. She sold her couch before she left. It was over-sized and almost too big for her bungalow as it was. Instead, she decided to move only her two grey armless side chairs and the coffee table that once belonged to her parents. Maybe she will be able to buy a sleeper sofa. Grant's big desk takes up almost all the remaining space in the den. His straight-backed—decidedly not office—chair is the last item to enter the space.

She signs the paperwork presented to her, looks with quiet resignation at the now muddy floors, and offers both men a cool drink. They decline—off to the diner for a bite before they return to Edmonton. She frowns as she starts to examine boxes. She's done it. She's here, and all of a sudden the hollow essence of homesickness overwhelms her.

After the moving van rumbles back down Poplar Street, rubbing the dry, late summer leaves off the few overhanging tree branches, she unpacks the boxes, stores away, rearranges, cleans floors, and finally settles on her front steps with a box of crackers and a cup of tea. The arrangement of her possessions comes together in no time. Gaby has a knack. Even with reduced furnishings and floor space, fewer odds and ends, and a cramped kitchen with her dining room suite now occupying centre stage, she manages to create quiet luxury and a lived-in atmosphere over the course of the next few days. She hangs her artwork. She places a picture of herself with Grant, taken at Niagara Falls a few weeks after they were married, on her bedroom bureau. It's been two years. She can manage to look at his photo without welling up, so she's improved—"moved on" might be too strong a phrase to describe her just yet.

Gaby meets the local antique dealer, Ben Tullis, and learns that she won't be able to buy a new couch unless she travels to a furniture warehouse in a nearby community known for bigger stores and rock-bottom deals. Hayworth has never managed to attract the "big" stores. Perhaps it relates to taxes. Gaby isn't sure. She manages to find her way to the warehouse and chooses a convertible sofa they will deliver sometime after the holiday. She will have to leave work to come home and let them in. She assumes that will be okay. Its cranberry and grey stripes will work well with the side chairs. She comes upon a silver shag area carpet that will almost fill the living room, and totes that home in the truck.

She spends the remainder of her Labour Day weekend exploring the neighbourhoods of Hayworth. Her goal is to get a closer look at the Regional Provincial Government Services Building. The rambling one story complex is known fondly as the Hexagon. It houses the six divisions of Addictions, Mental Health, Counselling, Child Protection, Adoptions, and Income Security. Pearl Markowski told her each division has a hallway of offices. Reception, the clerical area, and all the meeting rooms are in the middle. The building, framed by bushes and small trees, stands alone in a field of asphalt. It looks, if one had to describe the design, like a squared-off doughnut with continuous vertical rectangular windows along each edge. Gaby wonders if one of those windows might become hers on Tuesday.

****

Contemplating the commencement of a new job is exhausting. She hardly slept. She struggles with what to wear—first impressions and all that. She settles on navy linen pants with a hand-knitted cream sweater. Navy beads and loafers complete the look. She fusses with her fragile hair, wispy and curly with no style and less control. She knots it in a bun, knowing full well it will not last until noon. She adds a little blush and a swipe of lipstick. She doesn't expend any effort on make-up.

Gaby drives her truck to work. Although she could walk the few blocks from her house, she doesn't know about expectations as they relate to home visits, and her contract most definitely indicates she requires a current driver's licence and a reliable vehicle. As she enters the expanse of reception area, a barrel-shaped woman in a man's cardigan waves to her. Perhaps this is her boss. Pearl Markowski, the Assistant Supervisor responsible for the divisions of Addictions, Mental Health, and Counselling, stands round-shouldered and dishevelled in the centre pod of the Hexagon, chatting with a sparrow-like creature. When Gaby approaches the reception desk, the sparrow quickly scuttles toward her, releases the latch on the counter, and lifts it so she can enter this common area. A welcoming hand is extended. "Hello. Gabrielle, right? I'm Mimi Long, the secretary for Counselling Division. I'll be working for you." She turns and points at Pearl, currently lumbering across the expanse between them. "This is Pearl Markowski. You two have talked on the phone." She lowers her head and takes a step back as Pearl approaches.

"Gaby. Gaby. So happy you're here. Mimi and I were discussing caseload reassignments. We intend to have a little 'Welcome to Counselling Division' get-together later today so you can meet everyone."

"Hi! I'm excited, Pearl." She offers her hand. "I'm so happy to finally meet you both in person." She is careful to include Mimi who has managed the whole operation of contracts and contacts via telephone.

"Mimi will get you settled in your office. She'll ensure all that pesky paperwork is completed. You know the government—lots of paperwork!" She guffaws—a hearty snort without consideration of whom it might disturb. "Then she'll let me know so we can get together for a chat." Pearl waves to another worker entering the clerical area, and trundles off.

Mimi jumps to attention. "Come on Gabrielle. Do you prefer to be called Gaby?"

Gaby nods, unable to get any words out of her face before Mimi continues.

"Everyone is so relieved you're here. They all have too many files and are anxious to reorganize their caseloads. We work on a rotation system. New cases are assigned to a counsellor based on the referral list. Most clients come to the office, so territories aren't the primary focus, but two of the counsellors handle referrals from the south of town and you and Elliot will handle cases from the north." They have arrived at an office door, unlocked and slightly ajar.

Gaby is curious but gives Mimi the lead. The office is small and at the end of the corridor. Gaby knows the other three counsellors watched her walk by. They lifted their heads from their desks but did not attempt to interrupt the trek down the hall. The view from her window is the parking lot and street. Tips of bushes brush the outside lip of the window ledge. The space houses a desk with a chair on rollers snuggled in behind it, a file cabinet, a desk lamp, a telephone with a couple of buttons currently flashing, and a small Dictaphone machine. In the opposite corner from the desk are a low table and three additional mottled-looking stackable chairs. "We can get you any supplies you need. Do you prefer a blotter or a blank desk top? I can get you a blotter."

"May I move the furniture?"

The look on Mimi's face registers surprise, but she doesn't miss a beat. "This is your office, Gaby. What do you want moved? We could do it now."

"I'd like my desk to be up against the wall, across the window. I don't like to sit behind a desk when I'm in a session with clients. I'll move the chairs around a little, too, so anyone in the room is out in the open and not behind a piece of furniture. I need one chair beside my desk."

Mimi helps Gaby without comment, but Gaby saw all the other counsellors sitting behind desks. Maybe they move to another chair in the office when they talk to clients. Who knows? Gaby, as has always been the case, will carry on in her own way.

Her orientation with Mimi lasts until coffee break but she organizes her space, learns how to use the telephone system, and gets her necessary supplies, including a pocket calendar where Mimi has already entered a 10:30 AM appointment with Pearl, as well as the staff get-together at 1:00 PM. Mimi will notify Pearl that Gaby will be available for their "talk" after coffee.

It takes her a couple of minutes to traverse the centre hub of the complex and reach the staff room—a huge and windowless space off of the central clerical area, decorated with mismatched chairs of all descriptions. Gaby thinks everyone must have brought a discarded piece of furniture from home. One table holds four coffee pots and a kettle, obviously in deference to the tea drinkers. People smile and nod, but it takes a rather frazzled-looking older woman to break the ice.

"Hi there. Are you Gabrielle Ridgway, the new therapist starting today?"

Gaby forces an expression of confidence. They shake hands. "Gaby, please. My mother was the only person who called me Gabrielle."

"I'm Edith Finley. I know we'll meet more formally after lunch. I'm in the Counselling Division, too. Boy! Are we glad you're here! We're all swamped!" She looks around at the staff as they settle into chairs, talk to one another, and pour coffee into mugs that express sentiments like: I Hate Mornings or World's Best Dad. "This is Gaby Ridgway from Ontario. She's started today with us here in the Counselling Division. We are now, officially, fully staaaaaffed." She tries to expel the words like an opera singer. It comes off flat in more ways than one. "Here, sit down beside me. Let's get to know one another."

Compelled to include Mimi, Gaby turns to her. "Are you going to sit down, too?"

Mimi returns Gaby's look with one of surprise. "No. No. You take your break. I'll get coffee and then go back to my desk."

With no other obvious options, Gaby sits down in a flowered wingback next to Edith and tries to smile. She's worried it comes across as strained.

"So, everybody is swamped, eh? Well, I hope another body will help." She tries to look enthusiastic, but feels overwhelmed already.

"Listen." Edith leans over and, with a conspiratorial expression, glances about to make sure there are no eavesdroppers. "I figure both Elliot and Frank will give you all the cases they don't want—you know—the boring ones, or the especially complicated and time-consuming ones. Not me. I have a special case to give you. The referral came in a week ago and I haven't even called her yet. Three of this woman's children have died in the space of four years! Different circumstances, mind you. No hint of foul play, as far as I can tell. I think it should have gone to Mental Health Division but it was sent to us. From me to you—a case you can sink your teeth into, and brand new! Pretty good, eh?"

Gaby isn't quite sure. "I imagine Pearl will handle the reassignments, wouldn't you think?"

"No. No. She told us to each pick out three cases to get you started. After next week, you'll get assigned half the north-of-town caseload." She screws up her eyes as she attempts to calculate. "Maybe another eight to ten files. Elliot doesn't leave the office very much so I would guess they all have cars and can come in for sessions. By the end of the month, you'll be at full throttle!" She leans back in her chair and chortles as she takes a sip of her cooling tea. Someone passes around homemade chocolate chip cookies. Edith takes two and munches away while she continues to grin at Gaby.

****

The meeting with Pearl Markowski is not at all what Gaby anticipated. Pearl makes a point of preparing her. She explains that she expects Gaby to get all the cases that the other three don't want. With a surprising lack of professionalism, she disparages her staff by describing Frank as a religious nut, Edith as needy and insecure, and Elliot as too cute for words but chronically depressed. Then she adds, "You can make your own determinations."

Pearl supervises the four workers from Addictions and Mental Health, as well. Mimi does her clerical work in addition to that of the Counselling Division staff. There are other secretaries to handle the needs of the Addictions and Mental Health personnel.

Gaby mentions that Edith already indicated a case she wanted to transfer. Pearl reacts with a snide growl. "She's tried to dump that case for a week. She wanted to refer it to Mental Health Division. She hasn't called the woman yet. Look, Gaby, you don't have to take that case. The woman has an older son, hence the referral to us. Edith doesn't feel confident with the subject of death and dying. She doesn't feel confident with too much, if the truth be told."

Shocked that her supervisor speaks with such candor, Gaby merely states that the file has intriguing elements; she's here to work and she might as well start somewhere.

Pearl also makes it clear that she expects her staff to work without too much supervision. "You can come and talk to me whenever I'm free, but I expect you to do your job, schedule your appointments, have the mandated twelve to sixteen interviews per week, and keep your files caught up. Mimi is very efficient and, if you dictate your charts, she gets them typed in no time and ready for signature. I, on the other hand, hate paperwork. Don't be late with expense accounts, vacation requests, or sick day slips. She deposits them with me at a certain time each week. I review them then and I don't want to be bothered by that crap for another week. Once a year, I'll try to sit in with you on an interview to see how you work, but I don't get in your way. Any questions?"

Gaby has no questions.

Although she brought a ham and cheese sandwich to work, she jumps in her truck and speeds home to the safety and solitude of her quiet kitchen.

****

Mimi appears at her door a few minutes after she returns from her quick lunch at home. "Are you braced for the staff meeting? Thought I'd come and get you—first time and all that," she whispers as she peeks over her glasses.

Gaby reaches for a notepad, her agenda, and a pen. "Right behind you, Mimi. Thanks for holding my hand. I think I might need it today." They cross the open clerical space and enter a small meeting room designed for intimate gatherings of ten or less. Edith, her hair flying in all directions and telltale tomato soup on her beige blouse, is the first one there.

Edith almost upsets her chair as she rushes around the table, banging her hip on the corner in the process. "Ouch! Hi, Gaby. Glad you're here. At least I'm not the only one who's early. I've brought my referrals, including the one I told you about." She points at a somewhat imposing stack of manila file folders on the table. It looks like considerably more than three.

Mimi intervenes. "Three cases each, Edith. That was the deal." The look on her face is no-nonsense, and Gaby wonders why she seems to have delegated herself as Gaby's protector. "If you people dump on her, she'll decide to move south and find a job closer to the city. Give the girl a break."

So Mimi's afraid she'll quit before she gets started. Not any chance of that happening, but it feels nice to have someone in her corner. It isn't long before Frank Spencer fills the doorway. He's a mountain of a man. It appears he's pushing his overhanging stomach with each trunk-like thigh when he moves. As he throws himself into one of the meeting room chairs, it rolls backward and groans under his weight. He attempts to manage a cup of coffee in a mug the size of a mixing bowl, as he tosses three thin files on the table. Gaby notices a tiny gold pin on the lapel of his sport coat. It seems minuscule against his massive frame. It looks like little feet.

"These are all new referrals—haven't even called them to make an appointment—thought that would be the Christian way. No need for you to try to untangle problems you haven't worked with." He looks over the rim of his bowl of coffee. "I'm Frank Spencer. People call me The Pastor behind my back but I don't mind. Think of it as a compliment, in fact." He puts down the coffee and lifts his hand, but does not attempt to get out of the chair.

As Gaby leans over to shake Frank's hand, Pearl and the person she assumes is Elliot Banks crowd into the room. Elliot seems younger than the rest of them, except for maybe Mimi. He looks like he spends all his time working out; slight but muscular in his polo shirt that strains at the shoulders. His dress slacks are tight around his hips.

Pearl takes a seat at the head of the table and nods toward Gaby. "Let's make some introductions first, okay? Does everybody have their transfers?" Without waiting for a reply, she starts. "Everybody, meet Gaby Ridgway. She's from Ontario. Elliot, she will share the north caseload with you, so maybe by the end of the week you two can decide who wants what files. Gaby, have you met everyone?"

Gaby turns to Elliot, seated beside her, and tries to look engaged. "Elliot and I haven't been formally introduced. I'm Gaby. Nice to meet you." He avoids direct eye contact. She looks around the table. "I'm certainly pleased to be here and look forward to working with all of you."

Without additional preamble, Pearl instructs the staff to provide Gaby with three cases each, along with verbal overviews. Edith has five. Gaby offers to take all five but Pearl intercedes. "Pick three, Edith. Your caseload is the smallest to start with. Don't take advantage."

Chapter 4

Pearl's door is always open

Back in her office, with a cup of Earl Grey tea delivered by a thoughtful Mimi, Gaby begins to sort through her files in order to organize the upcoming week. As soon as she's about to ask Edith to come talk to her about the referrals she's generated, a soft tap on her door breaks her train of thought.

"Hi, again. Pearl says for you to go to Dr. Alden's office. She'll meet you there." Mimi's voice is a hushed whisper and she scuttles off like a little mouse. Gaby wonders why she didn't use the phone. Gaby couldn't have committed a wrong already. Only an introduction, she's sure. She leaves her tea to cool on the desk, and follows the bread crumb that is Mimi, who waits for her at the end of the hall.

"His office is over there." She points out a short corridor around the corner from the counselling arm of offices. "Let me know if you need me."

Gaby pats Mimi's shoulder, nods her thanks, and approaches the executive office. Clark Alden is the boss of her boss in the pecking order. She no sooner gets to the door which stands open, when Pearl sings out for her to come in. Clark, or Dr. Alden as Mimi calls him, is a frail-looking man with a pencil-thin moustache. He sits behind an antique desk cluttered with bound documents that resemble reports. A crystal ashtray, the size of a dinner plate, takes up the central spot. It's full. The air has a blue tinge. The telephone is covered in papers. Pearl stands like a sentinel—albeit a nervous one by the look of her one knee wiggling and rocking—right in front of the desk.

"Gaby, I wanted you to meet our fearless leader before you get too involved in your case files. This is Clark Alden—Dr. Alden—who is the overall manager of all six divisions here at the Hexagon, and a much respected psychiatrist in his own right." She gushes a bit.

It does not escape Gaby's notice that Dr. Alden winces when Pearl uses the colloquial term to describe the building. At this point, he stands up and produces a bony and ring-less hand for her to shake. "Welcome to our regional offices Miss Ridgway. I assume Pearl has managed to help get you settled in and you're ready to serve the fine citizens of Hayworth and surrounding area?"

Gaby continues to stand since Pearl continues to stand. She responds in as formal a manner as she can muster considering the atmosphere. "Thank you, Dr. Alden. Yes, I'm settling in and looking forward to meeting clients and getting to work. The community is fabulous, and Pearl helped me locate a sweet little house to rent."

He sits back down but doesn't suggest they do the same. "Yes, yes, I guess you need a place to live. I hadn't thought of that. Good job, Pearl." He nods up to her as she flushes pink around her ears. "Well, Pearl will keep me posted on how you progress. Her door is always open, so if you need any help, don't hesitate to ask her. It was nice to meet you."

And, that's that. Pearl's door is always open—not his, only Pearl's. Good to know.

****

As she reviews files at her desk, Gaby feels rather than sees Frank Spencer when he absorbs the open space where the office door has been left ajar. She turns in her chair and welcomes the big man. Frank lurches, it seems, through the opening and helps himself to a chair near the coffee table in the corner. "Thought you might like to look at the files I gave you," he huffs as he seats himself. Pleasantries appear to have been waived in favour of getting down to business.

"Sure, Frank. Let me pull them out. You said, in the meeting, they're all new referrals." Gaby doesn't quite understand what they might need to review.

"I wanted to talk to you about them. Hayworth is a small town. Everybody knows everybody."

Gaby gazes across at her new colleague. "No gossip, now Frank. I like to make my own assessment after I meet somebody. Since I'm new in town, I get to do that for a little while." She tries to sound casual. She doesn't want him to attempt to influence her opinion of people. In small communities, people are often judged by their family history before they even get a foot in the door. Knowing how it feels to be labelled, she intends to try and curb that in her caseload. "By the way, the lapel pin you're wearing is interesting. Significant?" She once again finds herself focused on the tiny gold feet positioned beside what appears to be a rubbed out mustard stain.

"Yes. My little feet." He tucks his big chin into his neck and squints over at the pin. "This is the size of the baby's feet when a woman has an abortion. I think it's important to show people what you believe in, don't you? I have posters in my office about anti-smoking and anti-drinking; about going to church and about our Saviour. I get lots of flack about it but the union says they can't make me take my messages down."

Gaby relies on years of experience to ensure she does not reveal her thoughts through her facial expression. "I always try to keep my personal views to myself, Frank. Different strokes.... Let's have a look at these new cases." She quickly pulls out the three files he'd turned over earlier.

"I especially wanted to talk about the referral from Mental Health Division. She's schizophrenic and her parents are upset. I don't like to work with the loony tunes. Mental Health Division should have kept her. Another one is a teenage girl who throws up every time she gets on the school bus. I figured you would have an easier time with her than me. And, there's one from Segue House. That place gives me the creeps, so you can have it, too."

Gaby is both uncomfortable and disturbed by Frank's judgmental attitudes toward clients. "Tell me about you, Frank. Are you a northern boy?"

"No, not me. My bride and I came up here twenty-five years ago. Thought a small town would be a good place to raise a family. Our kids are all grown up now and live back down south, but we'll stay here until I retire."

"Tell me about your wife, Frank. Does she work?"

"Good grief, no! I think the man should be the bread winner. No offence." He waves a pudgy hand like he's shooing away a fly. "We all know you're a widow, so you pretty well have to work, but really! There's no need for Edith to work. She has a husband. And there's Elliot's wife. She runs off to work every day. They should start a family! What's the matter with them?

Anyway...." He stops to take a breath after his tirade. His face is quite red and he's a little bit sweaty. "My wife's name is Margaret. She could stand to lose a few pounds but she's nice enough. Perhaps we'll have you over to dinner and you can meet her."

He starts to haul himself out of the chair and Gaby feels a measure of relief. "Thanks for the information about the files, Frank. If I have any questions, I'll get back to you." She won't have any questions.

****

Since she feels a wee bit of pressure to get appointments scheduled and clients moving, Gaby starts with a referral from Edith—the one of the young mother with the son. The phone rings five times before it's picked up.

"Yes?"

"Hello. May I please speak to Lorna Koski?"

"That's me. Who's this?"

"Hi. I'm Gaby Ridgway from Counselling Division here at Provincial Government Services. I have a referral from your doctor. It says you would like to see someone."

"Well, that took long enough! God, he musta' made that call two weeks ago! I've never heard of you."

"I'm new to Hayworth, Lorna. May I call you Lorna?"

"That's better than what most people call me. I'm sure you've already heard about me. I'm the one with more kids in the graveyard than at home. People say I'm jinxed and all my kids will die eventually—just the one left. Frederick Junior is my oldest."

"Lorna. I am so sorry. I would like us to meet and you can tell me your story." They schedule an appointment for the next day. When Gaby returns the phone to its cradle, she leans back in her chair and lets her gaze fall on the view outside her window. What a way to begin! A grief counselling case will be a challenge, considering she's still trying to make sense of her own loss, but she has to start somewhere.

****

Lorna appears the next day at the appointed time. Mimi alerts Gaby to her arrival and Gaby makes her way to reception. As she enters the waiting room, a quick nod from Mimi directs Gaby to her client. She appears to be quite young. She's perched in a corner chair by herself with her face focused on her lap when Gaby offers her hand. "Hi, Lorna. I'm Gaby." Her voice is soft so that anyone nearby cannot overhear. "Come with me."

Lorna gives a furtive glance around and ignores Gaby's outstretched hand. She scuttles a few steps behind, even as Gaby tries to walk beside her. She chooses a seat in the office as far away from the desk as possible. Gaby sits in a chair nearby, not returning to the desk.

"I'm glad you could make it. Can I get you coffee or tea?" Lorna shakes her head but makes no eye contact. "Your referral, from your family physician, says you need someone to talk to about the deaths of your children, and that your son might need to come in as well. Will you tell me about your children?"

Lorna looks up for the first time. "I don't know why you want to hear what everyone already knows. Three of my kids died. It was my fault. I told you on the phone, I'm jinxed." She sits hunched up in the chair, like she's cold. Although the calendar says September, she has on a heavy coat with a sweater underneath. She's dressed in jeans and runners. Her hair, long and in strings, looks like it could use a wash. Her skin is blotchy and pale. She sits with her red and raw hands in her lap. She twists her fingers one at a time, and with a force that makes Gaby wince.

"I don't want to know what everyone else knows. I want to hear your story from you, Lorna. Can you tell me your story?"

Lorna makes eye contact for the first time. "You want me to do that?"

"Yes, I do."

She leans back in her chair, as if she's making an attempt to start to relax. The coat remains on. The hair continues to obscure most of her face, and her hands continue to be tormented by the constant twisting. "I have given birth to four children in the past eight years. Frederick Junior, the oldest, is eight. The older girl would be six, now. The younger boy would be four, and the baby girl would be two." The last words are blurred by muffled gulps. "Sorry. I still cry, but I try not to."

"Crying is okay, Lorna."

"You don't know Frederick Senior. I am not to cry. He gets crazy mad and scares the boy if I cry."

"Cry here all you like."

She looks up again, a sort of sad expression of resignation in her eyes. Gaby thinks she has a way to go to gain this woman's trust.

"Three years ago, Frederick Senior took the children for a drive. I thought it was so thoughtful of him. I was a couple of months pregnant and sick as a dog all the time. It was a favour to me—to take the kids off my hands for a while—so it was my fault." She pauses, looking off into space like she's watching a movie.

"What was your fault, Lorna?"

"Why, the accident, of course." She looks incredulous. She must think Gaby is pretty stupid not to understand. "Frederick Senior took the kids for a drive. The little ones wanted to sit up front with him because it was a big deal to get to go in the car. Frederick Junior sat in the back. The kids were fooling around and he lost control. They hit the ditch and both the kids in the front were killed. It *was* my fault. I was the one with morning sickness that lasted all day. I was the one that needed a break."

"I am so sorry for your loss, Lorna, but it was a tragic accident." Gaby wonders about Mr. Koski. What kind of man would blame his wife for this?

"He told everyone it was my fault. He said I shouldn't have the baby I was pregnant with then. He said I would probably kill it, too." By now, her hands are shaking and they flame in their redness. She hunches forward, her face almost buried behind her hair. Gaby knows there's more. She's read the referral.

"Tell me about your baby girl."

"I don't know what to tell. I had her. One night I put her to bed. She was a month old—a good baby; such a little sweetie. She never cried. I went in to check on her an hour later. She was cold and blue. I called Frederick Senior. He was watching TV. I called the ambulance. I called the police. They took her away. They asked us questions all night. The boy was scared. Frederick Senior was mad as hell. They said she died of crib death, whatever that means. She was in her crib and she died. The doctor said some babies stop breathing for no reason. Some kind of syndrome, I guess. But why should that happen to my baby? He's right. It *is* my fault."

"We will talk about guilt, Lorna—yours, as well as your husband's. Thank you for telling me your story. What about Frederick Junior? How does he cope these days? Your doctor said you might want him to attend some appointments with you."

"I call him Freddie when 'he' isn't around."

"By 'he', you mean your husband?"

"Yes. Frederick Senior. When he's not around, I call my son Freddie but I'm not allowed to do that otherwise. No nicknames. Absolutely no nicknames."

She seems to parrot instructions given to her by her husband. "So, tell me a little bit about Freddie, Lorna."

"He's a good kid. He does okay in school. Frederick Senior always says he doesn't apply himself. Freddie isn't allowed to do sports because his father says he doesn't apply himself," she repeats, "and his marks would drop if he played sports. He spends a lot of time in his room. He remembers the car accident. He was five. He was a big brother. Maybe he feels guilty, too? The doctor thought that might be the problem."

"What problem?"

"Oh, he sees his brother and sisters all the time. He sees them in the car and in his room. Sometimes I find him asleep on the sofa in the living room in the morning because he says they're all in his bed. If I listen at his door, I can sometimes here him jabbering, most often to the girl that was closest in age to him." Lorna looks at Gaby while she talks about her son. "I think he's a good kid. I'm afraid he has problems, though."

"Do you ever talk together about the children who died?"

Lorna's expression is one of abject shock. "Talk? Out loud? Are you kidding? There will be no discussion of the children. Their names are never to be mentioned. We go on as a family without them. We must decide they never existed."

"Is that what your husband says, Lorna?"

"Those are the rules."

"Will you come back to see me again and bring Freddie with you? We can schedule an appointment for after school, if that works."

"If Frederick Senior says we can. Give me a time and I'll try to check with him."

"I'm happy to speak with Frederick Senior too, Lorna."

She stands and waits for Gaby to write down an appointment time. "Frederick Senior thinks talking about your problems is a waste of time. He only permitted me to come and see a counsellor because the doctor called him and insisted."

"Well, perhaps the doctor will have to insist again, but the referral was very clear about Freddie and his possible need for counselling, too."

"He won't care what the referral says, but I'll try." She reaches for the appointment slip.

"It was wonderful to meet you, Lorna." Gaby prepares to shake her hand for the second time, not confident in a response. "Don't worry, we'll work it out."

"I'm doubtful, but we can try." She lifts a rash-covered and rough hand just barely in Gaby's direction, so that Gaby must reach down in order to clasp it. With this, Gaby escorts her back to reception and enters their tentative next meeting in the master appointment book kept on Mimi's desk.

"Tough one, eh?" Mimi asks this while she remains focused on her typewriter; her voice a subtle whisper.

"Very sad, Mimi. I'll get my notes recorded for you as soon as I can." As she makes the trek back down the hall to her office, Gaby's thoughts are with the woman forbidden to use the names of her dead children.

Chapter 5

Your hands are tied

Gaby sits across from George and Rosemary Glover. She tries to keep her face devoid of expression. Rosemary has returned to their marriage counselling session after her short break to run to the washroom. What transpired after she left is the reason for Gaby's fight to keep her emotions hidden. She feels hoodwinked and doesn't think she has enough experience in this particular line of counselling to extricate herself from the quagmire created by George's private remarks.

Rosemary made the referral directly to the office almost two weeks ago. The case is one of Edith's transfers to Gaby. The background information stated that Mrs. Glover feels there are issues in the marriage and wants to get them out in the open. She said that Mr. Glover would come but she anticipated difficulties because he feels they have no problems at all.

When Gaby called to schedule a time, Rosemary started to confide in Gaby right away. "I want you to talk to him. He treats me like a housekeeper. He's never around, won't tell me where he's been half the time, and just doesn't talk!"

Gaby tried, without a lot of success, to redirect the conversation. "We will talk about all these issues when you both come in, Mrs. Glover. Marriage counselling is about your communication with your partner. We will not talk in private unless we're making or changing appointments. This is a rule I have when I work with couples. If you feel you need private sessions instead of couple counselling, we can arrange that."

"Oh, no, no! This is what I want, but you need to understand how I feel so you can tell George. He doesn't listen to me."

Gaby made another stab at explaining the process. "The primary task will be for you to communicate your concerns to your husband, Mrs. Glover. My role is to help you do that. I also have an obligation to help your husband communicate with you. We'll make it all work. You'll see."

After she reaffirmed the time and finally signed off, Gaby wasn't convinced she would be able to facilitate any mediation with this couple. One won't talk at all while the other seems to want her concerns expressed for her.

The introductions started off well enough. They encouraged one another to use first names, and the atmosphere in Gaby's office went from horribly tense to slightly uncomfortable during the initial fifteen minutes or so. George Glover described himself as an accountant. Rosemary told Gaby she was a secretary at a law firm. When each responded to the question about how they met, Gaby heard two entirely different responses.

"We're locals. We met in high school. I went away to university. One time Rosemary, here, came to visit me and ended up pregnant. I guess that's the way life happens. We were married. I finished my degree while she lived with her folks. I did right by her. Her parents had lots of money and a big house, so we never left. Rosemary took care of both of them and when they died, we inherited the place. Now she goes out to work which isn't necessary, but if that's what she wants...." While describing their twenty-five years together, he didn't so much as cast a glance at Rosemary, whose head was turned and tilted. She watched him with a soft, and what looked like tender, expression.

"Now, George." She patted his Oxford-cloth shirted arm. "We were so in love. Mom and Dad helped us so much. I was terribly grateful to them...and you were, too. Don't deny it. They offered to buy us our own home and we said 'no', we were happy to live with them. Before she became ill, Mom was a big help with the children. My parents were both sick at almost the same time. Dad had dementia and Mom had bowel cancer. Life was pretty rough." She looked at George and patted his arm again. His hands were clasped and hung between his knees. "George doesn't have much of a stomach for illness. I always managed the kids." Her expression was indulgent. "And he's a typical man—a difficult patient himself."

After some additional reflection on their life together, Gaby fielded the question that referenced the referral. "So what happened to result in a referral?

Rosemary, you go first this time."

Rosemary smoothed her navy blue pleated skirt that didn't require the attention. "We don't talk much. Now that the kids are away and my parents are gone, we need to talk more. I feel as if I looked up from all my responsibilities with my parents and the children to discover he had started another life. He works long hours. I understand that, but I need him to know how important it is to include me in his world."

"Have you told him that?" George was still focused on the floor, and glanced up at Gaby when she asked the question of his wife.

"My God! He must know that! We've raised two children and gone through the death of both my parents. There must be more to our life together than the odd visit out to the farm to visit with his father."

"Tell your husband, Rosemary." Gaby's voice was quiet but emphatic. "Communication involves the act of speaking directly to one another."

Rosemary hesitated but turned to George, who was reluctant to meet her eyes. "I want us to be more involved now, honey. The heavy lifting is over. The kids are doing well. I fulfilled all my promises to my parents. We have some money in the bank and no debt. Can't we spend more time together? Can't we take some vacations, just the two of us?" She looked back at Gaby, tears running down her face.

"George, tell Rosemary what you think about her concerns."

He turned to his wife, but looked past her toward the wall. His voice was flat, monotone and defeatist. "Whatever you want, Rosie. We can go on vacation if that will make you happy."

Rosemary stood. "What would make me happy is for you to want to spend time with me and talk to me. That's what would make me happy." She redirected her attention to Gaby. "I need to visit the washroom—out by reception, right? Didn't I see it there on the way in?"

Gaby nodded, although concerned about Rosemary's departure from the room at this particular juncture. It made her wonder if there might be more to the situation.

The silence, still heavy with Rosemary's tears and anxiety, was broken by George's rumbled murmurs. "Miss, I want you to know this—while she's gone. You can't tell her. This is in confidence, right?"

Gaby repeated the point she emphasized earlier. "I'm quite serious, George. I don't want you to speak about your wife or your relationship without her present. Tell me about your work. You're an accountant, right?"

"I've been involved with my secretary at work for over five years. She's divorced and her husband is obliged to pay support as long as she's single. Rosemary inherited a shit-load of money from her parents, and because of Alberta property laws, I wouldn't see a cent of it if we divorced." He's still bent over with his hands clutched between his knees, but he made eye contact for the first time. "I love my girlfriend. We have a great relationship. I don't want it to change and neither does she. The one reason I came here today was to see if you could pacify Rosemary. She thinks that since the kids are finally out of the house...." His voice faded as the door opened and his wife slipped back into the office.

****

Later that week, Gaby finds a minute to have a consultation with Pearl. "I need to bounce an idea around," she offers, after tapping on the edge of the open door permitting a clear view into the office of her supervisor.

Pearl is bunkered behind her cluttered desk. She looks up as she brushes sandwich crumbs from her pink sweater, and grey-streaked hair from her weather-beaten face. "Come on in," she bellows although Gaby isn't more than fifteen feet away. "What's on your mind? Work going okay?"

"Fine, I think." Gaby hesitates before she begins. The story of Mr. and Mrs. Glover is complicated. She doesn't often take her work home, because she learned years ago that if you permit that to happen, you'll burn out in no time. The Glovers have proven difficult to leave at the office. Gaby needs to know the best approach, as seen by someone with significantly more experience in the field of marriage counselling. "I think I should discuss a particular case with you. I need your thoughts—and maybe your guidance." Gaby takes the seat across from Pearl. She smoothes her charcoal cotton pants and adjusts her white blouse. The silk has a habit of drifting away from centre if she doesn't keep an eye on the buttons.

"Shoot." Pearl cups her chin in her hands and rests her elbows on the desk. "Do we need tea or can we manage without?" She has a "tell me everything" look. Gaby knows her boss is attempting to make her feel comfortable.

She begins. She explains her feelings about trying to assist a couple with their marriage when the husband has already stated in plain, albeit confidential, language that he has no intention of changing his current arrangement with his girlfriend. "I don't know what to do. They've scheduled another appointment, but it all seems like a sham to me." She knows her frustration escapes through the tone in her voice.

Pearl moves her hands down to her desk, clasps them together, and leans across toward Gaby. "I expect you won't have to do much, Gaby. They might come to a couple of appointments, but they'll give up on the process in no time. Your hands are tied. Both people have to be motivated. You know that. My guess would be that Mrs. will get fed up with the lack of progress and stop scheduling the appointments. Seen it before; will see it again. Remember, we don't fix people. We don't tell people what to do."

Gaby can't help herself. "The exception is the kid who kept throwing up on the school bus—the referral Frank gave me. Her name is Julia. I told her to stop it. I said she could come and talk with me every week, but she had to stop hurling on the bus. She was in yesterday and told me she's gone a whole week without puking. Now, we will try to find out what the real problem is and how we can address that. I like her. She's a nice girl."

"Exception proves the rule, I guess, but don't worry about this couple. They'll sort themselves out, for better or worse. Let's go scare up some tea. I'm exhausted. We were cattle branding all weekend and I'm still not back to rights—might actually be too old for this ranching business, I guess."

****

"Want a colour TV?" Gaby swivels in her chair to see Elliot Banks leaning against the door frame.

"Come in, Elliot. Do I want a TV? What are you talking about?" Gaby has a small TV—a black and white ancient contraption with bunny ears, poor reception, and two channels. She has not bothered to invest in cable because it would necessitate a new TV, which isn't one of her priorities right now.

Elliot Banks is about thirty-five years old. He's a tall man with wavy blond hair just starting to flash silver in the right light. He's very attractive and an exercise fanatic, having been an avid football player in university. He often talks about his home gym and about how he runs three times a week. He wears golf or polo shirts that highlight his arms and chest. "My wife tells me that our bedroom will contain either me or the TV by tonight. The TV's in the car and I thought you might like it. It's a pretty good size and practically new."

Gaby giggles. "This puts a new spin on marriage counselling, Elliot. You're telling me if I take a colour TV off your hands, this will save your marriage?" She tries to suppress another giggle but without much success.

He sighs. This is the typical Elliot-sigh that Gaby has grown accustomed to hearing. It can drown out conversations in the staff room or in a meeting. There have been times when Gaby has needed to ask to have a piece of information repeated because Elliot sighed and she missed part of a sentence. "Go ahead and mock me, but I can't take it home, Gaby." His head hangs down, like it often does when he talks.

The thought crosses her mind that Elliot may well be depressed. This TV could be a symptom of his troubled relationship. She knows few details about him or about his wife. They've been married for a number of years, do not have any children, and have been in the area for a decade. "Happy to take it off your hands. Can I pay you for it?"

"No chance! Are you done right at the end of the day? I'll deliver it over to your place."

"You can put it in the back of the truck after work, Elliot. I can take it home. No need for you to deliver."

"You could never carry it by yourself. I'll take care of it. Have you a space for it?"

"Yes. I have a sideboard in the living room. That will do for now. The wire where the previous tenants had cable is right behind. Pretty convenient, eh? I'll pop my head into your office when I'm ready to leave, how's that?"

He turns toward his office, emitting another huge expulsion of air. "I can't thank you enough, Gaby. You've helped me a lot." Head bowed and broad shoulders slumped, she watches his muscular back make its way down the corridor.

****

Gaby refocuses her attention on the Dictaphone one more time. She always tries to honour the initial commitment she made to herself—get her dictation caught up so she can go home for the weekend and have no loose ends held over until Monday. She knows she's somewhat obsessive, but it's a standard she's determined to at least try and maintain. Her internal phone line lights up.

"Hi there." She knows it has to be someone on staff.

"Gaby, it's Mimi. Are you busy tonight?"

"No, Mimi. What can I do for you?"

"I don't know. Can I come by after supper and talk over a concern with you. My husband will be at his parents' place for the evening and I thought I'd take the opportunity."

"Come for supper, Mimi. I'll stir up some vegetables and make some rice. It won't be fancy." She finds herself feeling enthusiastic. "We'll have a girls' night."

"Thanks, Gaby. I have dessert covered. There's a crisp in the freezer. Tim will never miss it."

"Okay, see you after work. Elliot intends to stop by for a few minutes to drop off a TV—long story—but come by anytime after 5:30 PM. I should be organized by then."

After she hangs up the phone, Gaby shuts her door with a quiet click. There's an unwritten rule around the office that a closed door means "do not disturb", and she wants to make the best use of her time before the end of the day. An open door is too compelling for Edith, especially, who insists on case-conferencing every new referral with Gaby.

Company for supper—a real social engagement!

****

Gaby leaps through the living room and flings open the screen door as Elliot, balancing a television that looks far bigger than he described earlier, starts to lean against the porch wall for support. "Hi. Put it right over here." She's cleared the buffet and covered it with a runner. "I can understand why your wife didn't want to share bedroom real estate with this! It's a monster!"

Elliot gives her a grimace-laced sigh as the back of the television presses into his broad chest. "I don't think it would matter what size it is, Gaby. No more watching sports highlights in bed. That's the bottom line. Let me plug it in and make sure it works. You don't have cable, right?"

Gaby nods.

"Well, no problem. I brought the ears and they pull in a couple of channels. Are you going to get cable?"

"Why? Want to watch the sports highlights with me instead of Celina?" Gaby chortles, but realizes Elliot thinks she's serious. "I'm kidding! I don't know about the cable. I imagine it would be good in the winter. We'll see."

By now, he has the television up and running. The colour is passable, although perhaps a bit pink around the edges. Maybe cable would be a nice treat. As he turns to leave, Mimi appears on the other side of the screen door.

"Hi, you two. Big TV, Gaby. It makes a décor statement." Gaby opens the door and she walks through to the kitchen balancing her casserole dish filled with some variant of a crisp, as Gaby thanks Elliot yet again and they say good night.

Gaby ensures Mimi is settled at the kitchen table with a glass of wine, and begins to concoct a stir fry for their supper. She looks so much different from when she's at work. At work, Mimi wears her hair pulled back from her face in a tight bun or a pony tail. She wears dark-rimmed glasses. Her wardrobe consists of longish, shapeless skirts and pullover sweaters. She wears no jewellery except her wedding band. Right now, she sports no glasses at all. Her long and straight brown hair hangs down around her face. She has on what can only be described as a fluffy white blouse and very tight blue jeans with wide, flared bottoms. She has a ring on every finger and big hoops in her ears.

"Contacts?" Gaby asks the question.

"I know I look a lot different when I'm not at the Hexagon. This is more me, but I was told I was a little too 'bold' for the work place. When I applied for this job, I thought I'd try to be more reserved. Yes, I'm wearing contacts." She smiles over the rim of a wine glass now almost empty.

"Well, I think you look great. How a person dresses shouldn't relate to how their work is judged."

"That's a great philosophy if anybody followed it." She cracks up at this point. "I don't think Elliot even recognized me. The last time he saw me like myself was at the Christmas party. He didn't come to the summer barbecue." She slaps her hand on her knee. "You know, I really don't think he knew who I was!"

"So...what did you want to talk about, Mimi?" Gaby sets two plates of rice and stir fried vegetables down in front of them. She refreshes both wine glasses and sits across from her friend.

"I want to have a baby, but I don't want to go out and live with Tim's parents at the farm. It's a complicated story. When his folks retire, they want us to take over. That won't be for years yet, unless somebody gets sick or dies or whatever." She munches away for a minute and then comments on how good the food is. "Tim wants to quit his job. He works as the produce manager down at the grocery store. He expects me to leave work, too, and then both of us would go live at the farm. He says I can have all the babies I want, but he wants me to stay home with them—home will be his parents' place." She stops to take a breath and another bite.

"Did you two discuss all this before you were married? When did you get married anyway, Mimi?"

"We've been married two years, and no—the one real discussion was that we would take over the farm and that we both wanted kids. None of that's changed, but I don't want having kids to be based on me leaving work for good and living out at the farm."

"How far away are Tim's parents?"

"Oh, not far—twenty minutes, tops. Tim's an only child and he helps out. My father-in-law farms wheat and canola so this is a busy time of year. He hires extra help, but he feels better if Tim is there with him. I don't mind. Tim has the heart of a farmer. I've always known that. I can hardly wait for you to meet him. You'll like him. He's a nice person." She pours herself a little more wine. "But that doesn't help my problem. I want to have a baby but I don't want to quit work."

"What does your mother-in-law say?"

"Tim's mother? I think she hoped I was pregnant before we were married!" Mimi guffaws. "She said she'd move to town if it meant she'd see more of her grandchildren."

"So maybe Mrs. Long has the key to a solution, Mimi."

Her friend looks back across the kitchen as she loads portions of her apple crisp into bowls Gaby has laid out for the purpose. Her eyes narrow. "We could move to the farm and I could go back to work if I wanted, while Lorraine takes care of the baby. Is that your solution?"

"No, Mimi, but it might very well be yours."

Chapter 6

Everyone knows this is your truck

"Gaby, there's someone here at the front desk who wants to pop down to see you for a minute. Shall I send her down?"

Gaby is focused on paperwork. She has no appointments scheduled today and her intention was to catch up on all the forms she needs to compile, and review a couple of new cases to be scheduled. "Who is it, Mimi?"

"Cheryl Nadler from Adoptions Division. She says she has a referral, and you're up."

"Okay, send her down. If the referral is appropriate, I'll do the introductory paperwork from here, Mimi. I'll let you know." Gaby has never met Cheryl but has oftentimes seen her in communal hallways. She spends very little time in the staff room so she must take her breaks and have her lunch at her desk.

Before assumptions can get ahead of her, a petite brunette knocks on the door frame. Gaby stands up and approaches the social worker. "Hi, I'm Gaby Ridgway. I hear you might have a referral." Gaby smiles, a natural and honest smile, as she extends her hand.

Cheryl smiles back—a reserved, professional version, or so it seems to Gaby. She responds to the extended hand with a measure of hesitation. "I'm Cheryl Nadler from Adoptions Division. Yes, I think I might have a referral for you. I've heard, via the grapevine, that you quite like to work with young women. This gal is at Segue House. Ava Burrway called me. She said the client is reluctant and someone might have to make a visit to meet her. She can't stay there forever."

"What's her name?" Gaby reaches for a referral form. She has already contacted a client there—a woman who may want to surrender her children until she can get back on her feet. That case has been referred over to Cheryl's neck of the woods, although Gaby hopes to continue to see the mother. She has always favoured team work.

"Valerie York. She's thirty and housed at the shelter right now because she feels her husband has cheated. She wants to leave him but seems to have nowhere to go."

"I have another client there, but I've never been in the place—only talked to the director on the phone. Don't they have their own counsellor?"

"Not yet. I'm sure Ava would love to hire somebody, but fundraising is always an issue." Cheryl is dressed in soft slacks that appear to be totally wrinkle-resistant. She crosses one scrupulously pressed black pant leg over the other. She's relaxing. Her matching silver and black striped sweater fits to perfection and sits on her shoulders with exacting precision. "Ava's goal is to encourage clients to move forward and make decisions, but she doesn't do the long-term relationship counselling process that you do. How about I give her a call and we can pop over this afternoon, if you can carve out some time? You can get the tour." She smiles as she starts to make her departure. This time it seems more open and honest. "I expect we'll do more work together, anyway. I received your referral for the resident at Segue who wants to explore temporary surrender."

About twenty minutes later, Cheryl calls Gaby's direct line. "I have an appointment for us at Segue House to meet with Ava at 2:00 PM. Does that work for you?"

"No problem, Cheryl. My truck is in the parking lot, so meet me at the front and we can go together."

Arrangements made, Gaby lets Mimi know her schedule. She looks forward to spending more time with Cheryl, although she feels akin to an unmade bed when in the other woman's presence. Every hair and every seam is perfect with that girl. Gaby wonders if her dark locks even move when confronted with the wind. Cheryl has all those attributes that Gaby feels she missed out on—petite with a nice figure, controllable hair, perfect skin. Instead, Gaby makes do with her scrawny frame and tube-like figure, her thin hair, and her skin that requires constant attention to avoid the inevitable break-outs she has suffered since her teens.

****

At the appointed time, Gaby sees no sign of Cheryl in the central reception area of the Hexagon. She trots down the hallway reserved for Adoption Services, but Cheryl's door is closed. After she looks around for a minute or two, she decides to go out to her truck, although she doesn't think Cheryl would be around because she doesn't know which vehicle belongs to Gaby. Of course, in small town Hayworth, everybody probably knows her little black Mazda truck and she realizes the power of this phenomenon when she catches a glimpse of Cheryl as she stands with stoic determination beside the passenger door. From a distance, she looks like a statue with her black slacks and her matching sweater now covered with a light fall jacket. Her purse hangs off her shoulder.

"I'm not late! I ran all over the office looking for you! How did you know this was my truck?"

Cheryl's face remains expressionless. "Everyone knows this is your truck, Gaby. I don't want to be late."

Suitably admonished, Gaby hastens to unlock the passenger door and then circles the box to the driver's side. She starts the truck and whips it around and out of the parking lot in short order.

"Do you know where to go?" Cheryl stares directly ahead and doesn't turn to speak to Gaby.

"Yes. I asked Mimi for directions earlier, after we talked. Wanted to make sure I knew the lay of the land." Her responses are hesitant. She feels nervous around this seemingly perfect creature seated beside her.

The drive only takes a couple of minutes before they pull up in front of a nondescript six unit apartment building located at the edge of an older residential area, not far from Gaby's rental. The building has no signage, but sports a chain link fence all the way around. The gate is there, but anyone can enter. When they reach the door in the front, Gaby can see actual attempts at security. The standard plate glass entry door that would come with a building such as this has been replaced with a steel door. There is a bell and an intercom.

Cheryl rings the bell and soon they hear the crackle from inside. "Yes?"

"Cheryl Nadler and Gaby Ridgway, Ava."

"Come on in." The buzzer sounds and Cheryl turns the knob on the door.

Once inside the glass vestibule and suitably identified, they are admitted into the building proper. Gaby finds herself in an open lobby with what looks like two apartments, one on either side. There are stairs that lead down to the basement and stairs going up to at least two more levels. Ava Burrway stands on the institutional green linoleum tile floor and waits for them. She is a tall woman, in a black pantsuit with a red scarf tied loosely around her neck. She would have to be considered plain with her short brown hair and features beginning the telltale sagging of a woman nearing fifty.

"Hi, Ava. This is Gaby Ridgway from Counselling Division. She's here to meet Valerie York and to set up an appointment with her...later this week?" She turns to look at Gaby who shakes Ava's hand.

"Nice to meet you. This is quite the place. Yes. I can see Valerie tomorrow morning, if she wants to come by the office."

"Come in and talk to me first, you two." Ava waits until her private office door is closed. There appears to be no other staff. "I hope Valerie will see you, Gaby. I've broken every rule in the book by letting her stay here. She isn't escaping any kind of acrimony at home. She doesn't want to stay with her husband. You can look at my file, although I haven't had time to write many notes—or you can judge for yourself after you talk to her."

"Do you still not have any help?" Cheryl looks around like she might start to clean floors and tidy counters. Gaby sees her eyes dart over the papers piled on Ava's desk, and the waste basket that overflows in the corner.

"Waiting on a grant. How do they expect me to keep up to four apartments with women and their children, organize building maintenance, do counselling, and then do paperwork? Isn't it convenient that I have no private life?" She is sad, defeatist. She looks like she has the burdens of the world stacked on her shoulders.

Gaby reflects that she could well have that same look one day. Now that she feels settled in the community, it's time to make a more concerted effort to develop friendships and interests away from work.

"Do you two want coffee or tea? It would only take a minute." Gaby had taken a quick peek at the kitchen in this apartment as they rounded the corner to the master bedroom Ava uses as her office. It looked pretty chaotic.

"Goodness, no!" Cheryl jumps at the opportunity to refuse. "Gaby, Valerie is upstairs in the apartment to the right. I think she expects you." She looks at Ava for confirmation.

"Yes, go ahead. I told Valerie someone would visit, but she doesn't know your name or any details. You can leave the office door open on your way out."

Gaby accepts instructions from her two more experienced colleagues, and leaves the director's unit to return to the lobby. The stairs need a sweep and the lighting isn't great as she makes her way to the apartment where Valerie has been holed up for almost a month. She knocks on the door, which is opened by a woman Gaby assumes is not Valerie. "Hi there. I'm looking for Valerie York."

"That's me." The woman moves her cigarette from one hand to the other and pulls the door wider. "You must be the counsellor Ava said would come over."

Gaby hides her shock. This woman looks forty, or maybe older. Her file clearly stated her age as thirty. She is emaciated and unkempt. Her very long and dyed black hair is a massive tangle of curls that fly in all directions. Her skin appears leathery and is deeply lined. Her teeth are yellow. She is dressed in skin-tight blue jeans and a burgundy man's cardigan over a loose-fitting T-shirt. The pockets in the sweater appear weighted down with keys, cigarettes, and probably a lighter. "Yes. I'm Gaby, Gaby Ridgway from Counselling Division over at the provincial building. They said you might like to talk to someone about your current situation, Valerie."

"I think they want me to get my act together and go home. Nobody's hit me, so I don't fit the profile of a client who should be here, right?" She says all this while she hunts down an overflowing jar lid to deposit the ashes she's flicked into the palm of her hand.

Gaby looks around the apartment—a two bedroom, one bathroom unit with a windowless galley kitchen and an open living room and dinette. Furnishings are sparse and all look like they came from a junk shop. The floors are linoleum like downstairs, but in basic beige instead of institutional green. The walls are white and liberally smudged. There are no lamps; just ceiling fixtures. Gaby expects the place is quite stark in the evenings. "Ava thinks the time has come for you to make a plan of some sort. I'm happy to help you, if you like." She ploughs on, not sure if this woman is even interested enough to make the effort to resolve her circumstances. "I have an appointment available tomorrow morning. Will you pop over to the Hexagon so we can have a visit?"

Valerie utilizes the lit end of her smoke in one hand to light a fresh cigarette held in the other. Her nails and fingers are heavily nicotine-stained, a condition Gaby has rarely seen on a woman before. Her sigh is heavy. The air rattles a bit as it departs her lungs. "Sure. Why not? You came all the way here to meet me. The least I can do is come to one appointment."

Gaby does not miss the inference. One appointment. Okay, if that's what she wants. "Tomorrow at 11:00 AM. When you come in the building, ask them at reception for me, and they'll call. I'll come to get you." She makes a valiant attempt to get up off the navy floral patterned sofa that feels like it sits flat on the floor without the benefit of legs. It isn't graceful.

"That sofa's a bitch. I never sit there. Sorry. I should have told you."

Cheryl and Ava are standing together in the foyer when Gaby comes back downstairs. "I thought I would have to send out a search party, Gaby. You weren't supposed to have a session, just meet her and see if she agreed." Cheryl's voice is a cross between a hiss and a whisper.

"I had to sit for a minute and try to connect with her, Cheryl." Gaby whispers back, but has trouble controlling the annoyance in her voice. She turns to Ava and, in a normal voice says, "We have an appointment for tomorrow morning, Ava. We'll see where it takes us."

Once outside, Cheryl starts to brush at her black trousers with an intensity that would suggest they were covered with cat hair or worse. They seem spotless to Gaby. "I'll be so glad to get home and have a shower. There's never enough hot water, but there you have it." On the drive back to the Hexagon in Gaby's truck, Cheryl spends her time running her finger, protected by a tissue, around the door and window handles. She gives Gaby the dusty tissue when she gets out.

✱✱✱✱

Valerie York, dressed in the same jeans and burgundy sweater she wore yesterday, sits across the room from Gaby. She is sullen. Gaby can sense her resentment. She rolls her office chair toward her client and leans forward as she speaks. "I'm very happy you made it, Valerie. How about you tell me a little about yourself and how you ended up as a guest at Segue House."

Valerie drags a clutch of black, unwashed curls, behind her ear and crosses one leg over the other so her left ankle rests just above her right knee. "Can I smoke?"

Gaby offers her an ashtray. In her two months on the job, it has never been used before. Clients seem to notice she doesn't smoke and so they don't ask. There are a lot of smokers in the building, though, so Gaby accepts this general state of affairs.

"Albert. He prefers Al. He's my husband. He's a truck driver. I think he sleeps with a different girl in every town where he stays over. He says he stays in the sleeper behind his cab but I don't think so. When he came home last week, I cleaned his truck and found a piece of paper on the floor with a phone number." Valerie's face has turned a rosy shade and she puffs on her cigarette like she'll never be permitted to smoke another. "I called the number and it belongs to some girl outside of Edmonton. I asked her if she knew Al and she said she's served him a couple of times at the Husky Oil truck stop restaurant where she works. I asked how he managed to get her number and she said she gave it to him; that he's cute! I asked if she knew he was married and she said that guys on the road are never married when they're away from home. Al told me he took the number because she gave it to him, and the reason I found it on the floor of the truck was because he missed when he tossed it into the garbage bag. Do you believe that?" She's breathless as she finishes dumping her issue into Gaby's lap.

"I think what you believe is most important, Valerie. Tell me about you and Al—how you met, your wedding."

"I first met him at a diner down south—kinda' like this broad I talked to on the phone—but he wasn't married. He told me he owned a nice house here at his base in Hayworth and invited me up. I never left. We got married about five years ago." The look on her face is wistful. She peers though a smoky haze at Gaby. "I suppose you think I'm worried this girl will act like I did—meet a guy at a truck stop and go home with him?"

"Tell me about Al, the person. What's he like?"

"He's a good guy, you know. I liked him from the minute I poured him a cup of coffee. He's respectful. He never yells or gets mad at me. I spend a lot of time alone. He calls before I go to bed. He trusts me, I guess."

"What makes you think that?"

"He's never once suggested I might see somebody on the side while he's away."

"What does it feel like to be trusted?"

Valerie leans back in the chair, uncrosses her legs, and stubs out her cigarette. "That's a funny question. What does it feel like to be trusted? Safe,

I guess. Safe in the idea that Al and I are good. He goes away and doesn't worry what I'm up to because he knows I wouldn't cheat. It feels good." She looks across at Gaby and her eyes begin to twinkle. "I know what your point is. You want me to feel bad that I don't trust Al. You want me to think of all his good qualities and remind myself why I liked him in the first place. Right?"

"No one comes to counselling with a goal to feel bad, Valerie. Having a look at the other side of a relationship is helpful, though."

"Well, I see the other side and now I feel bad." She nods as she says this and Gaby is pretty sure they have made a break-through.

"Are you interested in inviting Al to come in for a session with us when he's in town?"

"He gets home tomorrow night. I'll call and ask him. Do you think Ava will mind if I stay over there for a few more days?"

"Ask her. Maybe you can tell her what's on your mind."

"Will you call her?"

"Nope. I don't want your permission to talk to the director at Segue House because you are quite capable. You don't need me to run interference. You call me once you have Al's schedule and we can set up a meeting for the three of us."

Chapter 7

There will no doubt be changes

By the spring of 1979, Gaby has managed to settle herself into the rhythm of small town life in the north. Her friends, acquaintances, and associates are, by and large, those people with whom she works. Mimi has become her closest confidante. She attends all the staff parties, and has managed to carve out a small professional niche for herself. Certain referrals ask for her specifically now, and she has earned a reputation as someone who is frank and nonjudgmental. Her vacations consist of trips to her sister's. She likes to cover over Christmas, so her colleagues with family in the vicinity can take advantage of days off between Christmas and the New Year. She spends three weeks at Nina's every summer. She's managed to save a considerable sum, and finds herself tossing around the idea of home ownership once again.

Today, there is a staff meeting scheduled for 9:00 AM sharp. She dresses with care, choosing navy linen pants and a bulky grey sweater she knit over last winter. After many futile attempts made to hold her fine hair up with a jewel-encrusted clip designed for someone with much more abundant locks, she settles on the simple approach and tucks her curls behind her ears.

Dr. Alden, rarely seen outside his office, will attend the meeting. There must be an issue requiring his presence, and everyone has been on tender hooks all week. Gaby suspects there will be new rules related to how the office paperwork is to be completed. The Alberta Department of Health and Welfare has been called to task by the provincial auditor for poor documentation, so someone has to pay the price. Gaby has a very strong suspicion it will be them. Similar situations are happening in all the divisions. There will no doubt be changes. On top of this, she has a new referral to meet in the afternoon.

She trots through her kitchen and into the living room, stopping to grab her jacket hung on the coat tree by the front door. She moved the watercolour of the house to the wall by the entry some time ago. She smiles at the image as if nodding goodbye to a dear friend, and jogs down the porch steps toward her truck.

****

Gaby acknowledges Mimi as she manoeuvres her way through reception. "Big day, today, eh Mimi?"

"God only knows... 'cause nobody tells me nuthin'!" Mimi grins at Gaby. "See you in a few minutes."

Edith follows Gaby into her office and sits down in one of the client chairs, breathless, before Gaby has a chance to take off her coat or say "Good Morning".

"What do you suppose this is all about? Dr. Alden never comes to meetings! Maybe there will be cutbacks. Do you think that could be it?"

"If it is, then you don't have to worry, Edith." Gaby can't keep the irony out of her voice. "Last man in, first man out. That would be me, you know—not you."

Edith doesn't listen. "We might be forced to take on bigger caseloads! Maybe they'll close down the Mental Health Division and we'll have to take all their files! Oh my God, I can't do any more than what I do now! I'm swamped all the time! You know that!" She looks at Gaby through thick glasses. Her pant suit is dishevelled and her hair sticks out in all directions because she continues to drag her fingers through it.

"I know, Edith. Everybody has big caseloads. Everybody tries their best to manage."

"You never have any problems. I don't know what it is."

"I'm an organized person. We've talked about that before. It bugs me if I'm forced to use my time for search and rescue missions in my office, or in wondering what's on my schedule. I'm organized, Edith, plain and simple." All the while Gaby talks, Edith fidgets and appears not to hear a word.

Once Gaby has her day planner out and her files stacked on her desk, she turns to face her co-worker. "Let's go get some coffee so we can be in the staff room in good time. I need a coffee and you, my dear, need to relax. We can't worry until we hear what he has to say." She pats Edith on the knee. "Come on, let's go."

****

When they finally enter the meeting room, as it has taken considerable time for Edith to find her mug and make her tea, Pearl is already there. She isn't seated at the head of the table, but rather one seat to the right. Pearl is absolutely never the first person at a meeting, although she's always the one who calls them. This must be serious.

"Hi, Pearl. You look all bright-eyed and bushy-tailed this morning." Gaby attempts an injection of joviality to no avail. Pearl barely looks up from her notes as she grunts "Good Morning" at both women. Gaby sits at the far end of the table from Pearl, on the opposite side, so she will have a good view of the proceedings. This has become a habit of hers over the past twenty-two months. She left her knitting at home on purpose today. Gaby likes to knit in meetings. It soothes her. She is less likely to get caught up in much of the anxiety and chaos that invariably occurs as staff resist change, and exhibit their anger and anxiousness over all the typical government office politics. Although she misses the distraction, she felt this might be the day to avoid sticking out. Edith snuggles in beside her.

Elliot and Frank arrive together and hover at the door. The reason why becomes apparent when Dr. Alden, a single piece of paper in his hand, appears behind and pushes past them to the seat at the head of the table. The two men wait for Mimi before they seat themselves. Mimi gives Gaby a wide-eyed look from over the top of her glasses, which always slip down her nose. She drops into the chair to the left of Dr. Alden and places her notepad and two pens, with precision, in front of her. Elliot and Frank, with little grace and less organization, finally settle into the two chairs on the opposite side from Gaby and Edith. The room is small and without windows. Gaby feels a little flushed already, and the meeting has not even been called to order.

"So, are we all here?" Clark Alden looks around the room, reaches for the ashtray, and turns to Pearl.

Pearl is red in the face; flustered in Gaby's opinion. *Good God. Are they closing the place down? Maybe buying a house isn't such a good idea after all.* Gaby now wishes she had her knitting. Dr. Alden lights a cigarette.

"Dr. Alden is here today because he has some information to deliver from the Department of Health and Social Welfare. It covers all the divisions here at the Hexagon, so he is meeting with each group separately. Dr. Alden?"

As he sucks on his cigarette, he examines his perfectly manicured, although yellowed, nails and begins. "The Department of Health and Social Welfare will conduct audits of all divisions over the next six months. The priority is to reorganize as mental health institutions throughout the province are gradually down-sized and patients are integrated back into the community. As a result, the caseloads of those in the Mental Health Division will expand and other workers will have to absorb some of the overflow. There are many cases currently held by the Mental Health Division that could be managed by the Counselling Division." He reads all this from the piece of paper in front of him.

Edith raises her hand and coughs, in an attempt to interrupt with the beginning of a question. "Edith, let me finish and then I'll try and answer your questions. Furthermore," he continues, "we have never been vigilant about our documentation and that must change." He glances over at Pearl. "Pearl will provide you with a standard format, and a form which must be filled in each time you meet with a client. It details the reason for the session, what you did, etcetera, etcetera." He waves his cigarette back and forth toward both sides of the table. "In addition, Pearl will conduct performance appraisals on each of you. Your caseloads will, no doubt, expand. Our expectations as they relate to record keeping are being raised, and we want each of you to know clearly where you stand." He turns, almost reluctantly, toward Edith. "Now, I will try and answer a few questions. Edith?"

Gaby's co-worker gulps for air. She is red in the face and fidgety. Her voice whines as she attempts to formulate her question. "Will there be cutbacks? Job loses?"

Dr. Alden frowns and looks around the room. "I think I made myself clear. Caseloads will no doubt increase for this division. We will expect more from you and your work must be documented. I don't think we will get additional staff, but I am sure we won't see job losses. Are there any other questions?"

Edith jumps to the bait for a second time. "Dr. Alden, I don't know how I can see more people than the ones I see right now. I'm run off my feet.

Everyone knows that." She looks around the room for confirmation. Gaby is aware she has the smallest caseload; that she transfers any and all files where she feels the least bit out of her depth. She remains quiet.

Frank asks if he can make a comment and Dr. Alden nods. "In this line of work, I feel the client is more important than the paperwork. God knows how much work I do. Nobody complains."

Pearl interjects. "Frank, you rarely give a file to Mimi for typing. Your record drawer is filled with notes attached to files with paper clips. I don't like paperwork anymore than you do, and everybody here knows it, but times are changing. The government requires good records to prove we are actually doing our jobs. If anybody ever wanted to take you to court, where would you be?"

Elliot sighs—the kind of sigh that could probably be heard by someone passing in the hallway. Gaby tries to send a look of support his way, but he's focused on the table.

She is startled when Dr. Alden turns his attention toward her. "Gaby, what are your thoughts? You haven't made a comment."

She attempts to inject some levity into the situation once again. "I wish I had my knitting here so I could relax. This is all very intense, but as for record keeping, I was trained in the school system and records were important because we talked to people's children. I have no problem with record keeping. Larger caseloads are always a challenge, but I'm pleased to hear there won't be any down-sizing. I'm the last man on the ladder, as it were." She casts her gaze around at everyone in the room.

"Well, if that's all, I have two more meetings today and another three tomorrow. Please try to keep the information exchanged here confidential until I have had a chance to meet with all divisions." With this, Dr. Alden pushes back his chair and sidles his way behind Elliot and Frank as he takes his leave.

Once the door is closed, with the exception of Mimi and Gaby, everyone starts to talk at once.

"I can't take more referrals. I'm swamped!"

"Paperwork takes away from time with clients."

"How am I supposed to prove I do a decent job? How can you possibly appraise my performance?" Elliot looks straight at Pearl, who is instructing Mimi about the minutes of the meeting.

She turns toward him. "Don't panic. We'll work on this together. Mimi will have your file forms to you tomorrow and I am waiting for a performance appraisal guide from the department. When I get it, you can each have a copy so you'll know exactly what's expected, the same as me. For your information, Dr. A. has to do one on me, too. I have one more division meeting today and then one tomorrow. So we all have pressures." She attempts a smile for the first time since the meeting started. "Okay, folks, meeting adjourned. Go get some coffee. Remember, no public discussions until day's end tomorrow."

On her way back to her office, Gaby watches as Edith, Frank, and Elliot all pile into Frank's office and close the door. Right now she doesn't care if she's odd man out. She has a family to see. She thinks this will be the first of many mental health-related referrals.

****

Mimi leads the way as Ivan and Iona Baranski follow her down the hall to Gaby's office. They have left their eighteen-year-old daughter, Audrey, in reception. Mimi gives Gaby a "look". Gaby understands this must be the way the parents wanted their session with her to start.

Gaby seats them in her office and, as is her custom, rolls her office chair away from her desk and over closer to her clients. She proffers her hand. "I'm Gaby Ridgway. Please call me Gaby."

"Ivan. Ivan Baranski." His big paw grabs Gaby's hand and swallows it almost up to her wrist.

"I am Iona, Audrey's mother." She reaches for Gaby's hand but doesn't shake it, so much as hold it. "Audrey is still in the waiting room." Sometimes clients prefer to simply state the obvious.

"We want to talk to you alone first. Our daughter—she does not fully comprehend her situation. We sometimes don't understand either." The big man's voice shakes as he tries to maintain control in front of a stranger.

"Tell me why you're here, Ivan. I may call you Ivan?"

He nods. Gaby has read the referral. Audrey left home for the first time in September to attend university in Edmonton. When she returned at Christmas, she told her parents she had been gang-raped by the boyfriends of the three girls with whom she shared an apartment. The Baranskis immediately reported the rape to the police. Audrey told them, in great detail, about the incident. She was checked by a doctor who stated there was no evidence of an encounter of any kind, rape or otherwise. The police, in Edmonton, interviewed her roommates. They said no incident ever happened; that Audrey's paranoia increased throughout the fall. They said the more work they were given in classes, the more delusional she became. Only one of them had a boyfriend but he never stayed over. The story was all fabricated. She was sent for a psychiatric assessment, was diagnosed with schizophrenia, and placed on medication. She did not go back to school.

Ivan and Iona tell Gaby the story she already knows. They add that the pills make their daughter vague and shaky. She has always been a quiet girl, but now all she does is sit and stare at the television most of the day. They have such high hopes for their daughter. They want her to go back to university; to be a teacher like she's always dreamed. Perhaps the doctors in Edmonton have made a mistake. They don't want Audrey to be mentally ill. They don't want to renew these pills that make her act like a zombie. Ivan's voice cracks. Iona twists a handkerchief in her hands and dabs at her eyes.

"May I meet Audrey today?"

"Yes, yes. I will go and get her." Ivan starts to jump up.

"That's okay. I'll ring Mimi to bring her down. We can talk for a few minutes and then, if you don't mind and Audrey is amenable, I would like to meet with her alone."

Audrey's perfect skin looks like grey parchment; like old lady skin you can almost see through. Her long, light brown hair is pulled so tightly back into a pony tail that her face appears like canvas stretched over a frame. Her hands shake and she buries them in the coat pockets of a garment much too heavy for the April weather. It remains buttoned to her throat. Her eyes dart, like those of a cornered animal, from her parents to Gaby. "Come in and sit down, Audrey. It's very nice to meet you."

Her father gets up and moves to the chair on his left, so that Audrey is forced to sit between them.

"I wanted to talk to all of you, Audrey. Your parents, as well as the psychiatrist from the city, have told me a little bit about what happened to you, but I would like to hear from you."

Audrey sits on the edge of her chair and never pulls her eyes from the floor. "I thought those boys hurt me but the doctors said I imagined it all. Once they put me on these horrible pills, I don't imagine anymore. I want to sleep all the time. My mouth is dry and my hands shake, but I don't imagine anymore. Everyone should be happy now."

"Is someone not happy, Audrey?"

The girl looks at her mother but is quiet. Iona pipes up. "Perhaps your father and I will wait for you down the hall, honey. You talk to this nice young woman. Make another appointment and you can come whenever you like, right Miss Ridgway?"

"Gaby, please. And yes, we can make another appointment for next week, if you want." Audrey barely nods. Her parents shut the door with quiet precision on their way out.

"Mom knows who isn't happy."

"Who is it, Audrey?"

"My dad. He wants me to get off the pills. He says he wants his little girl back; that I'm not crazy anymore." The tears creep down her tissue paper cheeks. "He gets mad when I don't bathe; when I don't get out of bed. He stares at my shaky hand holding a fork and says he can't watch me eat."

"He doesn't understand that if you stop your pills, the hallucinations will come back?"

"The doctor in Edmonton tried to talk to him but he wouldn't listen. He said they should fix me; make me normal! I want to curl up and die."

"Shall I try to speak to your father about this, Audrey? Shall I try to convince him that you need to take your pills; that you work as hard as you can to be you? Let's make another appointment. I'll ask your parents to come and see me, too. We can also talk to the psychiatrist and see if there's a possibility of a medication adjustment so there are less side effects. Let's start with that, okay?"

Tears rim her eyes. "At least Mom understands." They walk down the hall together so Gaby can make the appointments with her parents.

****

A couple of months later, Mimi notifies Gaby she has a phone call. "Gaby, I have Audrey Baranski on the phone. She sounds really upset!"

"Put her through, Mimi." Gaby sighs. She thought the situation was on an even keel with this family. She has seen Audrey on a regular basis for the past two months and the girl has improved considerably. She wants to try and get a job in town.

"Audrey, it's Gaby. What can I do for you?"

"He won't buy me any more pills, Gaby." Her voice cracks and fills with tears. She tries to whisper. "I took my last pill four days ago and he won't go to the pharmacy and pay for another prescription!"

"Where's your mother, Audrey?"

"In the kitchen. I have the phone in the pantry."

"Let me talk to your mother."

Gaby can hear the pantry door creak open and then the muffled sound of Audrey as she obtains Iona's attention. "Hello? Gaby, is that you?"

"Yes, it's me, Iona. Audrey says she's run out of pills. Can you see to it that she gets her refill, Iona? The pills are important."

Iona's sigh is audible down the phone line. "Ivan insists she should stop taking that medication, Gaby. I must admit, I hoped she would be okay but I don't think she is." She sighs again. "I will see to it that she gets her pills. Thanks for speaking with her."

"Let me speak to her again before you hang up, Iona." With Audrey back on the line, Gaby emphasizes how important it was that she called and how Audrey can call her anytime.

Gaby can only hope that Iona follows through. She senses the mother's resistance may well be as strong as the father's, but hidden from view most of the time. Gaby expects she will continue to receive panic calls from Audrey—a case with no resolution in sight.

Chapter 8

Sorry if I messed you up

The letter from her landlord arrives in early August of 1979. She has been in Hayworth almost two years. The owners have decided to sell the little house now, and the letter offers her first refusal. She has until the end of October to make a decision—move, or secure financing and buy the place. As she sits at the table on a Friday afternoon after work, the sun streaks across the living room hardwood and drifts into the kitchen. She has often thought about buying. This house is small but would work for her in her current circumstances. Interest rates are on the rise. The price they want is high; there are very few descent homes that ever come up for sale in Hayworth. She could put down a fair chunk of change from the money she received when she sold her old house. That mortgage was insured so when Grant died, the loan was paid off. Now that she's single again, she doesn't want to put all the money from that sale into another property. She wants the security of funds in the bank...and there's no denying the pressure of skyrocketing interest rates. Her thoughts bounce.

She's off to Kingston to visit Nina and her family in a couple of weeks. She'll talk it over with her. In the meantime, she wonders who she could get to inspect the house and see if it needs a lot of work, or if the price is okay. She supposes that Mimi probably knows someone.

"Hi, Mimi? I didn't know if you'd be home yet."

"Hi, Gaby. Hold on. I need to switch Phoebe to my other arm." She grunts with the effort. "There. What can I do for you? We haven't talked for what—

an hour?" She giggles. Mimi and Tim have been residents at the Long family ranch for almost a year. Everybody seems happy. Mimi loves her work at the Hexagon and her mother-in-law dotes on her granddaughter. The situation is a win-win.

"Do you know any appraisers or contractors?"

"Now, what are you up to, Gaby? Gonna' build yourself a house?"

"I wish. My landlords have sent me a letter to tell me they want to sell and I have until the end of October before they put it on the market. I can buy or move. I like it here. I thought I might buy the place, if it's in as good a shape as it seems to be."

"Tim's dad could come and have a look. Listen—Cheryl Nadler moved to The Station, you know, at the far end of town? I'm almost certain one of the tenants in there is a carpenter. Maybe she could introduce you to him. Ask her next week."

"Maybe I'll invite her out to lunch at the diner. Good idea?"

Mimi finds this funny. Gaby can hear Phoebe giggling in the background. "She might come to meet you but she won't eat. In all the time she's worked at the Hexagon, I've never seen her eat food she hasn't made herself, but you can try. Let me know how it works out. And if you want Martin to pop over, give a shout back. He's no expert, but he can tell you what he thinks of the place."

"Thanks. You've been a great help, Mimi. I'll let you get back to your family. See you Monday."

Cheryl's phone number is unlisted, but she runs down Poplar Street every day at about the same time. On Fridays, she's a little later. Gaby takes a glass of white wine out to her front porch and patiently waits for the girl to trot around the corner from the bridge and up the street. She sits in the old rattan rocker she bought from the antique dealer in town and thinks about the idea of making this her permanent residence. Nina will be upset. She has never given up hope that Gaby will return to home turf.

Here she comes. Gaby steps down off the porch, crosses the patch of lawn, and waves to Cheryl as she approaches. Cheryl looks confused but stops. She bends at the waist and grasps her knees as she attempts to catch her breath. "Gaby? Is this your house? What can I do for you?"

"Well, I wondered if you would join me at the diner for lunch tomorrow. I want to pick your brain about a tenant in your building."

"I don't know anybody there that well. I don't discuss work outside the office, Gaby." Her tone is admonishing. Gaby is a wee bit offended.

"Oh, my question isn't about work. I need the advice of a contractor, or carpenter, or somebody, and Mimi told me there was a guy in your building."

"She must mean Joe Dodd. He's in the book. Call him. I'm sure he'll meet you and talk about whatever you want. I don't do lunch at the diner. It doesn't look like the cleanest place in town, now does it?"

Gaby shrugs. The restaurant is the only place in town other than the hotel, which costs a fortune and the food isn't great, but she refrains from voicing this remark in response. "Thanks, Cheryl. I'll let you get back to your run. Sorry if I messed you up." Gaby smiles. Cheryl doesn't. She continues down the sidewalk. Gaby returns to her wine and thinks, for a moment, about exercising.

After supper, she calls Joe Dodd. "My name is Gaby Ridgway. I hear you're a carpenter and I hoped you could have a look at a house I might want to buy. I'm happy to pay you for your time" She hears purring. He must have a cat.

"Sure. I can come by sometime this weekend if you like. Tomorrow morning? Around 10:00 AM? What's the address?"

"It's 15 Poplar. I'll be here. I rent the house now. Come to the front door. I rarely use the back."

"Right oh. See you tomorrow."

He sounds nice enough. After two years employed as a counsellor in Hayworth, she might even manage to meet someone who isn't a co-worker, a client, or a shopkeeper. She smiles as she curls up on her sofa to watch what she still considers to be Elliot's TV.

****

Saturday morning is hot by 9:00 AM. Gaby has both doors open. The old screens provide the necessary protection against the ever-present house flies. All the windows are open, too. There isn't a breath of breeze strong enough to move a leaf. She tunes her radio to the local station, makes coffee, and waits for Joe Dodd.

He parks on the street, which is too narrow for his truck—a rumbling monster. He couldn't have hoped to get it in her driveway, since she barely pulls her Mazda pick-up in far enough to clear the sidewalk. She guesses she could have parked all the way up to the fence. Oh well.

He's a big man who holds himself with confidence. He looks to be in his forties, barrel-chested, large hands, thinning brown hair, and a tan. Gaby jumps to the screen door as his hulk fills the space on the porch.

"Come on in. Joe, right? I'm Gaby. Nice to meet you!" She reaches out to shake his hand. Joe looks genuinely interested as he returns a firm grasp.

"Joe Dodd. Cute house. Owners want to sell, do they?"

He fills the living room just like he did the porch. Bigger rooms and higher ceilings would suit him better than this little shack. "Yes, they've given me first refusal. I think I might be ready to buy, but I need to know if I'll inherit any problems. I thought, maybe, you could help me with that." She smiles up at him. "Coffee?"

"Sure, coffee would be great. Let's look around a bit and see what the old place has to say for herself." Coffee in hand, he starts to roam, asking permission to go into the bedroom and bath, to go up the narrow ladder-like den stairs into the attic room, and out the back door to the rickety step Gaby uses to access the clothes line. The backyard is passable—fenced and grassy—but she doesn't use it much, preferring the front porch. The owners hire someone to mow the lawn, so she hasn't had to spend any time back there at all. The gate doesn't even lock. If she ever decides to get a dog, the gate will need to be fixed. He leaves his coffee on the kitchen table and goes down to the cellar. The basement is insulated and holds the gas furnace and the washer and dryer that came with the place.

"How are your heating bills?" he calls from downstairs.

"Not bad. Everybody wants lower bills."

"If the place was mine, I'd add more insulation around the foundation." He's back upstairs, now. "The back door needs to be replaced. It doesn't close properly and the weather stripping is almost gone. I bet you get snow coming in at the bottom corner if the wind blows from that way. The fence gate needs to be fixed." He grins over at her and reads the frown that is now etched on her face. "Don't worry. I haven't found any expensive issues."

"There haven't been any problems since I've been here. So, what do you think?"

"Depending on the price they want, I would expect it to be a good deal for you. There are projects you could do—besides the insulation in the basement and the new back door. This kitchen is way overdue for new cupboards and a new floor. The porch could use a coat of paint, and the bathroom should be gutted. The fence should be secure. None of these issues constitutes an emergency, Gaby, but improvements all add value."

She tries to insert enthusiasm into her nod, with little success. The owners want $69,000.00 for the house, which is much more than a house like this would be worth back home, but that's the real estate market in the north. If she buys it, she would finance half the cost so she would have mortgage payments of about $350.00 a month—less than her current rent. All the other expenses, like a lawn mower, would take a slice out of her nest egg.

"If I buy the place, would you do the insulation and door for me; maybe paint the porch and replace some light fixtures? The fence will be an issue if I decide to get a dog. I don't know what else I'll be able to afford—not a kitchen for a couple of years—but I think I might make them an offer."

"Great. Glad to see you'll be in town for a while. A lot of folks from the east move here for a couple of years and then leave. I'm one of those easterners who came here and stayed put. So, you're a dog-person, are you?"

"Yes, I am, but I don't know about taking the plunge. Work is a challenge by times. So, what do I owe you, Joe?"

He laughs. It rattles the pictures on the walls. "Not a dime. Give me a chance to bid on the work and I'm happy. Come down to the diner with me and have some lunch and I'm even happier."

****

Gaby makes her annual trek back to Kingston for three weeks. This trip to visit Nina, Craig, and their four kids is special. She will break it to them that she intends to consider Hayworth her home; that she intends to buy a house and make her new start official. They haven't been to visit her yet, and she isn't able to accommodate the six of them, but she feels comfortable and safe in the little house on Poplar. She's sure it will all work out.

Nina and all four children wait for her in the small terminal building at Kingston Airport as she makes her way down the metal stairs from the plane onto the tarmac. She can see them at the window. The airport is small. The day has been unending. Her suitcase is already loaded on the baggage cart. Thank God for small mercies. Gifts for everyone are secured in that bag. The kids change so much over the space of a year. Elly, at eleven, is tall now with long legs that seem to go all the way to her neck. She's the first one to run and meet Gaby. Young Craig, at nine, isn't far behind. He can't let his older sister get ahead of him by much. He looks like Nina. Josh is seven now. He seems all grown up. His hair is curly and blond. Gaby isn't sure whom he favours, although everyone says he looks like her. Freddie hangs back. He's only starting to get used to this idea of Aunt Gaby who comes to visit from somewhere far away. Gaby intends to try and convince Nina, now that the kids are at the age where they can be managed, to come out west next summer.

****

"I intend to buy a house when I get back to Hayworth, Nina." They're sitting, as they always do, at the kitchen table. They can watch the kids on the deck and in the backyard. The weather is hot and muggy. The sweat on the jug of iced tea runs into the cloth placemat meant to protect the new pine table.

"You always do this, Gaby. You spring stuff on me with no warning! I thought you were out west for a few years to clear your head, and then you'd come back to this neck of the woods!"

"I know you did. I might have thought that myself at first, but I like it there, Nina. I like the people. I adore the work, even though the job can be tedious— lots of government changes." She shrugs. "You know. Every new minister has to put their stamp on the affairs of their department. It pays to be flexible, but the position is secure. I'm not the guidance counsellor whose husband died. I'm Gaby Ridgway, a counsellor at the Hexagon. I like it." She finishes with a flourish and takes another sip of her drink.

Nina wordlessly accepts her sister's decision when she looks across the table and smiles. "So tell me about this house. Interest rates are on the rise."

Gaby, encouraged by her sister's support, launches into the details about the house, the costs, the mortgage, the down payment, and Joe's advice. She has decided to call her landlords when she returns to Hayworth, and get an idea about how they would like to work the sale—two lawyers and no real estate firm will be the best option. She's done it before. Mimi has given her the name of a lawyer, and she has already obtained preliminary approval for her mortgage.

As she chatters away, Nina waves her hand across Gaby's line of vision. "Joe? Who is Joe the carpenter? Tell me about Joe." She has a conspiratorial look on her face and she grins from ear to ear.

"Joe Dodd, Nina. One of the social workers from the Adoptions Division gave me his name. They live in the same building on the outskirts of town. He came over and checked the house out for me, and then we went for lunch at the local diner."

"You said all that." Nina sounds exasperated. "What's he like?"

"I have to get to know him first! I think you might have to wait until after I buy the house, and then I'll hire him to replace the back door and add some extra insulation in the basement. I also want him to paint the front porch and install some new light fixtures." She relents, then, and gives her sister a few details. "He's a big guy, in his forties. I think he has a cat." She screws up her nose at the thought, having never been a big feline fan. "He's nice; says he likes to cook; divorced, I think—at least not currently involved with anybody—and has a pretty good reputation, business-wise. He's okay looking—losing his hair, barrel-chested. Drives the biggest damn truck I have ever seen!"

Nina titters. "Sounds like you found out an awful lot for an assessment and a lunch. Who, precisely, was doing the assessing again?" She leans over and taps Gaby's hand. "It's time you met someone, anyway, Gaby. Keep an open mind. Cats aren't all bad."

"Easy for you to say." She responds with good nature to the teasing, but her heart lurches a little as her mind drifts toward Grant. "Let's go outside and see what those monsters of yours are doing, Nina. Nobody's crying, so they must be up to no good."

****

Back home in Hayworth, fall approaches fast. Gaby closes the sale on 15 Poplar Street. Joe is commissioned to do the tasks they discussed, and before the end of October and the first snowfall, she hosts a little office party where she can show the place off.

Mimi helps. She and her husband Tim are the first to arrive with lots of food including a slow cooker full of meatballs and a platter of veggies. Pearl appears at the door with Dr. Alden at her side. Gaby hears them coming up the steps. "Put that stupid cigarette out, Clark. You know the girl doesn't smoke! She's barely finished having work done on the place. Don't stink it all up." Gaby sees her plant a delighted look on her frowning face the second her knock is answered. Dr. A., suitably admonished by Pearl who appears to possess a significantly different attitude toward her boss outside the workplace, returns from stamping out his cigarette on the sidewalk. Each presents her with a bottle of wine.

Frank and Margaret are the next to appear. Gaby has met Margaret often over the last two years—at Christmas parties and summer staff gatherings. She runs into her in the grocery store on occasion and they always have a nice chat. She is sweet in her own way. Around Frank, she often just sits and sports a soft, vacant smile. Gaby whispers that she needs some help in the kitchen—not true—and gives Margaret a chance to visit with Mimi for a few minutes away from her evangelistic spouse.

Elliot shows up alone. "Hi." Gaby looks past him out on to the darkened porch, lit by new, frosted glass sconces on either side of the door. "Where's Celina?" There's a note of concern in her voice. Celina is by far the funniest woman Gaby has ever met. She is a tall, feathery blond bombshell, younger than her husband by what Gaby estimates to be about ten years. She talks in what seems to be a fake and squeaky baby-voice. She dresses like a streetwalker and looks like she's had a boob-job. Gaby likes her a lot, and her party will not be the same without the young woman's company.

Elliot sighs, almost loud enough to be heard over the music Tim has managed to organize inside. "She's on her way. We had a fight. She'll come in her own car." He looks first at the ground and then down the street.

"Good—not that you had a fight! Good that she will come anyway." She leans over and whispers in Elliot's ear. "We'll give her a couple of glasses of wine and then she'll be fine, Elliot." He purses his lips and shakes his head before he makes a beeline for the beer in a bucket by the kitchen door.

By all accounts, the night is a screaming success. None of her neighbours call the police even though there are cars parked all over the place. Celina is fabulous and, although they return home in separate cars, Gaby is convinced Elliot will not have to sleep on the couch. Margaret has a good time visiting with most of the staff, outside of Frank's line of vision. Pearl seems to relax even though Dr. A. is there, and before the evening is over, Dr. Alden tells Gaby she may call him Clark when they are outside the office. Apparently, if office gossip is to be believed, he only gives someone this privilege if he likes you. Mimi and Tim help her clean up and she goes to bed considering her house to be appropriately warmed.

Chapter 9

Grain dust on a windy day

It has been two years since Gaby purchased her house and four years since she first arrived in Hayworth. In all that time counselling in the small town, Dottie and Lyle Smythe have to be one of the saddest referrals she has received. She accompanies them down the hall to her office. Lyle holds his wife's hand and murmurs constantly to her as they make their way ahead of Gaby. She has seen them once a week for the past two months, since their referral to her from the visiting psychiatrist, Rachel Wilkerson.

Dr. Wilkerson asked if someone could try and help this poor couple deal with their anxiety and stress as they learn to face Dottie's diagnosis together. Dottie has early onset dementia. She is fifty-two. Lyle is fifty-four.

Today, the plan is to talk about the need for Lyle to perform more tasks. Dottie has almost forgotten how to cook; forgotten how to work the washing machine. Lyle does not cope well and says he's afraid he'll lose his temper. Gaby is suspicious this has already happened.

They settle in to her office. Dottie looks old for her age. She's chubby and frumpy. She has always worn her tired auburn hair in braids wrapped around her head—old-fashioned and severe. Every week, her hair is more untidy. Gaby suspects she can't remember how to take care of her exceedingly long locks and Lyle is not ready to take over this routine for her. It is July, but she wears a wool coat and shows no inclination to remove it. Lyle tries to take off his jacket but Dottie objects by holding his sleeve. He relents and sits down with it unzipped and hanging open. Lyle is tall and attractive in a Paul

Newman kind of way. His complexion is ruddy from hours on the tractor. He's in good shape because of all his outdoor work. One might assume Dottie to be his mother.

Gaby starts with Dottie. She leans over to touch her knee and get her client's attention. She stares at the window behind Gaby. "How are you, today, Dottie?" No response.

Lyle nudges her. "Say 'hi' to Gaby, Dottie. Mind your manners." He speaks to her as if she were a small child. He has had to learn this skill. They never had any children of their own.

"Hello." Dottie does not look at Gaby, but she responds to her husband's command.

"It seems she gets worse every week, Gaby. All she does is sit and stare unless I tell her exactly what to do. Dr. Wilkerson has upped her pills so she doesn't scream and cry anymore, but now she's like a zombie. I'm goin' downhill pretty fast." There are tears in his troubled blue eyes.

"What about help, Lyle? Can you get any help? Care givers need breaks. You've watched her slip over the last two years. You know you'll need to get some help eventually."

Lyle clutches his wife's hand, like he has to ensure she's still there beside him. "I hate to bring anybody else in, Gaby. It took me eighteen months before I even told the doctor. The referrals to you and Dr. Wilkerson are good, but what? I need to hire a babysitter, now?"

Dottie turns and looks directly at Lyle. "Are we going to have a baby?"

He gives her a gentle pat on her coat-clad knee with his free hand. "No, honey. Just an expression."

"Oh. I always wanted to have a baby." Dottie starts to cry.

Lyle fumbles for a tissue and Gaby offers the box off her desk. Dottie remains unaware of the snot that runs across her upper lip. Lyle mops her up. "Don't worry old girl. Bad choice of words. You'll be fine." He looks at Gaby and rolls his eyes again. "I deal with this all the time. She seems to listen, and maybe one word will register. Gets me into a lot of trouble." His voice cracks with grief.

They try to talk for almost an hour. Lyle expresses reluctance but knows, if he wishes to prevent institutionalization, he will have to hire a housekeeper to both be a companion for Dottie and manage the house so he can run the farm. He still can't cope with the idea of her dementia. "I feel like I'm watching her die, even though she's still right there in front of me, Gaby. She's drifting away, like grain dust on a windy day. Can't stop it if I try. Maybe I can find somebody who can do her damned hair!" It's the grumble of a man coming to terms with his loss.

After they leave, Gaby takes a stab at writing up her case notes. She thinks a discussion with Dr. Wilkerson might be in order. Lyle must soon face the inevitable and Dottie will have to be placed in a nursing home.

Edith appears at Gaby's door. "Are you coming for coffee? I want to pick your brain about our statistics. I can't seem to figure out what categories my files fall into. Types of counselling, diagnoses, number of times seen. I need some help to keep it all straight. Can you help?"

Edith has wiggled her way in and sits in the chair at the end of Gaby's desk, where she unabashedly peers at the notes Gaby attempts to compose about the Smythe couple. Gaby closes her file folder and reaches in her desk drawer for a piece of paper. "Try this, Edith. It's a copy of a table I keep under my blotter so that every time I see someone, I tick off the numbers, length of time, type of session, and major problem. Then, at the end of the month, I can write my report."

Edith grabs the data sheet. "Where did you get this? I book a whole day the end of the month to go through my files and try to make sense of the numbers. A whole day!"

"Well this is a lot easier than that, Edith. I made it up myself, but you are more than welcome to have this and make your own copies."

"I don't know." The older woman hesitates while she scrapes a sprig of unwanted hair off her brow. She shrugs. "The government pays me for the day, whether I review all my files or whether I see clients. I guess, if I do paperwork your way, they'll get more work out of me. Maybe my way is better." Her smile is barely discernible.

"Suit yourself, Edith. Keep the sheet, though. I have lots." Gaby knows she's the lone staff member not resisting the stats. She doesn't care. She would rather be ahead of the game and spend the time with clients. "Let's take a break and get some coffee."

****

"How's the kitchen project, Miss Rich Girl?" Frank Spencer lounges with legs up in a recliner as they make their way into the staff room. Interest rates are considerably higher than when she bought. Anyone whose mortgage has come up for renewal in the past couple of years has a huge payment, now, eating away at their disposable income. Gaby's mortgage is manageable because she put down half the money for her house and it's still not up for negotiation for another three years. She intends to spend the interest from her remaining savings to finance the kitchen. Frank can be obnoxious and pushy, sometimes.

"Joe's been at it for a couple of weeks. I think I'll like it when he's finished." She tries to be as vague as possible.

"I bet a new kitchen installation is expensive, and Joe Dodd isn't cheap either." Frank continues to rumble on.

"My motto is 'don't buy what you can't pay for', Frank. My house is tiny. You said so yourself almost two years ago when I bought it, so the kitchen isn't big, either."

The fact of the matter is the kitchen will be fabulous. The cabinets, counter-tops, floor, sink and tap, and all the appliances are brand new. Joe sold her original stuff so it didn't have to go to the dump. The new light oak cabinets, tile counter-tops, and vinyl flooring will add some glamour to the little house. He put pot-lights in the ceiling. He will add under-cabinet lighting and a small work island with real butcher block. Yes, renovations are expensive, but worth every penny in the end.

Joe has been great. They've even had supper together a couple of times at the diner. Most often, she picks up dinner and carts it home, though. Right now, the fridge resides in the middle of the living room floor. She can manage breakfast and lunch, but supper out of an electric frying pan is too much like work. It'll be over soon.

Elliot heaves a sigh—his normal opening before he actually remarks on a subject. "Saw you and Joe at the diner the other night. Are you two an item? Why did you hire him, anyway? There are cheaper carpenters around."

"No, we're not an item. Cheryl Nadler told me about him when I needed someone to inspect the house before I bought it. He was kind enough to do that, and then did a couple of updates for me before the weather turned cold. You guys know, price isn't the primary consideration. You need to trust the person who works for you."

Mimi appears at the door in all her glory—seven months pregnant with her second child and "as big as a house", as she describes herself. "Gaby, can you spare a minute? I have a referral I need to talk to you about."

"My turn already?" Gaby silently questions the timing as she rinses out her mug and follows Mimi back to reception. "Didn't you give me somebody this week, already?"

Mimi waits until they're out of ear shot of the staff room. "I thought this person might be right up your alley. No, you're not up next, but have a look at the referral and let me know if you'll take it."

Gaby sits down beside Mimi's desk and reviews the referral form. There isn't much to see. The person's name is Charlene Quinn. She's twenty-five, has been in Hayworth less than six months, and reports she moved from Halifax, Nova Scotia. She's far from home. The reason for the referral is vague. "What makes you think I need to take this one, Mimi? There isn't even a real reason for the referral. She says she has troubles. What kind of troubles?"

Mimi shrugs her shoulders and leans over as best she can with her big belly. "That's all I could get out of her. She wanted to talk to someone and I thought you'd be perfect."

"Okay. I can see her by the end of the week, Mimi. Set it up and then leave me out of the rotation until the others are caught up."

Mimi nods. Her voice is conspiratorial. "Don't worry. I won't put you in a position where you're taken advantage of. I know everybody's caseload numbers—at least I would if they handed in their stats on time. I told Pearl she would have to address the issue at our next staff meeting."

****

Gaby meets Charlene Quinn for the first time a couple of days later. Mimi calls to tell her the young woman has arrived and Gaby goes out to reception to escort her down to her office. Mimi watches as Gaby comes around the corner. Charlene is the one client in the waiting room. Without a missed step or changed expression on her face, Gaby introduces herself. "Charlene? I'm Gaby Ridgway. Nice to meet you. Let's go down to my office." She looks over Charlene's head and back at Mimi who widens her eyes.

Charlene presents herself to the world like no one Gaby has ever known before. She is a decidedly petite young woman, no more than five feet tall. Her hair is very short and dyed bright orange. Although July has turned out to be muggier than one would expect in the north, she wears a black leather bomber jacket covered in chains and zippers. Underneath is a white T-shirt with a plunging V-neck making it obvious she is braless. She has on shorts and black fish-net stockings. Her eyes are enhanced by black liner and a smoky grey shadow applied with liberal abandon. Her ears are pierced at least ten times each. Her nails are so long they seem to curl down over the pads of her fingers, and are painted with a shiny black lacquer. Her purse hangs from her shoulder. It's the size of a wallet and bulges with who knows what. It bumps her hip as she walks, and the attached suede fringe enhancements almost brush the floor.

"So...your referral was a little vague, Charlene. What makes you want to see a counsellor?"

Settled in the office chair closest to the door, Charlene cuddles her purse on her lap and looks at Gaby with confusion in her eyes. "I guess I don't know. I have issues. I don't like people very much. I feel like I should have been a vampire or a bat—coming out at night when no one's around."

Gaby peers at her client as they talk. She's very petite, compared to her remarkably large breasts. She has beautiful white, flawless skin. The combination of heavy make-up and plucked eyebrows, reapplied with black pencil, take away from her high cheek bones and deep-set eyes. Her teeth protrude—not like she has an overbite, but like she has her father's teeth in her mother's face. As a result, her lips looked stretched. With the red lipstick, they become the dominant facial feature.

"What brought you to Hayworth?" Gaby tries to encourage her to open up. "You told Mimi you moved here from Halifax about six months ago."

"That's right. Jumped in my old Land Cruiser and headed west. People said there were lots of jobs. I was hired on as a cleaner at the hospital. Now isn't that romantic?"

"What did you want to do?"

"That's the problem. I don't know. I thought I could find a good job and make a lot of money. Even work like mine pays more than it would down east, but I hate the lousy job of having to clean sick people's crap, and it costs more to live here. I think I need to find a way to like people better or I'll never have a decent job."

"Tell me about where you're living, Charlene."

"With three other girls in a rental house in town. I answered an ad on the bulletin board at the hospital. I'm pretty sure they don't like me, but I pay my share, so they shut up. I spend most of my time in my room—in the basement. They have the three bedrooms upstairs so, like the bat I am, I live in the basement. But hey, there's a positive! I have my own bathroom, at least. They all share the one upstairs."

"Do you have family back east, Charlene?"

"My mother's parents. Don't know about anybody else. I don't want to talk about them today. I'll tell you about them some other time."

After signing the standard consent forms and explaining her role as a counsellor including all the details regarding confidentiality, Gaby schedules another appointment for the next week. She needs to glean more background. She also tells the girl that they will set some goals together during their next meeting.

"What kind of goals? I thought we could talk. I have issues. I told you that. I want to talk!" Her voice is strained with anxiety; almost panicky.

Gaby attempts an explanation. "Charlene, part of the counselling process is to move forward. In order to do that, you and I need to set goals so we can talk together and work toward those goals. In my experience, the alternative is simply to go in circles. Try not to over-think this. You made the appointment because you said you have issues. We will reveal your issues, address them, and the process may create a better circumstance for you."

Charlene looks at the floor. She mumbles, "I wanted someone to talk to. The girl at the front said you would talk to me."

"Of course I'll talk with you, Charlene. That's a given, but positive counselling is based on establishing goals and working toward them. Are you willing to give this a try? We'll meet once per week for a couple of months and see how we do." She leans over and looks directly into Charlene's smoky eyes. "We will do our best to address those issues you want to talk about, Charlene. First, we have to determine what they are."

After she walks Charlene back down to reception and puts the appointment in Mimi's book, she retreats to her office in order to document the session. It proves as challenging as the session, itself. Charlene doesn't like people. She has grandparents with whom she has obviously had a falling out. She left Nova Scotia angry. She hates her job. She makes no attempt to interact with her housemates, and she describes herself as a bat. The discussion of goals will be Gaby's focus for their next visit—if the girl manages to turn up for a second appointment.

Chapter 10

She looks like a tough customer

As they settle into a booth by the window, Gaby realizes that eating out at the diner with Joe has become a habit since the kitchen was finished more than a month ago. They seem like dates but Gaby isn't sure. They have supper at the diner. She makes her own way there and her own way home. She would like to offer to make dinner for him, the new kitchen as the excuse, but she's afraid she might compromise their friendship as well as their professional relationship. Tonight, they talk about what the pros and cons are of a bathroom renovation at 15 Poplar Street.

"If you want me to do it before snow flies, we need to make a plan."

"Would I be without facilities for any length of time, Joe? The house has one bathroom. I don't want to get started and then be stuck running to the gas station." Her point is crystal clear.

"The biggest problem is the toilet, and I'd replace that while you're at work. It will have to come off to put down the new floor. That's one day. The tub will stay and I'll install a shower, right? So, you might be without your sink and tub for a couple of days." He looks across the table as he takes a sip of his beer. "You could use my shower." The expression on his face isn't quite a leer.

Gaby is secretly delighted. "Right! And how many tongues would wag over that?"

Joe looks down at his paper placemat advertising local mechanics, the grocery store, and oil field equipment operators. "People talk about us now, Gaby." He stops and looks up. He's amused.

Here it comes. Well, she might be ready to date again. He's a nice man; both feet firmly planted on the ground. "I'll make do, Joe. But, if people are talking anyway, how about we go to the movies some night?" Their food arrives before he can answer, but Gaby thinks he looks a little flustered.

"Hey, Patrick! Do you do all the jobs now—work the counter, take orders, bus tables? Where's Nancy?"

Patrick grins down as he sets their plates of meatloaf, mashed potatoes, vegetables, and gravy down in front of them. "Nancy has some family gig. I told her to take off. I can handle the tables by myself." He nods at Gaby.

"I bet you two haven't met before, at least not formally. Patrick, this is Gaby Ridgway. She works over at the Hexagon, where Cheryl works. Gaby, this is Patrick Hollinger, the 'almost manager' of the Hayworth Diner. He lives at The Station, same as me."

"Hi, Patrick. Nice to meet you officially." Gaby reaches up to shake his hand which he frantically rubs on his white server's apron first.

"I've heard lots about you from a friend of mine. She says you're her counsellor and you're nice."

Right on cue, Charlene Quinn pushes open the big glass door with her hip, sashays down the length of the diner, and plunks her behind unceremoniously in the staff booth at the back. Patrick, who flushes and looks almost embarrassed, nods to them again, turns on his heel, and scuttles toward the girl. There is hushed whispering and a considerable amount of head-shaking before Patrick disappears into the kitchen

Joe digs into his supper. "Well, I wonder who that is. You're not talking so that means you know so I won't ask." Gaby told him some time ago that if they ever met anyone out in public whom she didn't talk about or introduce, it was for a reason. Confidentiality is required at all times, even if a client feels they have permission to grab her attention at the post office or in the toothpaste aisle at the drugstore. "I haven't seen Patrick with anyone over at the apartment building, but I'm gone all day so who knows? He's a good kid. He's had a rough time of it and everyone at The Station has become pretty protective over the last years. She looks like a tough customer."

Gaby continues to eat her supper in silence. Soon, Joe's thoughts return to the subject that was interrupted earlier. "So...an evening at the movies? I'm a passable cook. Maybe I could cook you supper first and then we could go. Would that be a date? Do you want me to renovate your bathroom first so, in case we break-up, it'll be all done?" He chuckles as he mops up gravy with a piece of roll.

****

Gaby and Charlene have met four times. Gaby feels little progress has been made. Today, she plans to try and determine how Charlene interacts with her roommates. The young woman still maintains she doesn't like people and that she has unresolved issues. Gaby needs to find out the core reason for her problem, and what the actual issues are. If not, there's no more need for counselling because the client has no motivation to change her circumstances.

Dressed in the same extremes as always, Charlene thumps her way down to Gaby's office and tosses herself into the chair by the desk. She drops her fringed purse to the floor and plops her elbows on her knees. "So, I suppose you want to know all the gritty details about me and Pat." The words shoot out of her mouth like pellets from a shot gun. "I was disappointed you didn't come over to say 'hi' the other night."

"I never acknowledge clients in public, Charlene. Our relationship is no one else's business. Even if you had spoken to me, I wouldn't have let on to my companion how I know you."

"Your companion." She draws out the "pan" portion of the word. Her tone is mocking. "That was Joe Dodd, a carpenter that lives at The Station where Pat lives. Pat told me all about Joe. Do you like to slum it, or what? Isn't he a little beneath you?"

Client's often try to transfer the conversation. Gaby's discomfort doesn't impede her focus. "How about we discuss you and Patrick? He seems nice enough. Tell me about you two."

"Not much to tell, so far. He hates to be called Pat, so I call him that to aggravate him. I first met him when he was in the waiting room at the hospital. He sees Dr. Wilkerson. He's quite a loony tune but when I go down to the diner, he'll buy me food. I always tell him I don't have any money." She roars at what she appears to think is a big joke. "I've never been to his place, but I'll get there eventually." She grins at Gaby. "He collects toys. He says his mother killed herself but he won't talk about it except to the doctor. He says he has family, but won't talk to me about them either. He's a tough nut to crack." She laughs at her pun, although it sounds more like a sneer. "Nut, get it?"

"Do you consider Patrick to be your friend, Charlene?" Gaby wonders why Charlene appears so interested in somebody she seems to dislike, or thinks about with such contempt.

"Listen. My goal is to get out of this horror show of a house I live in. If I can convince Mr. Loony Tunes that I like him, he might let me move in—free rent and all the food I can eat at the diner. What could be better than that? He's harmless. I could put up with him, if absolutely necessary—if you know what I mean?" She grins again.

"Tell me about your roommates, Charlene. I'm interested in your description of your living arrangements as a horror show."

"Okay." Charlene readjusts herself in her chair and leans over toward Gaby. "Let me give you an idea of what they're like. First, there's Crystal. She works as an administrative clerk at the hospital. She is a prissy, religious fanatic. In my opinion, she needs to get laid. Then there's Ila. She must be six feet tall. She looks like a horse. She thinks she's smart. She's a nurses' aide. Let me tell you about her cat. She brought home this kitten. They all thought it was so cute. I hate pets. Waste of air as far as I'm concerned. I put up with it and its damned smelly litter box for a full week. Then I put it in a pillowcase and held it in the toilet until it was dead. I drove to the dump and threw it out. Ila thinks somebody left the door open and the stupid thing bolted."

She leans back in her chair. Gaby is horrified and applies every measure of control she can muster to ensure her feelings don't bleed into her expression.

"You see what I have to live with? The third one—and the most insignificant, if I do say so—is Roz. Roz looks like a mouse and acts like a mouse. She cleans all the time. She never talks, just runs around after people, polishing and picking up. She's a cleaner at the hospital, too, so I even have to put up with her bullshit at work. Now, do you understand why I need to get Pat to let me move in with him?"

"Is that the first time you've killed an animal, Charlene?"

"What? Killed an animal? I can't imagine what that has to do with the subject, but hell, no! If I didn't like my foster home when I was a kid, I killed their dog, or cat, or—once it was a parrot. Animals are easy to kill. They trust you. They can't think ahead and imagine what you might do. Can we change the subject for a minute? I have a question. What we say is confidential, right?"

"Yes. Within certain limitations, Charlene."

"What are the limitations?"

"Well, if a client tells me they intend to commit a crime or hurt someone, I am obliged to report this to the authorities in order to prevent a crime from occurring. That was in the document you signed when you became a client."

"Oh, I never read that shit. What about a crime I've already committed? Do you have to report that to authorities?" She says the word "authorities" as if she's poking fun at the gravity of the question.

"No. Events that have occurred in the past are confidential, although I am required to keep detailed notes that are available to other staff. They have the same confidentiality requirements as I do."

"Good. I have a story I might want to tell you."

"I hope you feel you can talk to me about whatever you like, Charlene."

"Well, maybe I can, but not today. Anyway, I have to leave early. Pat works the 3:00 to 11:00 PM shift today and I thought I'd go and keep him company."

"The owner doesn't mind that you are there to visit with an employee while they work?" Charlene has no sense of boundaries and respect for what others do. Gaby hopes to plant the seed that people need to work when they're at work.

"Are you kidding? Margo Johnson is almost never there. She works as an accountant. Has her own firm. I think Pat and Nancy pretty much run the joint. I've only seen Margo once."

So, it appears that as long as Charlene can get away with an act, then in her estimation, the behaviour is permissible by default. Gaby has serious concerns as she walks down the hall to reception with her client. They schedule another appointment, but Gaby remains doubtful about where their relationship is headed. Next time, they will have to re-examine their goals yet again. In the interim, it will be necessary to have a discussion with Pearl.

****

"Pearl, I need to talk to you about a client. Do you have a few minutes?"

"Sure, Gaby. You look tired. What's the problem?"

"No wonder I look tired, Pearl. I've been up half the night trying to figure out what I need to do about Charlene Quinn. I don't know if we're the right service for her. She might need to be with a mental health counsellor."

"Is she under psychiatric care, Gaby?"

"No. At least not yet."

"Well, you know the rules. No referrals to mental health unless the client is considered a mental health patient. Tell me about your Charlene Quinn." Pearl sits behind her desk. She takes off her reading glasses and has difficulty finding a suitable spot to put them down. The surface is covered in files, loose papers, and binders about workplace practices.

"Well, to start with, she seems to have no consideration for anybody but herself. She hates everyone. She was bounced around from one foster home to another. Right now, she's pretending she likes this one guy so that he'll ask her to move in and she'll get free rent and food. She uses everybody!"

"I worked with a guy once who said that no matter how terrible your client appeared, dig deep to try and find a redeeming quality. Focus on that. Does Charlene have a redeeming quality, Gaby?"

"I have difficulty seeing where somebody who can drown a defenceless kitten in the toilet can have any redeeming qualities, Pearl. She told me she lived in many, many foster homes as a kid. If she didn't like a family, she killed their pet and then they'd want her moved. I wonder if she has empathy."

"Do you think she's a sociopath?"

"Sociopath—no moral conscience, takes no responsibility, blames others, antisocial, and maybe criminal. She's certainly all of that. She even asked me if I was obligated to report criminal behaviour if it had already happened. I'm scared to death about what she might tell me next. I had trouble handling the kitten story."

"Document all the details, Gaby. Don't make statements that might be construed as judgmental in the file, but declare all the facts and be clear. Don't write so the reader has to peer between the lines. I know you try and protect your clients by avoiding too much detail, but this is not the file to do that. Sociopaths are difficult. They don't care who they hurt."

"Thanks, Pearl. I'm not sure if I feel better or not." She meets her boss' gaze as she lifts herself out of the chair.

Back in her office, she takes the remainder of the afternoon to research sociopathy and compile her notes regarding Charlene Quinn. Mimi will have a field day when she types these up.

****

Later on that evening, after a supper of cold chicken and salad, Gaby goes out to sit in her rattan rocker on the porch. August isn't half over, but fall has inserted itself into the cool air. She starts to relax with her cup of tea when the rumble of a truck motor slows down. She opens her eyes, as she thinks that Joe might be stopping by to say hello.

Instead, the vehicle is an old red Toyota Land Cruiser looking the worse for wear. It stops with precision in front of her house. The issue of clients turning up at your home is an understood hazard when you live in a small town and practise as a helping professional. It happens, but not often. Gaby doesn't get up.

The door opens and out pops Charlene. A flash of bright orange hair disappears momentarily when she jumps out of the seat and her feet hit the ground. She's wearing a red tartan short skirt and black patterned leotards. Her white T-shirt is pulled tight over what appears to be a black lace bra. She flounces up the walk toward Gaby. "Come on! I want to take you for a drink."

"Hi, Charlene." *Try and be polite.* "I'm afraid I don't socialize with clients. Thoughtful of you to offer, though." She makes a concerted effort not to ask Charlene to sit down or come in.

Charlene puts on a huge pout with lips that stretch from one side of her face to the other. "You know I have hateful roommates and Pat is working. He won't drink, anyway." She throws her hands up in the air. "Says it would disagree with his medication. Like I said—loony tunes. I want to go to the tavern, have a few beers, and dance!" She's whines, bending her knees to punctuate her sentence.

Gaby, now standing at the top of her porch stairs, attempts to take control. "Charlene, I don't socialize with clients. That's all there is to it. I can't be your friend."

"I'll stop counselling. Then we can be friends. How about that?"

"Even if you stopped seeing me as your counsellor, we couldn't be friends, Charlene. That's the way it is."

Charlene responds abruptly, almost before Gaby is finished her sentence. "That's okay. I don't want to stop counselling anyway. There's information I have to tell you. Never mind. I'll see you next week." As quickly as she arrived, she's gone.

The screen door bangs behind her as Gaby goes inside. She catches herself wishing Joe would call, but she knows his sisters from Nova Scotia are with him this week. She could always contact him about the bathroom, once his company leaves. He's right. It needs to get done before winter. By the feel of the evening air, that could be anytime now. She turns on the television and settles on her couch, which has become operation-central in the little house. Summertime shows are almost all repeats. Although her eyes are on the tail-end of an entertainment show, she realizes her focus is superseded by Charlene. The last intrusion she needs is a client like Charlene turning up on her doorstep at all hours. Is the young woman dangerous? Is Patrick able to handle someone like her? If, as Charlene says, he's a patient of Dr. Wilkerson and takes medication, then he has mental health challenges of his own. What does Charlene want to confide in her? What could be worse than drowning her roommate's kitten in the toilet because she doesn't like the smell of kitty litter?

With self-admonishment, she realizes she has brought her work home with her yet again—but this time it landed on her front porch all on its own.

Chapter 11

Maybe she took off

Charlene appears for her counselling session. She has a faded bruise on her right cheek. She's made an obvious attempt to mask it with make-up, but instead she looks more ghoulish than normal, with her heavy black eyeliner and bright red lips plastered against matte foundation and a heavy application of rouge. She has had her nose pierced since Gaby saw her on her front porch last week.

"What have you heard about Roz, Charlene? Has she come home?" It has been all over the local news. Roz Dover left the hospital after her shift ended at 11:00 PM on August 6, almost a week ago, and hasn't been seen since. The police are baffled. The community was asked to search their out buildings, garages, stored vehicles, and basements. Her heart pounded and her hand shook on the railing as she descended the stairs, but Gaby did as asked and managed to peek into every corner of her basement. She felt silly, like she was over-dramatizing. She could see the whole area from the bottom of the stairs, but she walked around anyway. Then she tramped around her backyard. In the end, she stood on her rear steps—the ones repaired by Joe—and studied the red and rundown garage, nee shed, on the property next door. Could Roz be in there? Would her neighbours check?

Charlene is blasé, even though the subject of her roommate's disappearance continues to consume the small community. Her eyes are steely as she meets Gaby's gaze. "Maybe she took off. Who knows?" Then she tips her head a tiny bit and continues to look straight at Gaby. "Maybe she ended up like Ila's cat."

Gaby feels a chill run down her back and she involuntarily clenches her shoulders in response. "Have the police talked with you and your roommates?"

"I thought, for a while, that two of those Mounties expected to move in. They went over every scrap of Roz's room. They searched the whole house. They asked lots of questions about who she hung out with; if she had a boyfriend. The one guy she ever mentioned was some hot mechanic who worked on her car. I always thought she preferred girls, so I kept my distance." She throws her head back and shrugs. "I couldn't answer most of their stupid questions. I didn't know her that well. Ila and Crystal talked about her family down east. I think everybody figures she went home."

"Almost a week has passed, Charlene. The news said she wasn't home."

"Maybe she was grabbed on the way back. Who knows? She was a mousy little creep. I never liked her anyway."

Gaby controls her feelings but wonders about Charlene's response. She's almost too disengaged, even for her. Suspicions aside, she moves on with the interview. "Let's talk, today, about how you managed to come to Hayworth, Charlene. Everybody from away seems to have a story about how they came to Hayworth. I want to hear yours."

"I'll tell you mine if you tell me yours." Charlene's expression challenges and her eyes narrow as she meets Gaby's gaze."

Gaby tries her best to push her concerns about Roz to the back of her mind, and to look indulgent. "Our counselling sessions are all about you, Charlene. What brought you to Hayworth?"

Charlene rearranges her short skirt and crosses her legs. "Well, since you asked, I'll tell you all about the real me. I was born in Cape Breton, a few miles outside Sydney. My parents were immature idiot kids and only took care of me until I was about two. My grandparents didn't want me for some reason. I don't know why."

This is new information to Gaby. Up until this point, Gaby was familiar with her history from the time she turned eighteen and was on her own. Charlene has referenced foster homes and her mother's parents, but only in vague terms.

"Have you contacted your parents or grandparents, Charlene?"

"I screwed up the courage to try and find family almost a year ago. I had no job and no money. I thought I'd have to sell my truck. I didn't want to go to the shelter, so I looked up my grandparents. They live in a fancy new house in a subdivision. I went to see them."

"What happened?"

"They said they hadn't seen my mother in ten years. I stayed for two nights, in a guest room with its own bathroom. My grandmother got all huffy when she saw me with her diamond studs in my ears. She asked for them back and then they told me to leave. They gave me a cheque for five hundred dollars and told me to have a nice life. They have a pretty fancy place—you know, with furniture that isn't made from cement blocks and old boards. The earrings are nice and big, eh? I swiped them on my way out." She tilts her head to the side so Gaby can get a good look at the studs.

Gaby ignores the earrings. "Then what did you do?"

"I had to stay at the shelter. It was gross. People cough and hack all through the night. There are mental cases there and they wander around and try to steal your stuff. I would have been better off in my truck. I met a guy. He needed a ride to Halifax, so I thought 'what the hell' and said I was driving to Halifax the next day and I'd take him with me. He had a few bucks that he gave me for gas. I never told him I had any money."

"So you drove all the way out here with no idea whether or not you could find work?"

"I'm not stupid! I can read a newspaper! Just because they're about to close hospitals in Nova Scotia doesn't mean that's happening in Alberta. Every small town out here seems to have a hospital! I already knew hospitals have trouble finding people to do the shit jobs. You don't have to be Einstein to figure that out."

She sounds incensed and Gaby's afraid she's offended the young woman, so she tries another tactic. "Tell me about the fellow you drove to Halifax. Was he a nice guy?"

"Why do you want to know about him? He was nobody. He could disappear off the face of the earth and no one would care—the same as me." Her voice falls. Gaby leans forward in order to hear her.

"Do you think that if you disappeared, no one would care?"

"Well, maybe you would—but, oh I just remembered, we're not friends, are we? We'll never be friends, so you wouldn't care either." Her look is defiant. Her eyes blister in their blackness. She reaches up and touches the bruise on her cheek.

****

All anyone in the office talks about is the missing girl. Local news has turned into provincial news, and Gaby caught a story on the national broadcast last night. She's been gone more than ten days. No one can remember a situation like this happening in the area before. The police say they have persons of interest, but no suspects. Women in the community feel uncomfortable.

Pearl asks to see Gaby following coffee break a couple of days after her last interview with Charlene.

"How are your sessions progressing with Charlene Quinn now? Is she coping with the disappearance of her roommate, or does she not care?"

Gaby plops down in one of Pearl's office chairs and crosses one baggy cotton-clad leg over the other. "In all seriousness, Pearl, she seems to have no feelings other than to say the cops are stupid and no one misses Roz anyway. I find it a challenge to get her to talk about it, let alone describe feelings—if there actually are any." Her frustration bubbles up; an emotion she would never reveal outside Pearl's office. She trusts Pearl.

"I am concerned about you. I think, although you will probably disagree, that this client may be dangerous. She has a sociopath's personality. We already know that. She killed this girl's cat, for heaven's sake! We don't know what she's capable of."

"She came to my house for a visit earlier in the evening of the night Roz went missing."

"Have the police contacted you, Gaby?" Pearl's expression has gone from annoyed to alert.

"No. Why would they? I can't discuss Charlene with them. If they asked if she was at my house, I would tell them she appeared at my door around 8:00 PM and was there for five minutes. I didn't even let her in."

"Good. They may track the whereabouts of each one of Roz's housemates. Charlene might tell the police she was with you. If that happens, tell them what you told me. She didn't say she wanted to hurt Roz, did she?"

"My God, Pearl, what are you implying? That Charlene hurt Roz or that I knew about it and didn't report it?" Gaby can feel herself shaking. Her eyes well up with tears, no matter how hard she tries to keep her emotions in check.

"No, Gaby." Pearl leans forward and stares into Gaby's eyes. "You have to be careful. This woman makes me nervous. I know you won't repeat details she's told you in confidence unless she provides you with information that might endanger someone else. She understood all that when you first met with her, right?"

"Yes, Pearl." Gaby's audible sigh is one of exasperation. "I explained all the rules. She signed all the forms. They're in the file and she was given her copies. The inappropriate and antisocial behaviour she revealed was about the kitten—and she tried to reconcile with a grandmother but stole her diamond studs instead." Gaby looks across at Pearl and shakes her head. "Do you honestly think she might have hurt Roz? She's a little spit of a woman. How is that even possible?"

"Stranger crimes have happened, my dear. I've been in this business for years. This girl scares me. Keep good notes. You might need them."

****

"Hi, Charlene. Come on in. Good week?"

"If you could call having the RCMP crawling around 'good'." She plunks herself down in the chair by Gaby's desk. Mimi, resplendent on swollen ankles and with just over a month left in her pregnancy, escorts Charlene down to the office. She widens her eyes at Gaby when Charlene's back is turned. This has become a habit.

"Still no news?" There are posters up all over town, of Roz and of her car, a battered and dilapidated olive-green 1975 two-door Ford Pinto. How hard could it be to find a Ford Pinto, for God's sake?

"You know...." Charlene appears thoughtful. "There was a case down east a few years ago. Some guy was driving down the road on the South Shore, going to work in Halifax. He vaporized. They looked for him all summer. When the leaves started to fall off the trees, they found him in his car, upside down, in some gully off the side of the road. They figured he went to sleep or lost control and disappeared until fall. Crazy, eh?"

"That's a sad story, Charlene. It must have been torture for his family, wondering what happened to him."

"Who knows? At least they found a body. Supposedly, that helps people cope. That's what they say." She examines her long black nails as she talks.

"Last week, when we finished up, you told me about how you left Sydney and came out west. I'm interested in your trip and in the young man you drove to Halifax. Do you keep in touch?"

"The trip out here was fine. I was forced to stay in Winnipeg and bus tables at some dive near the train station for two weeks, but I put together enough money to get the rest of the way. If you show guys enough tits, they'll give you a big tip. Guys are such assholes. There isn't much more to tell. I drove here, hired on at the hospital, stayed at the local flophouse until I saw the ad, and here we are. Satisfied?"

Gaby is not satisfied. Charlene started this whole process when she said she had issues but has never revealed too much. Pearl is correct about the cat incident, though. She expects there are a lot more similar stories. Might as well go back to the beginning. "Charlene, when you first came to see me, you said you had issues. How about we talk about those issues one by one? I know you don't like your job or your roommates. I know you had a rough time in foster care. We need to decide, as a team, what issues you would like to explore in more depth. To do that, you have to share details with me. Right now, as I see it, you gloss over topics to make them seem unimportant— perhaps, so you won't feel hurt again—but in order to progress, you have to want to get to the roots of your feelings. Do you understand?"

"I think you don't want to see me anymore."

"Not true. We have weekly appointments booked to accommodate your current work schedule. I manage to see you in the mornings when you work afternoon shifts and on your days off, if you work the day shift. In my eyes, we aren't progressing. What did you want to accomplish when you decided to come for counselling?"

"I told you from the start, Gaby. I don't like people. I don't like my job. I hate animals and I hate my life. I've thought about different ways I could kill myself. Are you happy now? Is that what you want me to say?"

"When are the times you wanted to kill yourself, Charlene?" Gaby hadn't thought of this girl as suicidal—without feelings, yes, but suicidal, no.

"When my grandparents didn't want me; when I was at the shelter in Sydney; on my way out west; when I was in Winnipeg. You name it. I think about it a lot. The guy who came with me from the shelter—he made me want to kill myself."

"What prevented you, Charlene?"

"What prevented me?" She almost shrieks. "Don't you want to know why I felt like killing myself instead of what kept me from doing it? I don't get you!"

"You've told me a lot of situations make you think about suicide, Charlene, but you haven't acted on them. To me, that means you see value in you. That's good. We need to look at what that is and expand on it."

"I haven't killed myself because nobody would notice or care. Satisfied? Why should I off myself? I get more satisfaction out of other people's misery. Nobody would give a shit if I lived or died." Her voice is still elevated, but her head is bowed and she examines her nails again. She no longer stares at Gaby. The challenge has ebbed.

"So, if you have suicidal thoughts, what happens?" Gaby thinks she knows the answer already, but won't reveal her insights for fear she might give her client ideas.

"Simple. When I start to think about snuffing myself, I hurt somebody else—like when I took my grandmother's earrings; like when I drowned Ila's stupid cat; like when I stole all the money from the cash before I took off from Winnipeg. What would you call that, Gaby? Do I redirect my ideation down another avenue?" Her voice is snide.

Gaby doesn't respond. She waits with practised patience for Charlene to get her annoyance off her chest.

"I'm not stupid. Surprised? I've read about people like me. I won't kill myself. There'll always be ways for me to redirect my anger away from myself. There! Self-awareness has occurred! Am I cured?"

"How did you redirect your suicidal thoughts when you were at the shelter in Sydney, Charlene?"

"Oh, let's leave that little nugget for another session, shall we?" Charlene wiggles into her tight leather jacket with all the zippers. "I have to go now. I imagine there's a nice cop at my front door and I can practise using my tits to their best advantage. Men—they're all alike." She chortles as she gets ready to leave.

Gaby feels compelled to accompany her down the hall to reception. Even after all the times she's been to the office, Gaby doesn't trust her to make a direct exit to the foyer.

****

"I'm glad I called, Joe. I needed some company for supper and I wanted to talk to you, yet again, about my ill-fated bathroom." They sit across from one another in a booth by the window at the diner.

"I was pleased to hear from you, Gaby, and we don't have to talk business. We can have supper as friends. You don't have to be one of my customers."

"I needed a break from co-workers and clients, Joe. It has been a tedious couple of weeks. All anyone can talk about is Roz Dover, and I have a bad feeling about all this."

"Well, if they find her car in the vicinity, then they'll no doubt suspect foul play, but until then, Gaby, she might have just driven away. Nobody knows."

Patrick comes to the table with their orders. As usual, they've both ordered the special tonight—turkey dinner with all the trimmings. "Hi, Joe. Hi, Gaby. Have you two started to make the diner a habit?" He seems delighted with the idea.

Gaby is anxious to set the record straight, but she isn't sure why. "Oh, we're discussing whether or not I can afford a new bathroom, Patrick. How are you these days?"

"Okay, I guess." He looks pensive. "I suppose this is a stupid question, but have either of you ever met someone that you liked at first and then didn't? I'm not sure how to get rid of her, now."

"We've all been there, kid. You have to stick to your guns. If you don't want to see her, you have to say so." Joe doesn't mince words.

"I wish it was that easy. I'll have to talk to the doc about it, I guess. I'll go get the water pitcher and be right back to refill your glasses."

Joe looks over at Gaby and confirms what she already knows but can't reveal. "He sees a psychiatrist, Gaby. He used to have lots of problems but he's been quite normal since around the time our friend, Ben, died. She was so good to him. He's come a long way."

If Patrick is attempting to extricate himself from Charlene, as Gaby suspects, she understands his dilemma better than most would.

Chapter 12

There were no signs of a struggle

Finally, after many dinners at the Hayworth Diner, Gaby has invited Joe for supper. As is most often the case, she plans to use the excuse of finalizing plans for her bathroom. They still haven't gone to the movies together, but she put it out there a couple of weeks ago, so she wants to leave the next step up to him.

She stands back to admire her kitchen for the thousandth time. Since it remains the biggest room in the house, she has been able to keep her dining room suite by locating the table against the far wall and placing two of the six chairs on either end of the sideboard in the living room. This arrangement effectively accommodates her little work island with the wooden top.

She's made a taco casserole. It bubbles away in the oven. A salad chills in the fridge. She bought crusty buns at the grocery store. She's always wanted to take the time to make her own bread again, but work always seems to get in the way. Maybe that can be her winter-works project this year. September means there are lots of apples around, so she's made an apple crisp that now cools on a rack atop her soft green tile counter. The table is set and all she has to do is wait for Joe to arrive at around 6:00 PM.

A knock on the screen door alerts her to the fact that her friend has seen fit to turn up about ten minutes early. His frame shadows the screen as she rounds the corner from the kitchen and makes her way toward him. "Come in, come in. The door's not latched." It creaks as he opens it and fills space.

"I'll fix that squeak for you the next time I'm here, Gaby." He grins and presents her with a bottle of German white wine. Almost as an apology, he adds, "I know supper is Mexican and red would be better, but neither one of us seems to have a taste for red, so I took a chance and threw tradition to the wind. It's already chilled, if you want to crack it open now. Do you have a corkscrew? We don't have much time before the news comes on."

"What?" Gaby is a little overwhelmed with Joe's entrance. He never talks this much. *And what about the TV? He came to her house to watch TV?*

"Let's turn on the news, Gaby. They found that girl's car today. One of the cops I know told me this afternoon."

"They found Roz Dover's car? Where?" Gaby pulls wine glasses out of the cupboard while Joe opens the wine. "Here." She puts the glasses down on the counter. "I'll go turn on the television."

"You won't believe this. They found her car at the end of some extended dirt road that used to lead to two old farms bordering the Wolski property. The story is that these bachelor brothers, long dead, owned the properties, feuded between themselves, and never got along with anybody in their family. I guess they had a few cousins." Joe carries the glasses into the living room and sets them carefully on the coffee table. "The Wolskis have tried to buy the land, but nobody left in the family would agree to do a deal." The supper news hour from Edmonton is about to start.

"The 1975 green Ford Pinto, belonging to Roz Dover, a cleaner at the hospital in Hayworth, north of Edmonton, has been discovered on an abandoned dirt road about ten miles outside the town. Miss Dover was reported missing on August 7, when she did not appear for her 3:00 PM shift at the hospital. Her roommates reported she did not come home the night before." A grainy picture of Roz, reproduced from her hospital personnel photo, is projected on the screen. "The local RCMP detachment is conducting an intensive search of the area which is described as including two abandoned farm houses and various outbuildings. They also report there was no sign of a struggle, Miss Dover's purse and car keys were located in the vehicle, and the driver's door was open. If anyone has any information as to the whereabouts of Roz Dover, or information regarding the night of August 6 when she left work at 11:00 PM, please contact your local detachment of the RCMP."

Gaby perches on one of her grey side chairs and stares at the screen as other news is read by the chisel-faced news anchor with the plastic hair. Joe gets up to turn it off. She breaks the silence. "It gave me the creeps to wander around my backyard and down in the basement when they asked everyone to search their properties last month. That fallen-down garage next door didn't help." She takes a sip of her wine. "Nice, Joe."

"One of my favourites. Glad you like it. Did they ever search that building?"

"Oh yes. Empty, thank God!"

"Well, the cops will be all over that property where they found her car. Let's hope there isn't some pervert on the loose. You have to remember to keep your truck doors and your house doors locked at all times, Gaby. Over at The Station, we used to lock the outside door when the last person came in for the night, but now we keep it locked all the time. It can be a hassle going in and out, especially for Amanda and Chester who manage the place, but we decided as a group that it would be worth it."

They eat together for a few minutes in comfortable silence. "We haven't talked about your bathroom yet, Gaby. Still want to look at doing a renovation?"

"Yes! That was the reason I asked you over." His look makes her regret the remark and she adds, "...and your fine company, of course."

"Of course." He glances over his shoulder at her as he moves their plates to the kitchen counter. "Let's take a trip over to Beaver Lumber in Carter River. You can pick out whatever you want and we can order what they don't have. They'll give me a contractor discount, so you'll save a little money."

"I bought my couch in Carter River right after I came here. Your neighbour, Ben Tullis the antique dealer, told me about the furniture warehouse. She was nice to me."

"Ben was nice to everybody. Too bad you never knew her better. She was a fine lady." Joe almost gets misty-eyed, so Gaby refocuses back on her bathroom. "Let's make a list and then we'll have dessert, Joe."

They spend the remainder of the evening with a measuring tape and graph paper. Suddenly, she realizes it's near 10:30 PM and they both have to work the next day. He hesitates at the door for a moment, which gives Gaby the opportunity to reach up on her tiptoes just enough to kiss him quickly on the cheek. "Thanks for the company, Joe. It was a great evening despite the news."

He lays his hand, with surprising gentleness, on her shoulder as he looks down at her. "Lock the door after I leave. I'll call tomorrow and we can arrange a time to go shopping on Saturday. I'm pretty sure I'm not scheduled to work this weekend. All I have to do is finish a client's walk-in closet by Friday."

After he's gone, and she's turned out her porch light and locked the doors, Gaby's mind returns to Roz's car. She'll stay up to watch the news at 11:00 PM. Perhaps there's more information. Regardless, this will be the focus of the office tomorrow.

****

Sure enough, the office is abuzz the next morning. Roz is all anybody can talk about. People assume Gaby must have information because one of her clients was a roommate of Roz's. She knows no more than anybody else who watches the news, although feelings of unease nibble around the edges of her denials.

She gets summoned to Pearl's office. "When's your next appointment with Charlene Quinn?"

"I have one scheduled for Monday afternoon. She works the 3:00 until 11:00 PM shift on Monday, so I see her right after lunch. Why?"

"I want you to be careful. Document every detail. The police have her, as well as the other two girls, Crystal and Ida, under surveillance."

"I assume you mean Ila."

"What?"

"The girls' names are Crystal and Ila. How do you know the police are watching them?"

"Dr. Alden received a call. It appears Charlene was quite forthcoming and told them she was seeing you professionally, so as a courtesy, they informed Clark."

"Do you think Charlene murdered Roz? Pearl, is that what you think? God! Charlene is so tiny! I wonder how she could actually hurt somebody. Really?" Gaby hears herself babbling and tries to calm down.

"We don't know details, but all of Roz's roommates would have to be considered suspects, I would imagine."

"Well, all I know is that Charlene turned up on my porch on the evening that Roz went missing."

"I know, but what the hell for?"

"She wanted me to go out for a drink. She thought we could have a visit, you know, be friends. Lots of clients think that. I explained to her that we couldn't be friends. She said she'd quit counselling and I told her it wouldn't matter, we still couldn't be friends. She said she didn't want to quit anyway, that she still had stuff to tell me, and then she took off. That was about 8:00 PM."

"Have the police contacted you?"

"No. Why would they? You asked me that before." Gaby begins to get nervous. Perhaps Charlene lied and said she was with her counsellor that evening.

"They will. They have to establish the whereabouts of anybody who knew Roz, and that includes Charlene. If they want to interview you, try and get them to come here and ask that your supervisor sit in. You can't talk about your conversations with Charlene, unless, of course, she told you she wants to hurt somebody—or, she gives permission, and I imagine that is quite unlikely." Pearl stares at Gaby, her expression full of unspoken questions and concerns.

"Pearl, she has never told me anything she might do or be contemplating doing! She told me she killed Ila's cat, but that was after the fact. She's never revealed a plan about what she might intend to do."

"Good. Let me know if you get a call from the police. Right now, they're tied up in the search of those properties where they found her car."

****

The trip to Carter River on Saturday, with Joe, is great fun. Gaby chooses a sink and toilet, new taps for her tub and shower as well as the sink, a vanity, vinyl for the floor, and tiles for around the tub and vanity. The colour combination will be black and white. It will look quite modern, but with a 1940s flair. They laugh a lot. It takes her mind off her upcoming session with Charlene. They eat lunch at a restaurant that isn't a diner, and tease one another about not understanding how to order when the tables have chairs and tablecloths.

When they get back to Hayworth, they end up at the diner for the Saturday night special—meat loaf and mashed potatoes. Nancy serves them and remarks that they're now a local fixture in the place and will soon resemble an old married couple. She says there are lots of older folks around who don't cook that much and eat out there a lot. They accept Nancy's good-natured kidding. She thinks they're a real couple.

"How would you like to spend Thanksgiving at The Station this year?" Joe lingers over his tea and acts like he doesn't want to call it a night even though it has been a very long day.

"Is this a dinner invitation?"

"Sort of. I expect to host Christmas dinner at The Station this year again—and you're more than welcome to come to that, too. We all got together last year after Ben died and decided we would do it again. Other than Cheryl, none of us knew you then, I guess. As for Thanksgiving, the gal who moved into Ben's apartment—you might know her through your work—Ronny Étang, thought she might like to do a Thanksgiving potluck and everyone in the building is invited. One more won't hurt. You want to come?"

"I know Ronny. Cheryl introduced me to her over at Segue House. Poor Ava Burrway finally qualified for more funding and additional help. When did Ronny move here? In the spring, wasn't it?"

"Yeah, that's right. So, will you be my date for Thanksgiving potluck, or what?" He grins at her over the rim of his cup—a habit Gaby has noticed on more than one occasion.

"I need to be able to contribute. You ask Ronny if I can come and then I'll call and see what she needs me to bring. Deal?"

"Deal."

****

"Like my new earrings?" Charlene wiggles her head so the dangling hand-painted glass orbs bounce around. Gaby is still struggling to absorb the hair colour change. Charlene has bleached her short thick hair to a platinum rendering. With her heavily drawn dark brows and smoky black eye make-up, the result is quite dramatic, and to Gaby's more moderate tastes, not in a good way.

"They're beautiful, Charlene. I don't imagine you found those around here."

Charlene stretches out her arm and shakes her wrist. "The bracelet matches." She winks at Gaby. "Don't tell, now. They were Roz's. I doubt if she's gonna' need them anymore." She smirks down at the jewellery. "The cops are never gonna' find her."

Gaby's stomach flutters and she tries, with difficulty, to keep her voice even and her words benign. "What makes you think that, Charlene? I understand the police intend to explore the area inch by inch."

"Nobody's found the guy I was supposed to drive to Halifax. What a loser! He thought I would give him a lift and have sex with him, too! Can you imagine? He was such an idiot!"

"What happened, Charlene?" Gaby's voice is soft. Her mouth is dry. She crosses her legs and reaches for her coffee, now cool from sitting on her desk far too long.

"This is what I've wanted to tell you about." Charlene leans toward Gaby. Her voice is filled with enthusiasm, like she's ready to tell her about a great place she's discovered to shop for shoes. "I forget his name, but it doesn't matter. He never made it to Halifax." She leans back and giggles. "Serves him right. He tried to feel me up while I was driving! I pulled into a dirt road and drove about a half mile. He got all excited; thought we were going to do it in the car! Can you imagine? What an asshole! I told him to get out and followed him down the road—quite far in the end. Finally, I put the wire loop around his neck and snared him like a rabbit!"

Gaby, stunned, tries to maintain her composure as she watches the young woman in front of her, remorseless, discuss the act of terminating someone's life. It is a challenge to keep her thoughts focused, but she asks the obvious. "You're a small woman, Charlene. How did you manage to control this guy?"

She's off-handed; cavalier, almost. "Oh, he wasn't *that* much taller than me. You'd be surprised how little size matters when you have a snare around your neck, and somebody twists a tightening stick as fast as they can. Here, I'll show you." She reaches into her fringed shoulder bag and pulls out a wire loop with dowels twisted into the wire at each end. "No big deal. This is all you need. I think the actual term is garrotte." Her voice is calm, but she widens her eyes as she looks up at Gaby.

"Are you shocked? This isn't the wire I used on the guy. Don't worry. That's long gone, but a girl has to be prepared." She tucks it into her purse, pats the flap closure, and leans back into her chair. "Man, I am so glad to get that off my chest, but you see what I mean? They'll never find Roz."

"Now," all business, Charlene continues. "I know you can't tell anybody about this and all my records are confidential, right? You can't go to the police about me."

"No, Charlene. I can't go to the police, but I have to document our discussion sessions. Other people see the files."

"But they're bound by confidentiality, too, right? I looked all this up after my first couple of times seeing you. I know I'm right." Her tone of voice is leaden with challenge and her smoky eyes hold Gaby's.

"Yes, all that's true, but if I, or my files, were to be subpoenaed to court, my hands would be tied."

"I know. I know. You won't get called to court. They would have to charge me and that won't happen. Remember what I said. Cops are stupid."

Gaby decides she will not ask Charlene if she killed Roz. If Charlene killed her like she did this poor guy from Cape Breton, the police will find the body at the farm where they found her car.

Charlene adds as an afterthought, "If the police question you because you are my counsellor, you can't tell them about this."

"No, that's true. I expect they would ask me about the night Roz disappeared, and I have to tell them you were at my place in the evening and then left in a huff."

"That's okay. I already told them that. I went over to Pat's when I couldn't find him at the diner, but he didn't answer his bell. He might have been in somebody else's apartment. His lights were on and his car was there."

"Charlene, I would like to refer you to Dr. Wilkerson. Would you accept a referral to meet with her?"

"Why would I do that? I don't want to take pills. I don't hear voices like poor old Pat. I don't want to see her. Besides, if you refer me to somebody else, you have to tell them all our dirty little secrets. No, I want to come here." She leans over and pats Gaby's hand. "We make a good team."

Chapter 13

It kept me up all night

Greta Seeley deserves more in her counselling session. Gaby knows this. She has never before, in her professional career, permitted one client's issues to be superimposed onto another, although today she continues to struggle to keep her mind on Greta instead of Charlene. After this appointment, Gaby will meet with Pearl to go over, yet again, the details of the Charlene Quinn case. Today, Gaby will tell her supervisor about the man in Nova Scotia presumably murdered by her client; strangled with a snare of some sort for God's sake!

"I can't stop feeling guilty. I know they're being well cared for. I go and see them every weekend. They haven't forgotten me, but I feel like such a bad mother!" Greta, a short and chubby young woman of twenty-two, is the mother of two young children. Her crying is uncontrolled as she sputters out her feelings. Her long hair needs a wash and hangs down over either side of her face. Her ears peek out between the stands.

Greta came to Gaby, via a third-party referral, when she presented herself at Child Protection Division seeking temporary placement for her children. The case is exceptional. Her children did not need protection from their mother. The family was abandoned by Greta's common-law partner. Apparently, in a drunken rage, he threatened all three of them and then took off for parts unknown. Greta was left holding the bag with no money, rent due, and two children in her care. Amy is three and Joshua is six months. They made their way to Segue House, but Greta required a permanent solution so a plan was put in place. With her lack of education after grade twelve, she could not hope to get a job that would support her children and pay for a sitter while she worked. In the end, and after three months of unbearable stress, she has managed to put her kids in temporary custodial care and get a job pumping gas at the local filling station. She's also enrolled at the community college to take a course in bookkeeping. Her goal is to get her children back once she completes the course and lands a better-paying job.

Very few parents volunteer to surrender their children, even short-term. She is overcome with guilt and her feelings of self-worth are suffering as a result. No matter how Gaby attempts to rephrase her circumstances by pointing out she is making the best decision, her children are safe, and she is moving forward, Greta still sees herself as a bad mother. Periodically, she slips into thinking that she should simply try to survive on a minimal welfare cheque, and retrieve her children back to her rundown apartment; that this option would be her only alternative. Gaby's role is to assist her in making the best decision she can make while ensuring she explores all options and consequences.

"The greatest mothers are the ones that do what's best for their kids, regardless of how they, themselves feel." Gaby's voice is soft.

Greta lifts her head as more tears stream down her flushed cheeks. "I want to think that a year from now I'll feel like the best mother ever; like I've done this for them, but I've never done anything so hard!" Her voice cracks as she starts to cry once more.

"How about we make a plan, Greta? Let's write down your goals and your time-lines. Start with when your course ends and give yourself some time to land a job. What are we looking at?" Gaby picks up her pen and reaches for a sheet of paper.

"My course ends in June. I can do a placement one day a week during the course, and sometimes the office where you're placed will hire you when you're done. The gas station said I could do my placement with them, so that's pretty good, right?" She looks across at Gaby.

"So...here we are in September. You have nine months to get through. If your current employer does in fact hire you, you'll be able to get Amy and Joshua back by early summer. That's not bad, Greta!" Gaby tries, with quiet desperation, to make her voice sound enthusiastic. She can't imagine if she were to ever have a child, surrendering it to a stranger for even a day. "Your other option is to retrieve them now. The problem becomes how to pay for their care while you're in school, correct?"

"Yes. Welfare won't pay for babysitting or daycare. Child Protection says the foster family will be my babysitter while I complete the course. I wish there was another way, but I think this is the best I can do for them, so we have a future."

"Exactly. Know, in your heart, that you are going to make life better for your kids, and that the situation is temporary"

"I'll see them every spare minute and can even have them visit on the weekends, you know. I have to find a way to balance when I study and when I have them with me." All of a sudden, Greta's words sound like she doesn't feel quite so guilty.

"Tell me some more about your decision to take the bookkeeping course, Greta. What prompted your choice?"

Greta starts to talk about how good she was in math when she was in high school and if she hadn't become pregnant, she would have gone on to college.

Gaby continues to try and focus on the situation at hand, but she has become increasingly nervous about Charlene. Last night, Gaby rearranged the furniture in her living room so she could curl up on her couch and have a clear view of the front street. The advantage of this position is that she can see out the window, but someone driving or walking by would be unable to detect her there. Charlene keeps driving up and down the street. You can't miss that Land Cruiser.

"In the end, I thought a bookkeeping course might be good in case I ever wanted to do people's books from home. With two kids, it'll mean I can be home more if I want to. Good idea?"

Gaby looks across at Greta, and for a fraction of a second her mind sees Charlene sitting there. "Yes, yes, your choice seems very wise, Greta. Our time is almost up. Do you want to continue on with counselling? We decided after the first month, we would reassess." She leaves the door open for her client to determine if additional support might be required.

"Can I fly on my own for a few weeks and call if I need to come in?"

"That's a good idea, but call me regardless in a month and tell me how you're doing. I'll write to Child Protection Division and let them know your status. The file will remain open until then. Okay?"

Gaby walks Greta back out to reception. She will complete her notes and compose a letter to the other division after she meets with Pearl.

Out in reception, Mimi hands her phone messages that have been taken during the counselling session. Two are from clients rescheduling and one is from Ronny Étang, hopefully to talk about Thanksgiving because she doesn't need another referral right now. She has enough problems coping with her current caseload since Charlene appears to monopolize all of her available head space.

****

"Good afternoon. This is Maggie. How may I direct your call?"

"Hi, Maggie. It's Gaby Ridgway, over at Counselling Division. Could I please speak to Ronny?"

"Sure, Gaby! How are you? I hear you might be coming over for Thanksgiving at The Station. Are you and Joe an item?" She giggles.

Gaby is always struck by how child-like Maggie can be. Ava, the director of Segue House and Maggie's boss, thinks the world of her, and she is quite good at her job. "No, but Joe and I are good friends. He's helped me a lot with my house—first the kitchen, and now the bathroom is almost done. I think he feels sorry for me because I'm by myself, so he asked me to join all of you. That's why I'm calling Ronny."

"We'll see about the Joe-business." Her voice has a teasing quality. "Anyway, I'll put you through to Ronny."

After a few seconds, the phone clicks and Ronny answers. "Hi, Gaby! Joe said you would be calling about Thanksgiving. Of course, you are more than welcome and you don't have to bring a thing! We are going to have enough food to last a week!"

"Hi Ronny. Listen, I'm so pleased to be invited. How about I bring dessert?"

"That might be my one loose end, Gaby, now that I think about it. Patrick will likely bring a pie, but everybody else will be doing main dish stuff, so dessert should be perfect. I'm very pleased to hear you will be there."

"It sounds like The Station is a pretty close-knit group. You won't mind me butting in?"

"Not an issue! They welcomed me with open arms when I arrived on the bus at the diner back in May. Everybody will be there. I don't know, as yet, if there's anybody else invited. By the way, we need to meet soon and do follow-up on the referrals I've made. Let me know a good time and I'll come over."

"No problem, Ronny. Right now I'm managing a rather challenging situation—professionally, that is, not personally. In any event, I hope it will all sort itself out in the near future and I'll have more time." Her minds slips back to Charlene and she remembers her appointment with Pearl. A few minutes remain to say goodbye and make a cup of tea. "I'm looking forward to your get-together with everyone. Talk to you soon."

"Take care, Gaby."

Now her singular concern, given that Patrick Hollinger lives at The Station and has been in some sort of relationship with her client, is that he doesn't intend to invite Charlene to Ronny's for Thanksgiving dinner. He did mention, when she and Joe were at the diner a while ago, that he wanted to get out of a relationship. She hopes she assumes correctly and it was the one with Charlene.

****

After she makes tea and has a quick chat with Mimi—with a two-year-old and a new baby, it's all kids, all the time—Gaby traverses the hallway to Pearl's office. The door is ajar, so she knocks softly and pushes it open. Pearl is on the phone, looking out the generous window behind her desk. Her voice is low. Gaby doesn't want to disturb her so starts to back her way out again. Pearl turns around and motions her in as she says her goodbyes to whoever occupies the other end of the conversation.

Today, Pearl looks like she just climbed down off a horse and made her way to her desk. She's in blue jeans and a soft navy denim shirt. Her greying hair is pushed back behind her ears. "Sorry for my attire, Gaby. We're trying to get as much of the hay stored as we can before the weather starts to get out of hand. I intended to take the day off, but wanted to come in and talk to you about this whole Charlene Quinn affair. You know the police have her under observation?"

"Well, not in so many words." Gaby moves to sit down, although she doesn't expect this will be a good time to reveal the information about the admission of murder in Nova Scotia, especially if Pearl is in a big hurry to get back to her ranch. "Charlene told me she thought the police were following her, and they've been to her house a number of times, but...you never know with Charlene. It could all be made up."

She heaves a sigh. "I don't know if you have time today, but she told me quite the story yesterday. It may not be true, but it kept me up all night and I'm having trouble focusing on my other clients. This could be bad."

Pearl leans across her desk and peers at Gaby over her glasses. "Don't worry about my time. What did she tell you, Gaby? Did she admit to hurting Roz Dover?"

"No. Not in so many words. But she told me she killed a guy in Nova Scotia."

"What! My God, Gaby, tell me what she said!"

"Well," Gaby begins. She still feels pressure to be brief "I've written detailed notes, but the short rendition is that she met a guy at a shelter in Sydney. She was mad because her grandparents wouldn't let her stay with them. She stole her grandmother's diamond earrings even though they gave her five hundred dollars. I think I've already mentioned that. She met this guy who seemed to her like nobody would care if he went missing and so she killed him on the way to Halifax. She said she was incensed that he made a pass at her." Gaby meets Pearl's gaze. "From what I can determine, the body hasn't been found. We would have to talk to the RCMP in Nova Scotia to know for sure, and I sure as hell can't do that!" She takes a breath before she continues.

"In any event, she's wearing pieces of Roz's jewellery, telling me she thinks cops are stupid, and saying they'll never find Roz."

"Do you think she did it?"

"I don't know. I think she wants me to think that she did. She reminds me, over and over again, that I can't tell. For someone who said she doesn't read forms, she can quote the ethics rule book like a pro."

"This whole situation could go sideways in the blink of an eye. I can't believe they won't ever find her—her body, at least—since they're going over those farms with a fine tooth comb. How many ways can you hide a body on a prairie?"

"Well, if there's a way to do it, Charlene knows. She claims she killed the guy in Nova Scotia with a snare wire and a stick. She said she kept tightening the stick until he died. I found it hard to believe. She's such a small person. When I said this, she was quite adamant that when someone has a wire pushing through their windpipe, size doesn't matter very much." She shudders as she thinks about the conversation again—the reason why she can't sleep. Every client leaves an impression, makes a dent in your life, marks you somehow, but Charlene is not like other clients. This has gone from being experiential, from expanding her insight as a counsellor, to threatening, life-changing, and downright scary.

"When do you see her again?"

"Next week—Tuesday right after lunch, before her afternoon shift at the hospital."

"What if I sit in with you? We can make it a supervisory interview. Call it part of your evaluation." Pearl chortles at Gaby's shocked expression. "I know, I know. I never manage to do those sessions when I'm supposed to. What am I—two years behind? Anyway, it will be an excuse for me to sit in and do my own assessment of her. I think you need some added support with this, kid. And on that note, you don't see clients on Fridays, do you?"

Gaby shakes her head. "I reserve Fridays in case of emergencies and to do paperwork."

Pearl nods. "You're never behind in that department. Stay home tomorrow. Take a personal day. You need a break. This could get a lot worse before it gets better, Gaby."

"Maybe I will, Pearl. Joe Dodd is finishing up my bathroom. All he has left is the tile work. He has another job to start next week, so he's bound and determined to get the tile and grouting done before the weekend is over. Maybe I can help him with clean-up. Thanks. I'll let Mimi know."

Back in her office, and grateful for a boss who understands and appreciates the pressure of a case like this, Gaby tidies up what paperwork she hadn't completed already and makes her plan for the weekend. She'll call Joe tonight and let him know she'll be around tomorrow. Perhaps she'll score a dinner at the diner. He's always up for that. She might get that movie date, yet.

****

"Need an assistant tomorrow?" Joe answers the phone on the first ring, so Gaby takes the opportunity to jump right in after she hears his hello.

"Maybe. What do you have in mind?" His voice is soft and playful. She thinks he must be smiling. As usual, she can hear Blanche purring somewhere close by.

"I have been given the day off. Been working on a hard case and Pearl thinks I need a break so she insisted I take a personal day. How's that for a nice boss?"

"I think I need one of those. My boss wants me to work all weekend."

"Now, you can't blame that on me. You're the one who promised somebody you'd start their hardwood floor on Monday. I would have waited to get my tiles done."

"I know, Gaby. I'm my own worst enemy. Do you have particular tasks to do tomorrow, or do you want to help?"

"I want to help. I want to get as far away from counselling as I can."

"Okay. I'll be there at 8:00 AM. I won't even stop at the diner for coffee."

"Is that a hint?"

"Absolutely! If you intend to assist, the helper always takes care of the coffee." He laughs, now. "Wear old clothes and I'll teach you how to install tile. You never know when you might need another skill set."

After she hangs up, Gaby thinks that he could be right. Too many more cases like Charlene, and she might be ready for a change. She is surprised at herself for even contemplating such an option. The phone rings again and it's Mimi.

"Hi, Mimi. What's up? Are you still in town?"

"No. I was worried, though. You never take time off. I know how hard this case has been for you. Are you okay?"

"I'm fine. Weary, I guess, and not sleeping very well. Pearl suggested that since I didn't have anybody booked for Friday, I should take a personal day, that's all. I'm good. I'm going to spend the day learning the craft of ceramic tile installation here with Joe and then, if he doesn't have plans, take him to the diner for supper."

"Do you need some company tonight? I can come back into town for a couple of hours."

"Aren't you sweet, but no, I'm fine. I think there's a movie on TV tonight and that will take my mind off my problems, Mimi. You stay home with your babies and husband."

"Okay, but if you want company, you call me. Tim or I could come and get you if you didn't want to be there by yourself."

"Don't fret. I'm fine and I feel quite safe in my little house. Also, if anybody asks, say I'm off, maybe for an appointment. No big deal. See you Monday, Mimi."

She locates the 9:00 PM movie and settles in. If Charlene worked the day shift, Gaby expects to see her red Land Cruiser go by before the evening is over. It has become a habit that she intends to address with the girl on Tuesday, while Pearl is in the room.

Chapter 14

Keep your hands off my husband

Heidi and Mitch Kelly sit across from Gaby who attempts, with unsettled desperation, to focus on the task at hand. Two RCMP officers are coming to see her as soon as she's finished with the couple, and Charlene is scheduled for this afternoon. Mitch is explaining his wife's current condition and Gaby observes the pair.

Mitch Kelly is a man with a big build and a soft, rolling voice—like thunder in the distance when the sun is still shining. He is dressed in what Gaby guesses is an extraordinarily expensive suit. He's hung his camel hair topcoat with extreme care, on the tree for that purpose located in the corner of the office. His posture is slanted away from his wife who is seated beside him. While conversing with Gaby, he never takes his eyes off Heidi.

Heidi appears to be absorbed in a romance novel. She stares at the open pages. Her lips move, so it looks like she's reading, but they've already been in the session for ten minutes and she's never turned a page. She is dressed in a pinstriped business suit with a white blouse. Although the outfit looks to be designer, the hem of the skirt requires repair and the blouse has cosmetic stains around the neck opening. Heidi's hair is flat on the side where she slept and her make-up is applied in such a way as to suggest she wasn't looking in a mirror. It looks mask-like, with the marks of pancake foundation along her jaw line. Her eye shadow is uneven.

After initial observations, Gaby knows for sure she will refer this couple to Dr. Rachel Wilkerson. Heidi has a very serious problem. Heidi presents as much older than her chronological age, and as if she is suffering from a form of early dementia.

"Although I started to notice strange behaviour at home about a year ago, the staff began reporting odd behaviour to me about four months back. She was confusing files and getting clients' details mixed up. She came right out and told me she didn't want to go to court any longer because all the judges were against her." He turns his gaze to Gaby. "You have to understand. She is a highly respected lawyer in Hayworth. Everybody likes and admires her, including the judges."

"You said problems started at home almost a year ago, Mitch. Would you give me some details about that, please?"

"She seems to have gone downhill at a brisk pace. She's stopped taking care of herself. She won't have a shower unless I insist. She wears the same clothes every day. She won't go to the hairdresser anymore. Says the woman is trying to hurt her." His voice cracks a bit as he turns back to his wife. "She's gone to the same hairdresser for ten years. I think she's having a breakdown."

"What is she like at work with the staff, Mitch?"

"She tells me every day that she doesn't want to go to work, but I'm reluctant to leave her home alone. I don't trust her in the house. I don't even let her cook because she turns on the stove and then walks away. When she's at the office, she behaves much the same as she's doing right now. She sits behind her desk and acts like she's reading, although she never turns a page in that bloody book! God, I don't know what to do! Is she mentally ill? Does she have a brain injury of some sort I don't know about?"

His voice has elevated in pitch a tiny bit, and this evokes a reaction from Heidi. She looks up from her book, reaches out a hand, and pats Mitch gently on the knee. Then she turns back to her book without saying a word.

Mitch and Gaby talk at length about options. Gaby feels Heidi will no doubt be diagnosed with a rare form of early dementia. Her family history, as reported vaguely by Mitch, indicates her father was institutionalized when he was in his mid-forties because he was "crazy". Gaby gives Mitch the task of talking with his in-laws to try and tease out additional details. She will make a referral to Dr. Wilkerson, and they will proceed from there.

Mitch reaches out to shake Gaby's hand. When Heidi sees this behaviour, she closes her book and places it with undue care in her purse, empty except for some tissues. She stands, and with an elegance and grace that has served her over many years as she practised law, presents her limp-wristed hand to Gaby. "You are a lovely young woman, but keep your hands off my husband. He isn't yours for the taking, you know."

Gaby is at a loss for words. She looks at Mitch, standing behind his wife, as he shrugs his shoulders. Without another word, Heidi glides out of the office, after she waits patiently for Mitch to open the door for her. Gaby quickly regains her composure and adds, "I'll call your office with the appointment time for Dr. Wilkerson, Mitch. Goodbye, Heidi. It was nice meeting you." The other woman neither turns around nor acknowledges the remark.

****

Later on in the morning, Gaby's phone rings. Mimi, in her secretive voice, tells her there are two RCMP officers in the reception area to see her.

Once in the waiting room, Gaby is reminded of her mother when she looks at Mimi behind her desk. Her mother often used the expression: "her eyes were as big as saucers". "Thanks, Mimi. Please call Pearl and let her know she can come down to my office any time."

She approaches the officers and introduces herself. "Hello. I'm Gaby Ridgway. How do you do?" She shakes hands with them both in turn.

"I'm Constable Fiona Werbowski and this is my partner, Constable Sean Knox. Nice to meet you."

Constable Knox nods and shakes hands but remains silent.

"Follow me. We'll go down to my office. My supervisor, Pearl Markowski, will join us in a few moments." As a means of explanation, she adds, "Pearl thought it wise that I have someone with me. There is no problem with that, is there?" Nervousness creeps over her all of a sudden and she now very much wants Pearl in the room.

"Not a problem." Constable Knox speaks for the first time. His voice reverberates down the hallway. Gaby is relieved office doors are all closed.

By the time they reach her office, Pearl is waiting at the door. She introduces herself, motions for the two to enter ahead of her, and follows them in. Gaby pulls up the rear.

Once everyone is settled, matters are addressed both swiftly and methodically. Yes, Gaby saw Charlene Quinn at her home at 15 Poplar Street the night Roz Dover left work at 11:00 PM and has not been seen since—

August 6. No, she did not invite Charlene in and the young woman left after a few minutes. It was evening—about 8:00 PM. Charlene came by to say she wanted to take Gaby out for a drink. Gaby explains to both officers that, oftentimes, clients want to become friends with their counsellor. This is common but never encouraged. The other extreme is clients who refuse to acknowledge their counsellor, even in a social situation. They don't want to be associated. Two sides of the same coin. She explains that Charlene was annoyed at first, suggesting she would quit counselling so they could be friends. When Gaby clarified that they could never be friends, whether she quit counselling or not, Charlene acted like she had somewhere else to be and left, saying she didn't want to stop seeing Gaby professionally.

"We understand you can't tell us what she talks to you about," Constable Werbowski points out, after giving her partner a withering look. He had already tried, twice, to get Gaby to reveal the nature of the sessions. "Can you give us any opinion as to her state of mind when she left your house?"

Gaby looks over at Pearl, who has been sitting with her chin on her chest, examining her cuticles with narrowed eyes. She will get no help from her boss, who seems to have somehow distanced herself from the process all of a sudden.

"I can't tell you what Charlene was thinking or feeling, Constable. You will have to ask her those questions. I can tell you that when she was at my home, I did not let her in, and did not spend any appreciable time with her that evening."

The two officers rise together. "Thank you for seeing us, Ms. Ridgway. We appreciate you taking a moment from your day." All of a sudden, Sean Knox has become quite congenial. He turns to Pearl. "Nice to have met you, ma'am."

"I'll see you out." Gaby jumps from her chair, opens the door, and leads them back to reception.

Mimi runs out from behind her counter. "Are you okay? Do they think Charlene hurt that girl?"

Gaby shakes her head. "I have no idea, Mimi. I told them about that evening last month when she showed up at my door. I don't believe it to be important. They're trying to account for all the time. See you at noon. I have to go talk to Pearl for a minute. She intends to sit in with me when I meet with Charlene after lunch." Gaby dashes back down the hall and around the corner to Pearl's office.

Pearl replaces her phone in the cradle and looks up at Gaby. "I think Dr. Alden needs to be involved in this, Gaby. This situation could get out of hand and I don't want to be in the middle."

"What? Do you intend to sit in on the interview this afternoon like you said you would?"

"Yes. Clark reminded me that I made a commitment to you and I should stick to it." She looks up at Gaby with an expression akin to annoyance. "Everybody has a boss, so I'll be there, but don't expect me to say much."

"What's the problem, Pearl? Was I out of line this morning? I looked at you a couple of times for support, but you studied your fingers the whole time." Gaby is incensed and now her annoyance bubbles up.

"Listen, Gaby. This is a mess. Charlene Quinn is a sociopath. Hell, for all I know, she's a psychopath. She's a murderer for sure. The police are suspicious. I don't want this broad to get the idea that one of us betrayed her to the police. She's already killed somebody." In a calmer voice, she adds, "I live way the hell out in the country all by myself, Gaby."

Gaby is flabbergasted! Pearl is afraid of Charlene. She doesn't want to be involved because she's afraid this client will...what? Come and search her out in the night? Threaten her in her own bed? "Pearl, Charlene isn't interested in hurting us. I'm sure of that, but if you don't want to be involved, that's fine. I was feeling quite confident that if the situation goes sideways, as you so aptly phrase it, at least there would be more information than merely me and my notes; that you would have interpretations as well. But, if you don't want to take part, that's fine."

"No, no. Alden says I have to attend and then provide a full report to him, so that's what I'll do—but I'm not happy about it. And I hope the cops won't come back any time soon. Their presence is bad for business."

Gaby doesn't understand Pearl's sudden and bizarre change of heart. Police officers come into the Hexagon all the time, especially as it relates to the Child Protection and Mental Health Divisions. "So what's changed, Pearl? We've talked about Charlene before. You know what I have been forced to deal with here. There were no surprises."

Her boss' voice is quiet. "I read your notes this morning before the meeting with the police. She is one scary woman. I don't want her to set her sights on me. After today, she'll have one more person to focus her anger on. I hope she makes a mistake and tells you she's thinking about committing a crime. That way, you can report her without breaking any ethical rules."

Gaby returns to her office before she wanders down to the staff room for lunch. There should be no reason for Pearl to be afraid for her safety, or should there? For the first time, Gaby allows herself to think about the Land Cruiser driving past her little house on a regular basis; about Charlene, defiant on her front porch; about Charlene's fixation with Patrick and her descriptions of multiple attempts to find him at the diner or at The Station. Maybe she should be more nervous, but what good would that do?

****

Charlene arrives right on time. She's dressed in her hospital cleaning clothes—drab green top and baggy pants. They look like surgical scrubs. Her eye make-up is extra heavy, her earrings extra big, and her hair colour is almost shiny in its whiteness. She was told, when Gaby called to confirm their appointment, how Pearl would sit in on this session. She was told it was a supervisory visit for observation. It looks to Gaby that, despite her work attire, Charlene hopes to shock Pearl somehow.

She plunks herself down in the chair right beside Gaby's desk, shrugs off her leather jacket, and runs her fingers through her hair. It has a metallic sheen. "Where's your boss? You said she was going to be here. I have stories I want to tell her. Information I want her to know." Charlene simpers in her secretive and knowing way, exposing teeth that seem to protrude from stretched lips. Her large mouth doesn't relate to the rest of her.

"Never mind about Ms. Markowski, Charlene. Her role is to simply sit in on our session and observe how I work. All you have to do is be yourself. Ah! There she is now." Gaby looks up as Pearl appears in the doorway.

"Hello, Charlene, correct? I'm Pearl Markowski, Gaby's supervisor. I'll join you for a little while. You don't mind, do you?"

Pearl offers to shake Charlene's hand, but Charlene appears to ignore the gesture and opts for a flighty wave of her fingers instead. "I was telling Gaby that I was anxious to meet you. She's a great counsellor. She's a good person." She leans toward Pearl who has perched on the edge of a chair near the opposite wall, close to the door. "She's managed to get me to open up. I've told her almost all my secrets." She leers a little. "I imagine you've read my file. I should write a book, right? Anyway, I know you can't tell anybody about what I've done, so I don't care what you've read. Did you meet with the cops today, too?"

Pearl looks at Gaby.

"I told Charlene about my upcoming appointment with the police. I was clear about what I would tell them and what I could not." This part of Gaby's response is focused on Pearl. She turns to Charlene as she tries to regain control of the session. "Yes, Pearl was there."

"So how did it go? They expect me to have an alibi for the whole evening Roz went missing—to prove I didn't kill her, of course. I can't account for a few hours. They're suspicious, but they're stupid, too. Stupid and suspicious won't get you anywhere, will it? What do you think, Pearl? May I call you Pearl?"

Pearl nods. Gaby thinks she looks like she would prefer to shrink into the woodwork. Charlene plays with her like a cat with a mouse.

"Have you seen Patrick lately, Charlene?" Gaby attempts a subject change.

Charlene crosses her legs and sticks her chin out while she squares her shoulders. "I manage to find him at the diner every now and then, but his boss had the nerve to ask me not to sit in the staff booth anymore! She told me that Pat is there to work and not socialize. I wonder if he asked her to say that to me. Anyway," she shakes her head a tiny fraction, "I wait for him down the block." She snickers then. "He's such a schizo—I think he's convinced himself I want to hurt him. He's so paranoid. It's hysterical to watch how nervous he gets when he sees me outside the diner. All I have to do is sit there and he almost runs to his car. Last night, a guy in a big-ass blue truck came and picked him up at 11:00 PM. Pat's car must be in the shop. Anyway, I think that's the same guy that hangs out at your place—Joe somebody?"

"Tell me about your relationship with Patrick, Charlene. How is a relationship with him important?"

"There's a fancy Thanksgiving dinner being planned for The Station, you know. I hear you're invited." She stares at Gaby, her eyes defying Gaby to deny her statement.

Gaby refuses to be baited.

"Well, one of my roommates heard Chester Wolski...." She turns to Pearl to explain. "He and his wife manage The Station and he works at Ford. Anyway, my roommate heard him chatting with Joe, in the big blue truck, and Joe said you would be there, too. I thought Ila would piss her pants if she didn't tell me! She wanted to know if Pat had invited me. Well, he hasn't, if that's what you're wondering. He should invite me. We've been dating for a while. So will you go?"

"I don't discuss my personal life, Charlene. On the other hand, this is the time set aside for you to do exactly that. Let's talk some more about Patrick. Tell me the reasons you think the two of you are a couple?"

****

At the end of the session, Pearl bolts for her office. Gaby makes a cup of tea and drifts down later in the afternoon. She stands at Pearl's door. "Do you want to talk about Charlene and share your impressions with me?"

Pearl looks up from her desk. "She is one frightening character, Gaby. You need to be careful. She could try to hurt you somehow."

"I'm careful, Pearl. She drives up and down Poplar Street almost every night. That's creepy. I have to admit I'm more comfortable when Joe's there."

"Drives up and down your street? What do you do?" Pearl's eyes are wide.

"I rearranged the furniture in my living room so I could see out but she can't see me. I watch. What else can I do at this point?"

"I don't know how you can even sit in the same room with Charlene Quinn. I wanted to run down the hall and call those cops and tell them to come back and get her."

Gaby is shocked by Pearl's behaviour for about the fourth time that day. "Pearl, a friend of mine gave me a piece of advice. She said that to succeed in this business, you must find a way to uncover at least one redeeming quality from every client. You must focus on that quality, so you can deal with all the other terrible stuff. Do you know who told me that, Pearl? It was you, and not so long ago. Charlene is responsible in her job. She never calls in sick and always arrives to work and our appointments on time. That's the redeeming feature I focus on."

As Gaby makes her way toward the office door, Pearl mumbles behind her. "She's a murderer, for the love of God! Who cares if she has a positive quality?"

Chapter 15

Past acts cannot be revealed

The workdays immediately prior to a long weekend are always brutal. This is what Gaby thinks as she opens the small meeting room door to allow her most recent clients to exit. She has spent the first two hours of her Monday morning dealing with six adult siblings. They argue so much about the care of their mother that the nursing home referred the whole lot for family counselling. This was their third visit. Gaby's head spins. She tries to imagine what their mother must have suffered through when they were all children in the house.

Her counselling role is not without its challenges. The nursing home wants them to declare a spokesperson to represent the family. In other words, they want the Moffatt siblings to do their brawling before they arrive at the facility to discuss care plans regarding Mrs. Moffatt.

As they file out, Gaby's gaze is captured by the ever-alert Mimi, as she attempts to telepathically reach her before the family departs. Mimi makes her eyes huge, raises her brows, and casts the merest glance toward a chair in the corner. She doesn't move her head. Gaby looks over. Charlene, in all her platinum hair and leather jacket glory, is curled into a chair with her booted feet somehow tucked beneath her. She is thumbing through an old *Time Magazine*. She doesn't look up but Gaby knows Charlene knows she's completed her session. There appears to be no easy way to avoid a meeting, even though their appointment isn't scheduled until Thursday.

She heaves a sigh, thinks fleetingly about the cup of coffee she craves and deserves, and then takes a couple of steps closer to her client.

"Hi, Charlene. Why are you here today? We don't have an appointment."

Charlene, with slow and calculated precision that seems designed to absorb precious minutes, leisurely closes the magazine, places it carefully on the table, tidies the stack of reading material sitting there, and lazily looks up at Gaby. "I called early this morning asking for an appointment, but your secretary...." She takes a moment to toss a glare across the room at Mimi—a look dripping with dislike—and then returns her hooded and shadowed eyes upward to meet Gaby's. "She said I had to wait until Thursday. I'm afraid that will be too late, since I want to talk to you now." She sounds pouty; an emotion Gaby hasn't witnessed in the past.

Gaby gives Mimi a quick glance. "Mimi tries to keep me on schedule, Charlene. And, may I say, she does an excellent job." She nods at her friend and produces an expression to convey to Mimi that none of this will be interpreted as her fault. "I have ten minutes, Charlene. You may come down to my office for ten minutes, but I have other clients expected soon. Will that do?"

Charlene is up and flounces down the hall immediately, the fringes on her jacket and purse match her rhythm. When they get to the office, she ploughs in and drops into the chair beside Gaby's desk. "Do you like my boots?" She lifts both legs and twists at the ankles to give Gaby a full view of her above-the-knee, heeled, black patent leather boots.

"You didn't come over here to show off your boots, Charlene," says Gaby as she thinks how expensive, impractical, and unflattering they actually are. "What did you need to see me about?"

"You haven't told anybody about what I told you, have you?"

"Charlene, we have been over this before. I have talked to my supervisors because the police came to see me. I write notes on all my cases and you are no exception. Your past acts cannot be revealed by me. I thought we were clear about all this." She can't keep the tone of exasperation from leaking out between her words. Charlene is starting to get under her skin, and Gaby figures Charlene already knows this.

"Yes, yes, I know you can't talk and neither can anybody else. I like to be sure, you know. Can you get your friend, Joe Dodd, to ask Pat to invite me to Thanksgiving?"

"Oh, Charlene! Is that why you barged in here so early on a Monday morning? You know I can't and won't do that. If Patrick hasn't invited you, then that's the end of it."

"But Sunday is my birthday! I'll be twenty-five! It would be like a special party for me, if he asked me to come. Come on, Gaby. Ask Joe to talk to Pat." All of a sudden, Charlene's voice has changed and become softer, but darker, somehow. Gaby feels threatened but she can't quite put her finger on why.

Gaby stands up. "Charlene, we have an appointment for Thursday right after lunch. You can tell me about why this is so important to you, then. I will not discuss this with Joe. Besides, to talk to anyone outside the clinic about you would be a violation of your confidence. I would not do that."

Charlene stands as well. "I'm going down to the diner to ask Pat one more time about going to The Station on Thanksgiving. I'll tell him it's my birthday. He won't be able to say no." She leaves Gaby in her wake as she flies back down the hall and through reception.

An inconsistency nibbles away at Gaby. She pulls Charlene's file from her cabinet and takes a quick look at the referral. Charlene Quinn's twenty-fifth birthday was May 10. It was on her driver's licence.

****

"Hi, Joe! What can I do for you today?" Gaby is secretly pleased that Joe has chosen to touch base over her lunch hour. "I returned from the staff room a minute ago; had a bite to eat."

"I have someone with me I'd like you to meet. Any chance I can pop by after supper tonight?"

Gaby takes a chance. "How about coming for supper? Bring your friend. We might not eat until seven, but I'll cook."

"Sounds great, Gaby, but I need to tell you about my friend. Her name is Martha. She's six months old. She has one icy blue eye and one brown eye." He's giggling a bit as he talks.

"Is this a kitten, Joe? Are you trying to find a home for another stray?" Gaby knows the story about Blanche, Joe's cat; about how she turned up on a job site, all scrawny. He is convinced someone threw some sort of liquid at her and she's blind as a result. He took Blanche home that day and she has been with him for years.

"No—a pup. One of the carpet guys showed up at the job today with this little girl in his truck. Said his wife didn't want a puppy and he didn't know what to do. I said I knew someone who might like her so he handed her over. You said back when you bought the house that you might want a dog someday."

"God, Joe! I don't know. A puppy? What will happen if I don't take her? Will you keep her?"

"No. Blanche's nose would be out of joint, for sure. I guess she would have to go to the pound."

Gaby's mind races. She's wanted a dog. Her backyard is fenced. She can go home for lunch to let it out. She often goes home anyway for the break. "Bring Martha—is that her name? Bring Martha over for supper. Does she have gear—food, dish, leash, collar?"

"Oh yeah. The carpet guy brought all her stuff. Said he couldn't go home without getting rid of her. What a sin, eh? Thanks, Gaby. I'll bring wine. See you after work."

Gaby leans back in her chair for a minute and thinks about what her life will be like with a dog. Joe said she's a blue heeler and Siberian husky cross. How big will she get? Who cares? It'll be nice to have the company and another set of ears. Charlene has started to make her nervous as she drives up and down the street with predictable frequency.

Gaby calls the diner. "Good afternoon. Hayworth Diner. Patrick speaking."

"Hi, Patrick. It's Gaby Ridgway. What's the special tonight?"

"Lasagna with Caesar salad and garlic toast. Are you coming over for supper, Gaby?"

"No, Patrick. I was hoping I could pick up supper on my way home. Can I get two specials to go? I'll be there shortly after five."

"Great. By the way, I hear you're coming to The Station for Thanksgiving."

"Yes. Joe invited me. Are you bringing anyone?" Gaby can't help herself. She needs to know if Patrick plans to give in to Charlene.

"No. I'm really not seeing anybody, in spite of what some people might think, so I'm going alone—well, except for the pecan pie. Everybody always wants me to bring a pie from work."

"Sounds fabulous. I'll see you later, Patrick." Gaby decides she will justify the take-out from the diner because she wants to meet Martha and not work in the kitchen. The more she thinks about having a dog, the more excited she gets.

The afternoon flies by. Darkness is barely beginning to shadow the vehicles as she crosses the parking lot to get into her truck and go get supper. She sees Charlene's Toyota sitting in the fire lane and prepares herself for a confrontation of some sort.

Charlene rolls down her window and yells across the cold and dusky space. "Are you going home? I want to talk to you again."

Gaby stops in the middle of the lot, about halfway to her vehicle. "Charlene, we have an appointment on Thursday. We can talk then. I have to go. I'm meeting someone." What else would you call picking up take-out and having company for dinner when you don't want to provide details? "See you Thursday."

With an assertiveness she doesn't feel, and a cold foreboding she most decidedly does feel, Gaby takes the last ten steps to her truck. By the time she opens the driver's door, Charlene has pulled up right behind her rear bumper. She has effectively blocked Gaby's vehicle.

"I need to know you're not tattling to anybody, Gaby. I need to know you can keep your mouth shut. I want to tell you other things about me, but I need to know you can keep a secret."

Gaby stands with her hand on the door of her little black Mazda. "Charlene. You know the rules. I am not at liberty to repeat details you have told me after the fact. We've been over this again and again. Move. I have to go."

"I need to make sure. And, will you ask your friend Joe to talk to Pat about Thanksgiving? It's my birthday, Gaby. Be a sport." She smiles, but it looks like a sneer.

"Charlene, we'll talk on Thursday and I've made it clear I will not intervene on your behalf about Thanksgiving. You have to accept that fact. Now, move your truck. There comes Elliot and you have blocked both of us." Thank God Elliot parked right beside her this morning.

Charlene guns the motor of the old Land Cruiser and takes off. Gaby shouts out to Elliot. "Off to hit the gym before going home?"

"Yes." Elliot looks worried as he watches the red vehicle exit the parking lot. "Who was that, Gaby?"

"One of my clients. I needed to remind her we have an appointment on Thursday, but she seems to want to talk every day."

"Too needy, my dear. You have to let them go. When a client starts to act like that, it might be wise to transfer them to someone else."

All of a sudden, Elliot's caustic and mercenary ways of managing his caseload start to feel reasonable to Gaby. If only she could actually do a transfer, but the situation is way too advanced for that.

****

Gaby hears Joe's big blue monster pull up in front of her little house. The truck, a Ford crew cab with tandem wheels in the back, is a fixture in Hayworth. Poor Joe. Everyone knows when he's at the diner, home at The Station, or at work on a particular job site. There are lots of trucks in the community, but this one certainly sticks out.

Lasagna is staying warm in the oven with the garlic toast wrapped in foil. The salads have been merged into one, and it is safely chilling in the fridge. Gaby is surprised at how excited she is all of a sudden. She bounds to the door.

Joe lumbers up her stairs, Martha clutched in his arms. She's the oddest looking dog Gaby has ever seen. She has one brown eye and one icy blue eye, exactly as Joe described. The latter reflects the yellow glow from the porch light. She is a blotchy concoction of white, grey, and black with grey legs and white paws. She looks like she's wearing grey leggings and her white paws are dangling at the ends. Her head is speckled like her back. Her little face looks so sad.

Joe lifts her across to Gaby, who is balancing the screen door open. "Martha, this is Gaby. Gaby, this is Martha. You take her and I'll go get all her paraphernalia."

Off to the truck he goes while Gaby nuzzles the puppy and croons in her ear. She's an armload. "Aren't you a pretty girl? Your feet are quite big, Martha. Are you going to be a big dog? We will have to wait and see, I guess. Maybe you'll take after your mama and be smaller. Wasn't she a blue heeler?" She strokes Martha and continues to chat. "Now, I'm told your daddy was a Siberian husky but I think you inherited your mama's coat, too. That's good. Those husky-types are big shedders."

Joe returns with a dog bed, a couple of bowls, a leash, a bag of food, and a bottle of wine. He piles it all on the floor by the front door and gives Gaby a big grin. "Isn't she pretty? I've looked after her all day and we've been back at my apartment for a couple of hours already. Blanche wasn't too enthusiastic. The carpet guy said she's house-broken and she'll bark at the door when she wants to go out. That's good, eh?" He gives Gaby a little punch on the arm.

"Well, you must be happy you have a sucker like me for a friend! I expect she'll be big, Joe. You know that." She looks up at him as she lowers Martha to the floor. "I'll let her explore a bit while I tend to supper. Want a glass of wine?"

"Smells like Italian in here. You didn't come home after work and make spaghetti, did you?" He grins while he says this. They both know Joe is a far better cook than she could ever hope to be.

"Nope. Special tonight was lasagna, and Patrick made sure he had dinner ready for us when I stopped by the diner an hour ago—even garlic toast and Caesar salad. Not bad, eh?" She hands him a glass of wine and looks down at Martha. The puppy has unceremoniously collapsed on top of Gaby's sneakers beside the front door.

"I think she likes you," Joe notes as he follows her gaze. "She loves the vehicle, so she'll be good company for you, both at home and when you're out doing stuff. I already talked to Ronny, and Martha is more than welcome for Thanksgiving. Mason, Amanda and Chester's little boy, will love her."

Before they eat, Gaby attaches Martha's leash and they wander around the backyard for a few minutes. She puts a little food in one dish and water in the other before she sets the table and serves supper to herself and Joe. It crosses her mind that this is a very domestic situation. She likes it.

After supper, they clear up the kitchen and decide it might be fun to take Martha for a walk to let her get to know the neighbourhood. As they meander up the block, Gaby spies the Toyota Land Cruiser as it pulls up to her house. Her heart races. Charlene is starting to make her nervous. She's glad Joe is with her.

"I think you have company," he says.

"No I don't. I'll try and make this quick." *What in the world is Charlene up to now?* She's standing by the truck, in the soft glow of Gaby's porch lights, waiting for them.

"Hi there. You must be Joe Dodd. I've heard a lot about you from my boyfriend, Pat Hollinger. I saw your truck at my friend Gaby's, here, and thought I'd stop by and say hello." She throws her hand into Joe's space. He has no choice but to shake it.

"Nice to meet you." His voice is cautious and he glances over at Gaby who is glaring at the young woman.

"Charlene, what can I do for you tonight?"

"Not much. Is this your puppy? You never mentioned a puppy." She immediately crouches down and starts to pet Martha, who backs up and places one white paw firmly on Gaby's foot.

"Charlene, I have company. What do you want? Joe, would you mind taking Martha inside, while I talk to Charlene for a minute?"

Joe reaches down for Martha, as Charlene interrupts. "The *real* reason I stopped was to talk to you, Joe. When I saw your truck, I figured you were visiting my counsellor." She gives Gaby a conspiratorial wink. "Don't be shocked. It doesn't matter if I tell my new friend Joe, here, that you're my counsellor. I'm going to be like Pat. He doesn't care who knows he sees a shrink and takes pills. That's why I stopped by. It's cold, Gaby. Are you going to invite me inside?"

Joe stands still with Martha in his arms. Charlene has moved closer and slowly rubs one of the dog's ears while she talks to Gaby. "No, Charlene. Whatever you came to say, you can say it right here. You know I don't socialize with clients."

"Yes, yes." Charlene winks again, this time while she looks up at Joe. "She's such a stickler for the rules. If I come to Thanksgiving dinner with Pat, you'll have to socialize with me then, won't she, Joe?"

"Are you coming with Patrick? I didn't know that. He never mentioned it to me."

"Well, that's the point of my stopping to meet you. I want you to ask Pat to invite me to Thanksgiving dinner at The Station!" She returns her gaze to Gaby. "See? That wasn't so hard, was it?"

Gaby tries desperately to remain silent. She hopes Joe chooses not to intervene on Charlene's behalf. Martha has wiggled her head away from Charlene's hand. The pup leans back as far as she can into the crook of Joe's arm. "Charlene, you and Patrick have to make your plans together. Patrick has never talked about you to me. If he wants you to come to dinner, I'm sure he'll ask, and Ronny will be happy to have you."

"You could ask him for me—a little favour and not that big a deal." Her voice has an edge to it that Gaby recognizes as the voice Charlene uses when she's unreasonable and not getting her own way.

"Charlene, I will see you at the office. I'm cold and I want to go inside now. Joe has been clear. You have to let this go." She hooks her arm in Joe's, a behaviour she has never done before, and makes a move for the stairs. "Good night, Charlene."

When they get inside the house, Joe puts Martha down on the floor. Gaby makes a fuss about finding her a treat. "Tea?"

"Absolutely. You know, she's sitting right out there in her vehicle. Does she do this a lot?"

"She cruises up and down the street almost every night she isn't working evenings—checking to see if my truck is in the yard."

"Have you talked to the police about this? She's creepy, Gaby. What's her problem?"

"I can't talk to you about her problems, Joe. Let's have tea. She'll pull out eventually. I'm happy you're here, though."

"Listen, Gaby. When you take Martha out at night, take her into your backyard. I'm going to get a lock for the fence. I'll put it on tomorrow. Don't ever go out back and leave your front door open." His voice has a level of anxiety she hasn't heard before, even during the most stressful events of her renovations. "I wonder if poor old Patrick is having trouble getting rid of her. If she makes *my* skin crawl, I can't imagine how he must feel."

She knows her mouth is hanging open. "Joe, I don't think Charlene is out to hurt me!"

"Don't leave Martha alone in the back, either. That woman has a problem. I'm no counsellor, and I know you can't tell me what her issue is, but she is one scary lady. The way she looked at the dog.... Promise me you'll be careful."

While Joe is speaking, Gaby thinks about Ila's kitten.

Chapter 16

What harm would it do?

The first two hours of Tuesday morning are absorbed by a pair of marriage counselling sessions scheduled back to back with barely enough time in between to scratch down a few notes and run to the bathroom. All Gaby wants is a cup of coffee. She counts down the minutes until noon, so she can run home and tend to Martha who's spending her first workday alone.

"Got a minute to talk?" Pearl pokes her head into Gaby's office on her way to the staff room.

"Sure. Coffee first, or while we talk?"

"While we talk. I have to meet with Clark after I talk to you." She continues down the hall.

Gaby's heart starts to thump. There's a stinging pain behind her eyes. Tension? Does she need her eyes checked? What the hell could Pearl want, anyway? In the staff room, she pours her coffee. Pearl exhibits unusual patience as she stands at the door and waits for her.

As if she can sense Gaby's anxiety, she lifts her head up a fraction to be level with Gaby's ear and whispers, "I have to clarify some details for Clark. Don't worry. I know this whole Charlene issue hasn't been easy for you."

Safely back inside Gaby's softly-lit and cozy office, Pearl closes the door and sits with a heavy thud in the chair right beside the desk. "No point in wasting time. Mimi told me that Charlene Quinn showed up unannounced yesterday. I'm told, although I won't reveal my source, that she waited for you in the parking lot after work last night."

Gaby can't control a sharp intake of breath. "Is everybody keeping an eye out for me, or what?" She shakes her head a tiny bit. "It doesn't matter anyway. She showed up at my house last night, too. Joe was there. I have adopted a puppy that needed a new home, and he was delivering her—Martha, a Siberian husky and blue heeler cross. I'll take some pictures and bring them in. Better still, I'll bring Martha in the next time I have a day off."

"Yes, yes, I heard about Martha." Pearl shakes her head. "It was only a matter of time. I knew you wouldn't let that fenced backyard go to waste, but what about Charlene? What's going on?"

"I can't get a handle on it, Pearl. She saw Patrick Hollinger for a time. I'm pretty sure they're no longer an item but she isn't happy. I'm going to The Station for Thanksgiving dinner as Joe's guest. Ronny Étang is hosting. Charlene is bound and determined to wangle an invitation. She tried Patrick, then me, and now Joe. She stopped to ask Joe if he would intervene and get Patrick to invite her. She seems obsessed with the whole idea. She even said the date is her birthday, even though I know it isn't." Gaby can feel her anxiety build as she verbalizes her challenges.

"You know she's now considered a suspect in Roz Dover's murder? The RCMP sent a letter to Clark. He wanted me to tell you. The office has a great deal of information about this girl, although we're not able to share it. Clark told me he strongly suggested to the RCMP that they dig deeper into Charlene's background. I thought he went too far, but he's the boss." She closes her eyes and shakes her head. "I feel sorry for the other two girls in the house. What are their names?"

"Ila and Crystal. I don't envy them. Charlene makes me nervous. She has an air about her. Joe freaked out last night." She leans over toward Pearl. "Now, Joe has no information except that she's a client—and Charlene told him that when she introduced herself to him out in front of my house. After we went inside, he told me to never leave Martha alone in the backyard, or take her out back without first making sure the front door was locked. He was going over to my place this morning to put a reinforced bolt on the back gate. He said Charlene gave him the creeps and that he didn't know why she needed counselling but he thought she was a very scary lady—Joe's description, not mine." Gaby looks amused as she says this.

Pearl doesn't. "Does she come around often, Gaby?"

"No. She's turned up a couple of times. I don't let her in and I don't go anywhere with her. She drives up and down my street almost every night she isn't working evenings, though. It bothers me, but what can I do? I can't call the police because a client makes me nervous. She said at one point that she needs to keep a close eye on me. I assume that's because of the hitchhiker business." She sighs as she looks across at her boss.

Pearl's face is tense. Her lips are pursed. "It's almost lunchtime. You go home to your puppy. I'll talk to Clark. When do you see Charlene again?"

"Thursday morning. Mimi said she called and changed her appointment from right after lunch to early morning. She must have a schedule change because our routine is to meet before her 3:00 to 11:00 PM shift."

"If she contacts you at any other time before Thursday morning, or if you see her drive by your house, you document every detail. She's dangerous. The police don't know that yet, but they will in time. I have to be honest, Gaby, I think she hurt the Dover girl."

After Pearl leaves, Gaby takes a few minutes alone in her office so she can relax enough to feel able to make her way home. She feels unhinged; troubled by her almost visceral reaction to Pearl's fears. They collide with her attempts to be rational.

It is certainly possible that Charlene regrets her self-revelations to Gaby. Now Charlene is trying to control the situation with attempts at inserting herself into Gaby's life. In her mind, she must constantly be nearby. Gaby wonders if she talked about the Nova Scotia murder to Patrick Hollinger. That could be why she's so obsessed with him as well.

****

Martha is the perfect distraction. When Gaby pulls her little black truck into the driveway, she can hardly wait to get inside the house. Martha waits on the mat by the front door, all wiggles and whimpers as she scoops her up, hooks on her leash, and makes her way through the kitchen to the back door. At the last second, she spins around and runs back to the front and locks the door behind her as Joe instructed. "Sorry, little girl. We'll go now. I bet you have to pee."

Outside, she places Martha down on the grass. Gaby notes that a brand new and very shiny deadbolt has been installed on the gate. There is also a note attached. *I have the keys and will drop them by after work. I didn't want to leave them here, or barge in at the Hexagon.* "Are you done already,

Martha? That was fast. Let's go in and have some lunch."

In the midst of her giggles as Martha makes a giant effort to chase a fly, Gaby is distracted by a voice from the other side of the six foot tall privacy fence. Due to her height advantage on the back stairs, she can see Charlene as she rattles the gate.

"Hi, Gaby. I knocked at the front and tried the door. I saw your truck but thought maybe you'd walked to work. Can we talk?"

Gaby sighs. The rush of air is audible. She doesn't try to hide it. "Charlene, I came home to let Martha out and have some lunch. We can't talk now. We have an appointment day after tomorrow."

"I quit my job! I need to talk to you. I may have to leave town. I want to talk to you about it. Can't you let me in?"

"Charlene. You need to call the office. See if I have a free appointment before Thursday. Mimi will set you up."

"But I quit my job, Gaby! That should be important enough for you to talk to me right now. I even brought a present for your puppy. I made it myself."

Gaby considers admitting her into the backyard. What harm would it do? Then she remembers the gate is locked and Joe has the keys. Her mind slams back to Ila's kitten. "Charlene, I'm going in to eat now. Call Mimi. I'll see you at the office." She opens the door, hustles Martha inside, and locks the door behind her. Joe would be happy to hear how important the locked fence turned out to be.

Charlene is gone when she returns to work. Gaby checks her yard and house before she leaves. There is no sign of the woman or her vehicle. When she arrives at the Hexagon, Mimi says Charlene was in and insisted she see Gaby early the next morning. Mimi did the necessary juggling. Gaby goes to find Pearl.

****

"Wait until I call Clark, Gaby. He'll want to hear this, too." Gaby has located Pearl and attempted to tell her about her noon visit from Charlene. She slumps down into one of Pearl's office chairs. She can smell the tobacco before she has a visual of Clark Alden, stooped and frail-looking, shuffle into the office. He looks like he's recovering from a bender. It wouldn't be the first time.

His opening sentence is abrupt. "This client of yours has turned into a stalker."

Gaby tries to be funny. "Someone who hides in the bushes outside a movie star's house?"

"She torments you and invades your privacy, Gaby. I think she's a stalker, as well as a murderer, and from the looks of her file, an abuser of animals. Would you diagnose her as a sociopath?" He lights a cigarette and crosses his legs. He faces her in the second chair opposite Pearl's desk.

"Not my area of expertise, Dr. Alden. I would like to refer her to Rachel Wilkerson, but I know Rachel sees Patrick Hollinger so I'm doubtful if she would accept the referral. Charlene went out with Patrick—and if she's stalking me, then for sure she's stalking Patrick. I wondered, on my way home today, if Charlene told Patrick about that hitchhiker, too, and now she's afraid of what he'll say."

"Too bad he doesn't talk to the police, if that's the case. You can't, but he could."

"Patrick, according to Charlene, is a paranoid schizophrenic controlled on medication. All I know is that he's a sweet young man who works at the diner. He lives at The Station and is a neighbour of my friend, Joe. I'll see him at Thanksgiving, for dinner over there."

Clark waves his hand, having lost interest in Gaby's social explanations. "I think I should see her. I want to assess her and see what we're dealing with here. When are you scheduled for a session with her, Gaby?"

"Tomorrow morning, and then again Thursday."

"Okay, I have meetings tomorrow. Tell her she has to see me for some reason. Create a reason. I don't care. Document it in the chart. I'll see her Thursday." He leans toward Gaby. "I think you are in danger, Gaby. I don't want to alarm you, but this girl has admitted to killing someone. Her roommate is missing, and she has both you and this Hollinger guy in her sights. I'm nervous."

Gaby looks at Pearl, who sits at her desk with her head down as she examines a pencil. "Pearl, what do you think? She hasn't come right out and threatened me or done anything specific."

"I know that, but you're in a bad spot. If you were Patrick, you could report her. As her counsellor, you can't. I don't want to be a part of this. I asked Clark to intervene because I don't like this one bit!" She lifts her head. Her face is flushed. Gaby notices she has locked her fingers together, but her hands still tremble.

****

Joe turns up at about 8:00 PM to bring Gaby her keys. She's happy for the company. She and Martha have been for a short walk already, but she suggests they do a trudge around the block and then have tea. She's nervous. She wants to call Nina later, after the children are in bed.

"What do I owe you for the lock, Joe? By the way, I should tell you both your lock and your advice came in handy today."

He looks down at her with a frown on his rugged and square face. "Are you okay? The lock assembly was less than ten bucks. Don't worry about it. Buy me dinner at the diner some night."

"I'm fine. Charlene is keeping up the pressure on me. I can't talk about it, Joe, but suffice to say, my supervisors are now involved."

"Is she dangerous?" His eyes are wide.

"I can't talk about her, Joe." Both her voice and her expression are resigned.

"I must ask Patrick about her. He can say whatever he wants. I already know he was trying to get rid of somebody, and judging by how many times I've seen her at the diner or parked down the road from The Station, I assume she's the one. I feel bad for the kid. He's starting to act like he did a couple of years ago—you know, awkward around people and all weird. He's started looking at the floor again when he talks to you. I hope he isn't having some sort of relapse. No amount of pills can solve a problem like that girl."

They continue their walk in silence. It's dark with only the soft glow of the occasional street lamp serving to illuminate the treacherous sidewalk, badly in need of repair. Martha wanders along. Gaby thinks she won't need to be tethered with a leash as she matures. She already watches Gaby and sticks close to her leg.

When they get home, Gaby makes tea and they talk about the upcoming potluck at Ronny's. The whole building will be there, and Joe rattles off the names and identities for Gaby. "First there's Chester and Amanda. They have a little guy, Mason. They live in the basement suite and manage the place. Ronny lives in Number Two, where my friend, Ben, used to live. That apartment still has the kitchen peninsula I made for Ben. Rose and Maggie Woodward live across the hall. Rose works for Dr. Gunton and Maggie does the books at Segue House. Maggie was institutionalized for most of her life; has been with Rose for a bit better than a year, now. She's an odd duck, but nice enough. Cheryl Nadler lives above Ronny. You already know her. Man! Has she ever changed since Ben died, but nobody knows the reason. I live across from Cheryl, and then Patrick lives up in the attic. He'd started to change for the better, even before Ben died. Ben had a big influence on everybody. I hope he isn't going backward because of this Charlene-character."

"How has Cheryl changed?"

"Well, to be blunt, she was an obsessive, compulsive diva in my opinion. Then, after Ben died, she mellowed somehow. She's still Cheryl, but not so extreme. Both she and Patrick are different. Patrick—don't call me Pat, that's a girl's name—used to be totally paranoid. He worked as the dishwasher at the diner and never talked to people. He wouldn't bathe, either. His hair looked like he'd dipped it into the grease at work, and he always smelled like the garbage bin behind the restaurant."

"I remember him as the dishwasher at the Hayworth Diner. You're right. His improvement is remarkable." She doesn't mention his relationship with a psychiatrist, although she suspects Joe knows a lot more than he shares. She also doesn't mention her dealings with Cheryl and how she's seen subtle changes in the social worker's behaviour over the past year as well. "I'm looking forward to the get-together."

Joe makes a move to leave. Gaby walks him to the door, Martha close to her ankle. Joe leans over and gives Martha a little pat on the head. A gentle kiss whispers past Gaby's cheek. She's not sure it happened. "Thanks for the tea. If you're scared, you call me, understand? You could always come over to The Station if you don't want to stay here alone."

"I'll be fine, Joe. Thanks again for the lock. Maybe we can do supper Friday night? My treat?"

He turns to wave as he makes his way to his truck parked on the street. "We have a date, Gaby. See you later." With a roar of the engine, he's gone.

The street goes eerily quiet. Gaby locks her front door, hooks Martha up to her leash, and goes out to the back so her pup can have a quick pee before bed. She changes her clothes and settles in on the couch to watch some TV before she calls Nina. Martha climbs up beside her.

Gaby can see the street from her favourite spot. Charlene has gone by at least once. All the house lights are off except for the table lamp in the living room. At about 9:30 PM, she turns off the television, drags the phone over to the sofa, and turns out the light. After a minute or so, her eyes adjust and she can see the shadows of her home's interior, visible thanks to the reflection of the street lamp outside.

"Hi, Nina. I thought the kids would be in bed by now. It's 11:30 PM there, right?"

"Are you okay? Why are you calling on a Tuesday night?"

"I have some news—good and bad, I guess—and I didn't want to wait until Sunday to call. I have a puppy!"

"What? That's great! When did this happen?"

"Yesterday. Some guy at my friend Joe's job site said his wife didn't want her, so now I am the proud owner of a blue heeler, Siberian husky cross named Martha. She has one blue eye and one brown eye. She's six months old and a sweet dog. She's quiet for a puppy, like she's worried all the time; like she's an old soul. I don't think the guy's kids were very good to her"

Nina's voice is quiet. "So, what's the bad news?"

"Even though we were planning on me coming home for Christmas this year, I don't think I want to leave Martha with anyone. I think I might stay here and do office coverage the same as always. Joe did Christmas at his building last year after their friend died. He says he wants to host again this year and he's invited me."

"Is the relationship getting serious?"

"You know, I'm not sure. We like each other a lot, but that's it so far. He's a nice guy and is always anxious to help me, so I guess that's a start. How are the kids?"

"Everybody's fine. Growing like weeds. Craig's never home. Working like a dog before winter sets in, and then I'll have him underfoot for three months." Her voice is soft. "Not that I mind."

"You could always come out here for a week when he's off. I could take some vacation and we could have sister-time. Hold on, Nina." Gaby hasn't managed to prevent the anxiety from slipping out between her words. She crouches down into the sofa and then peeks up over the sill. Charlene's truck has pulled up outside and she's turned out the lights.

"What's going on, Gaby?"

"Honestly, Nina, I'm in a bit of a fix. I have a client who has revealed bad, unlawful, behaviours to me. Now, she seems to think I'm going to report her, which, of course, I can't, but she won't leave me alone. She turns up at the house at all hours. She wants to go to a Thanksgiving dinner I'm invited to. She even showed up here the day Joe brought me Martha, wanting Joe to invite her to the party."

"Is she out there now? What did she do?"

"Yes, she's parked out front. She's in her vehicle. All my lights are out, so I would presume she thinks I'm in bed." Gaby cuddles a sleeping Martha in closer. "I shouldn't reveal to you what she did, but you have no one to tell. You don't count in the grand scheme. She killed some hitchhiker back in Nova Scotia a few months ago. Here in Hayworth, she was living with three other girls. One of them owned a kitten and she drowned it in the toilet and then threw it on the dump. One of her roommates has gone missing and she, along with her roommates and some others, are being investigated for that. She knows I can't tell the police about what has already happened. She reminds me of that every time I see her, but my skin crawls whenever I'm near her now."

Silence settles between them. Nina is quiet for what seems like minutes. "Quit and come home, Gaby."

"I can't do that, Nina. I've started to feel like I belong here. I'm making friends that aren't in this business—people outside the office. I love my house, too."

"Is she still there?"

"Yes. It looks like she's slumped down in the front seat ready to stay all night. She has a white cup in her hand—coffee? I don't know."

"What do you plan to do, Gaby?"

"I'm not sure, but I'm worried. To be honest, I wonder if she's sat outside like this before and I've been asleep so never realized it. I'll stay where I am by the window, out of sight, and keep an eye on her. We have an appointment tomorrow morning and I'll confront her about it. I'll be okay. I'll call Joe if she tries to come up on the porch."

"Can't you call the cops?"

"And tell them what? Somebody is legally parked on the public street in front of my house? That's the trouble with this whole issue. All she's doing is playing with my mind. Thanks for the company, Nina. Call me later, in a few days, maybe."

Gaby reaches for the blanket on the back of the couch. She expects it will be an endless night.

Chapter 17

You need to stop

Gaby pulls her truck into the parking lot at the Hexagon on Wednesday morning. She can't help but notice Charlene's red Land Cruiser occupying two spaces across the back corner. Charlene is behind the wheel. Yes, they have an appointment early this morning, but that means 9:00 AM, not an hour earlier when Gaby arrives. *At least give me a chance to get my coffee!* She is aware of losing her patience. Charlene must have left her post on Poplar Street last night after Gaby finally fell asleep on the couch, and that was well past 3:00 AM. She's exasperated and overtired.

As Gaby traverses the reception area, Mimi, already with a full head of steam, hands her a phone message. "Dr. Wilkerson called. She asked if you two could meet to talk about one of her clients. I told her you were pretty busy, but if she came over here tomorrow before your first appointment, you would have some time. I hope that was okay." Her eyes are round, reflected behind her dark frames.

"No problem, Mimi." Gaby is rattled and more than a bit prickly. "I need to get organized. Charlene Quinn is out in the parking lot. I hope you told her 9:00 AM."

"Of course!" Mimi sounds incensed. "You do not see clients before then, Gaby. I know that."

"Sorry, sorry. She was out in front of my house most of the night." She leans over closer to Mimi. "I hate to think she's crawling under my skin, but the fact of the matter is, her behaviour is getting tiresome. Don't be surprised if she comes in any minute."

Gaby sets off for her office and then the coffee pot. She dreads this morning. She takes a minute to call Rachel Wilkerson—mostly to satisfy her curiosity.

"Hi, Rachel. Mimi tells me you're coming by for a visit tomorrow morning. Do I need to prepare?"

"Not at all, Gaby. This relates to one of your clients. I know you can't talk to me about Charlene Quinn, but I have a release signed by my patient, Patrick Hollinger, so I can talk to you. I was hoping I might get your help to determine Patrick's status without you revealing information about Charlene, okay?"

Gaby hesitates before responding. It sounds like Dr. Wilkerson wants information about Charlene without having to ask for it. "I guess we'll see what we can do, Rachel. I'm hesitant, and I can't reveal the reason."

"Don't worry. I know the reason and I won't put you in a compromising position. Thanks, Gaby. See you tomorrow."

****

The phone rings almost as soon as she's hung up and the light has gone out. Mimi reports that Charlene is in the waiting room, but she has told her Gaby will not be out to retrieve her for another half hour. "Don't wander down to reception. If you need me, call."

Fresh brewed coffee wafts its way up the hall as Gaby drifts into the staff room. Elliot, Frank, and Edith are already there, watching the coffee finish perking. Edith appoints herself representative of the Counselling Division and speaks first. "We want to know what's going on. You have a client that's mixed up in this Roz Dover case, don't you?"

Gaby acknowledges her colleagues as she pours her coffee. "Good morning, folks. Listen, Edith. I have a busy day today. If you think case-conferencing this tricky case I have might be enlightening, suggest it to Pearl. Perhaps she'll agree. The Quinn case is a challenge. It makes me tired and a bit cranky, so if you want more information talk to Pearl."

"We heard old man Alden is going to see her tomorrow. Is that true? He hasn't seen a client in years! We figured this must be bad." Frank nods at the group, looking for general agreement as he waits for Gaby's response.

"Dr. Alden wants to interview my client. I'm not sure what he expects to accomplish. I have an appointment with her, myself, in a few minutes, so I have to go."

"Maybe we'll see you for lunch?" Edith tries to find out when she'll be able to ask more questions. Gaby has this figured out.

"No. I have my puppy. I need to go home at noon. I like the break. See you later." She bustles out of the room before anybody has a chance to argue. She can hear the three of them mumbling, as she returns to her office.

Her watch shows exactly 9:00 AM when Mimi accompanies Charlene down the hall and taps softly on the door frame. She stays, with singular determination, in front of Charlene as she pokes her head through the opening. "I have Charlene Quinn for you, Gaby." This time her eyes are narrow slits. Mimi is decidedly not impressed.

"Come on in, Charlene. Thanks, Mimi." She turns around in her chair when her client comes through the door. The girl looks like hell, which stands to reason considering she was up all night, too. Today, Charlene will not be driving the conversation. Gaby must make the rules crystal clear.

She starts with the obvious. "You look as tired as I feel, Charlene." She ignores her client's attempt to speak. "Your truck was parked in front of my house most of last night. When you're not parked on Poplar Street, you're driving up and down the block. You need to stop, Charlene."

"I need to make sure that you're safe." Her tone is whiny and her lips are turned up in the merest ghost of a smile. "I don't trust that Joe Dodd. I like to make sure he's not pestering you."

"What? Joe is my friend! You do not have any role in keeping me safe, Charlene. I don't need protection from my friend, Joe." *What I think I need is protection from you!*

Charlene attempts to control the interview. "I told you I quit my job. Aren't you even a little bit interested?" The mask that reflects her conjured expressions reverts to a pout.

"What do you intend to do, Charlene? It costs a lot to live this far north without a job."

"Oh, I'm not worried. Crystal and Ila will carry me for a while. They're such idiots. By the time they figure out I'm ripping them off, I'll have disappeared. I want to come and see you every day, not once or twice a week. If I'm working, I can't come see you every day."

"Charlene, you can't come see me every day, regardless. I have other clients; other responsibilities."

"Well, I'm coming to see you again tomorrow, so we'll go from there." She juts her chin out in a challenge for Gaby to disagree.

"Tomorrow's session is with Dr. Alden, the Divisions Supervisor here at the Hexagon. He feels it's important to meet with you." Gaby sees no point in trying to be creative. "He's seen your file, Charlene. He's a psychiatrist. He thinks it's imperative that he talk to you himself."

At first, Charlene argues. She suggests she won't turn up if Dr. Alden conducts the interview. After a couple of minutes, Gaby notices a change in her demeanour, like she's figured out some kind of angle and is busy putting the whole situation to her advantage. "Does he know about Roz?"

"Of course he knows about Roz, Charlene. He knows she was one of your roommates. He also knows about Ila's kitten. He knows about the hitchhiker. He's read the file."

Charlene plays with the fringes that trim her shoulder bag. Her gaze is on the carpet. Her heavily made up eyes appear bruised, since all Gaby can see are the smoky lids. "But does he *know* about Roz? You think I killed her. Have you put that in the file?" She hasn't looked up.

Gaby can feel her heart beat. She can hear her breath moving in and out. She's not sure she wants an answer to her next question. "Are you telling me that you're involved in Roz's disappearance, Charlene?"

Again, the ghost of a smile crosses Charlene's face as she looks up at Gaby. "I guess that's for me to know and you, or your Dr. Alden, to find out. I told you the stupid cops would never find her. I need to see you every day. I need to talk about my problems every day." Her voice starts to rise in pitch.

Gaby pulls back. "Charlene, you and I will meet with Dr. Alden tomorrow. If you have any information about Roz, I think we need to contact the police. Would you like me to ask Constable Fiona Werbowski to come over to the office? She interviewed me regarding the fact that you came to see me the night Roz went missing. You and I talked about that."

"No police. I'll tell you all about the night they say Roz disappeared, but not here and not now. How about I come to your house?"

"No, Charlene. You cannot come to my house."

"Okay, okay. I know. I was trying to rattle you. You're so skittish, Gaby. You need to relax." She chuckles. Her eyes are empty, like peering into a room with no windows. "So, tell me again why I have to put up with some old psychiatrist named Dr. Alden. Is he going to try and analyze me?"

"Charlene, I feel as if you need more help than I am able to provide. I asked if you would see Dr. Wilkerson and you said no, so Dr. Alden has kindly agreed to a consultation. You have told me you killed a man in Nova Scotia. You told me how you did it. You drowned your roommate's kitten. You have indicated that you could be involved in Roz's disappearance. You stalk me by driving up and down my street, or parking outside my house all night."

Charlene's voice is steely calm. "...and you can all write in my file but none of you can tell anybody else about this. I know my rights, Gaby."

"All that's true, but I don't think I can help you. What you need is therapy from someone with more expertise than me. I want to refer you for better—more appropriate—help."

"I want to talk to you." She leans over and puts her elbows on the knees of her skin-tight pants, plunking her chin in her hands. "I want to come and talk to you every day. I think if I do that, I won't hurt anybody else."

Gaby recognizes the "pity me, you're the only one I trust" tactic. "There are many people more qualified than me, Charlene. Besides, you can't keep coming around my place. I've been clear. We cannot be friends. We cannot socialize."

"Today is Wednesday. There's still time for crazy Pat to ask me to Thanksgiving dinner at The Station. Then we would socialize because you would be there, too."

Gaby feels there isn't even a slim chance Patrick will ask her, so starts to wind up their discussions without responding. "You'll be here tomorrow to meet with Dr. Alden?"

"Will you be at the session, too?"

"I will be there, but Dr. Alden will conduct the interview."

"Okay, if you'll be there." She gets up and turns toward the door. Gaby rises to follow. On the way down the hall, Charlene tries to hook her arm into Gaby's. Perhaps with more force than necessary, Gaby dislodges herself from her client's grasp. Charlene's look is disarming. Gaby swallows hard to fight her fear.

At the glass door leading out of reception, and since there is no one within ear shot, Gaby emphasizes her concerns one more time. "No more cruising by the house or sitting out front, Charlene."

Charlene pats Gaby on the arm before she leaves. The fringes on her shoulder bag and her jacket swing back and forth, making time with the rhythm of her hips as she sashays out the door.

****

Gaby begins to put her notes in order—Dr. Alden will want them by day's end. Edith wanders in. She plunks herself down beside the desk and heaves a great sigh. "Come on in, Edith. Have a seat. Make yourself comfortable." She can't keep the slight whiff of sarcasm out of her voice, although she tries to exercise patience.

"I need to talk to you about a couple I'm seeing. I think they might be a better fit for you."

"Edith, I'm swamped right now. I have a very demanding case. Dr. Alden is getting involved. I have a new client to see this afternoon. I'm afraid I can't take a transfer from you right now. I'm sorry."

"I heard about this troublesome case, Gaby. Everybody's talking about this girl you see; that she's under investigation by the police." Edith leans over close enough that Gaby can smell stale coffee and egg salad on her breath. She must have eaten lunch early. "What's the latest?"

"I can't talk about it right now, Edith. I have to get home to let Martha out. Can we talk about this later? Tomorrow, or Friday? Yes, I should have more time on Friday." She sees the stricken look behind Edith's polite smile. "I'm not trying to put you off—believe me, I'm not. I'm swamped, Edith." As she talks, she gets up and reaches for her purse and jacket. "I have to go. We'll talk later."

Edith pushes herself out of the office chair by bearing down on the arm rests like she's prepared to ram them through the floor. "We'll talk Friday, Gaby. Sorry I bothered you." She hustles herself toward the staff room without a backward glance.

After this many years of working together, if Edith wants to feel slighted, well, too bad. Gaby races to her truck and the momentary solace of her house and Martha, for a well-deserved lunch break.

As she mounts the front steps to the porch and unlocks the door, she gives herself a little lecture. There is no need to scope out every jeep-looking vehicle she sees. Charlene will not lurk in the bushes. She said she wouldn't cruise by anymore. She did say that, didn't she?

Martha is so funny when Gaby opens the door. She wiggles from head to toe. She pulls back her lips and creates this goofy smile. They race across the living room and kitchen before they pile through the back door together, out into the yard. Martha doesn't need a leash out here now that she's safe inside the locked fence. She runs and runs. Gaby throws a ball for Martha to chase. The young dog could spend the day galloping after the ball. Eventually, Gaby retrieves them both and takes Martha inside.

Martha charges into the living room. She usually sticks quite close. *What's gotten into her?* "Martha, what are you up to? Come on. Let's get you some...."

She stops mid-sentence. Charlene is crouched down near Martha, offering a fuzzy blue dog toy. She looks up and smirks. Gaby hates that expression. "Hi, Gaby. I want to talk to you. I saw your truck and your door was unlocked."

Damn it! The front door! Joe is going to kill me! "Don't give that to Martha, Charlene." She knows she's abrupt. She doesn't care. She forces herself to move closer to the girl in order to pick up her dog. She backs toward the kitchen doorway. "Charlene, you have no right to be here; no right to come into my house, whether the door is open or not. I need you to leave."

"What are you going to do, Gaby? Call the cops? Those idiots! They'll arrive. I'll be sweet and tell them I dropped in to tell my counsellor that I don't want to see some old psychiatrist tomorrow. The phones were busy at the office. I saw your truck and I ran in for a second."

"I'm not discussing this with you now, Charlene." Her heart bangs as she tries to control the tone of her voice. "If you are going to cancel your appointment for tomorrow, cancel it. Call Mimi. Now, please go."

Charlene sits down on the cranberry and grey striped sofa. Gaby is still holding Martha, who feels extra heavy now that she's settled in Gaby's arms. "If you want me to stop tormenting you, you need to get me an invitation to dinner on Monday." She crosses her legs and examines her long nails. Gaby notices they are in desperate need of a manicure.

"I'll do what I can, Charlene," she lies through her teeth. "I'll call Joe and have him talk to Patrick. How's that?" *Whatever it takes to get her out of the house.*

It's a surprise to Gaby, but Charlene buys the lie. "Okay, okay. I'm sorry I disturbed your lunch. You call Joe tonight and then let me know what happened when we talk tomorrow."

"I thought you were going to cancel your appointment."

"Changed my mind. I'll be there. It'll be fun to give an old shrink a run for his money. You watch what I can do!" She stands up and turns toward the door. "Now remember, you promised to talk to Joe." She points her index finger in Gaby's direction. "Don't forget to lock your door, Gaby. Anybody could walk in when you're out in the back with your dog."

She watches Charlene get into her vehicle. She locks her door, sits down on the sofa, and starts to shake. She presses her cheek into the silky softness of Martha's ear, and suddenly discovers her thoughts have turned to house fires. "Okay, sweetie, let's get ourselves a snack. How would you like to come to the office with me this afternoon?"

Chapter 18

You can't live like this

Martha sits up on the front seat with Gaby, obviously thrilled to be going somewhere, anywhere. Her tail bangs a steady rhythm on the upholstery. As they drive through Hayworth, Gaby spies Joe at the gas station and pulls in beside his truck as he fills up.

She leans her head out the open window. "Hey, Joe! Feel like having supper at my house tonight? Who knows? I might even cook!" She tries to sound upbeat but the effort is exhausting. She knows she doesn't want to be alone but isn't quite ready to admit it.

"Who's in there with you, Gaby? Is Martha getting into the counselling business?" His head is tilted to the side as he looks into the cab while he finishes pumping his gas. "I might be late tonight, but I can pick us up the special from the diner. People are going to start to talk about us, Gaby. Either that, or they'll think I'm stalking you."

She can't prevent the cloud that crosses her face. "Let's not talk about stalking, Joe, but your company would be greatly appreciated."

"Is that client bothering you again?"

Gaby nods. "I'm nervous. That's about all I can say. When will you be finished tonight?"

"I'll be there by 6:00 PM, don't worry."

She nods her thanks and continues on to the office. She hopes her new client, not to mention staff and supervisors, won't mind a dog hanging around.

The minute Martha arrives in reception, the office is all aflutter. Mimi creates a big fuss. Workers turn up from all directions to see the beautiful heeler and husky mix with the unusual markings. Then, Pearl wanders into reception.

"Do we have issues, Gaby? You know we don't bring pets to work." Her eyes contain an element of softness upon which Gaby intends to capitalize.

"I have a client scheduled in half an hour. Can we talk?" Gaby knows her voice sounds strained as she continues down the hall with a leashed Martha, in the hopes that Pearl will follow her back to her office.

"Let's get out of the public eye, then. God! What a cutie! And she's so quiet, Gaby, but what's going on?"

They trudge to Gaby's office. She closes the door. Martha sniffs Gaby's chair, wanders around the office, and then crawls under the desk to lie down. "Good girl!" Gaby leans over and scratches Martha's ears before she returns her attention to Pearl.

"I don't want to sound too melodramatic, Pearl, but Charlene is making me so uneasy, I didn't want to leave Martha home alone. The thought crossed my mind that she might actually burn my house down. I know—melodramatic!"

Pearl's expression doesn't change. "Go on. Tell me what makes you feel like this."

"I saw her this morning and then she turned up at my house at noon. When I went into the house after being in the backyard with Martha, she was standing in my living room. She was so nonchalant! She even suggested that if I called the police, she'd say she was trying to cancel our appointment, saw my truck, and popped by to tell me in person. Honest to God, Pearl! She sat on my street last night until past 3:00 AM. I slept on the couch and that was the last time I looked at the clock. First she said she wouldn't see Alden. Now she says she will. She indicated she would tell him details about Roz Dover that would shock him!" Her voice softens a little as she reaches under the desk to give Martha a pat. "I'm scared of her, Pearl. I imagine that's what she wants." She looks across at her boss. "I even stopped Joe Dodd on the street and invited him to supper so I'd have company this evening. I had to promise Charlene I would try to get Joe to influence Patrick to invite her to Thanksgiving at The Station!"

"If she's going to that dinner, you stay the hell home!"

"She won't be going. Patrick, it appears, does not want her around. Rachel Wilkerson is coming over to see me tomorrow to talk about Patrick and

Charlene. She knows I can't talk, but she has consent from Patrick, so I'm puzzled about what she wants. Rachel's very professional. She won't put me in a potentially unethical position, I'm sure."

"After the session with Clark tomorrow, we will all regroup and discuss next moves. I'm honestly not sure where to take this. We can remove you from the case, but that won't stop her behaviour outside the office. What if I contact Constable Werbowski and ask if they can cruise by your house more often?"

"That would ease my mind a bit, but are we breaking confidence to do that?"

"I don't think so. They already know she's a client. They questioned you about her whereabouts the night Roz disappeared, and that information came directly from Charlene, herself. I'll do that, Gaby—right after I go get Martha a bowl with some water."

****

Laura Creighton is shown into Gaby's office at 2:00 PM. The referral came from her family physician, who feels she needs counselling in order to better prepare her for the progression of her disease. She has been diagnosed with Parkinson's.

Miss Creighton is sixty-five and has been retired from teaching for five years. She is a big-boned woman with long grey-streaked hair pulled into a tight French roll. Her glasses are heavy, black-rimmed, and much too big for her face. Mimi leads her in. She nods at Gaby and takes a seat on the far side of the office, beside the table. This is the area Gaby more often uses when she sees a group of people. Most clients, when alone, sit in the chair beside her desk.

Gaby stands and approaches her. She offers a hand, as is her custom. Miss Creighton stares straight ahead. "Would you be more comfortable sitting over here by my desk? I could take your coat and hang it up, if you like." She's wearing a black winter coat that hangs mid-calf, and her shoulders are covered in a blanket like shawl. It appears to be handwoven, angora, and is a rich mixture in burgundy plaid.

Miss Creighton sits with her hands folded in her lap and pressed down on a flat, shiny black patent leather purse. "This is fine," she says as she continues to focus on the wall opposite.

Gaby moves her chair toward her client and sits across from her. Martha pokes her head out from under the desk and rests her nose beside the leg. "I hope you don't mind my dog, Miss Creighton. She was a little under the weather today, so I brought her in to keep an eye on her. May I call you Laura?"

"You may. Well-behaved dog." When she turns her head, she moves her shoulders as well, almost as if she has a stiff neck. She allows herself the merest glance downward to get a glimpse of Martha.

"Some days she's pretty crazy, Laura. She's still a puppy. What brings you to see me today? Your doctor said in the referral that you recently received a diagnosis, and you want to get some assistance making plans on how you will manage your illness?"

"That's right. I have no family, so no one to take care of me. I gather I will need a lot of help. I have a little money, but no one." She still hasn't looked directly at Gaby. Instead, her neck remains rigid and her focus remains the wall to the right of the desk.

"I can help you with that, Laura. Let's start by you telling me about your diagnosis, the prognosis, and other details the doctor may have told you."

About fifteen minutes into the discussion, Gaby notices a difference in Laura's demeanour. She appears as if she's watching a movie and no longer has any interest in their dialogue. "Laura, what's going on?"

"The children won't sit still. Look at them, running around! Listen to them shouting and howling! There's no discipline. I need to find my strap! There will be punishments now!" Her head is moving from side to side. Her neck no longer seems stiff. Gaby knows, right away, that Laura is having hallucinations, and she waits for the images to subside.

"How long have you been having the hallucinations, Laura?"

"A while, now. Maybe six years. I retired early because of them. The kids said I went into a trance. I also thought they were stealing from me. I kept all this to myself, but I quit work." She's sitting poker-straight again.

"Have you told your doctor?"

"No. He would say I'm an old woman with time on my hands. Alex Gunton has no patience with the elderly. He told me that Parkinson's disease sometimes has hallucinations and delusions that come along with it, so I assume that's what I have."

They talk together for an extended session. Gaby will help Laura make a plan for long-term care, which she will require sooner rather than later. She also convinces Miss Creighton that a referral to Dr. Wilkerson is important, because the psychiatrist will be able to help with medications. Before she goes, Laura asks if she can pet Martha. They sit together while Gaby holds Martha's collar. For the first time during the ninety minutes, the older woman appears to shed her formality. Her face loses its rigidity as she talks to Martha in a soft voice.

****

Before the afternoon is over, Gaby manages to snag Pearl for a quick update regarding Charlene. They both return to Gaby's office because of Martha. "Our meeting with Dr. Alden is tomorrow after lunch. I think she might tell him that she's the one who killed Roz! The more I think about it, the more sure I become."

A troubled and frustrated expression is planted on Pearl's face. "Have you finished your summary for Clark? Did you include what happened today?"

"Yes. I tried to be professional. I stated the facts: she came to my house and entered without permission; she tried to manipulate me into getting her invited to a local party; I agreed to intervene as a matter of necessity, in order to extricate her from my living room. I hope Dr. Alden can read the chart and we can have a chat beforehand. Rachel Wilkerson is coming by in the morning. I have no other appointments. If I have your permission, I'll bring Martha with me tomorrow and take her home at noon. I don't want Charlene to see the dog in my office. She'll know she's succeeded in making me afraid."

"Right now, whatever works best for you is fine with me. Go home. It's been a long day." She reaches for the file sitting on Gaby's desk. "I'll take this down to Clark and give him an update. I'll tell him you want to meet with him before the session—tomorrow after coffee, say? Will Rachel be gone by then?"

Gaby jots down a note in her day planner. "Rachel will be gone. I'll meet with Dr. Alden any time after 10:30 AM."

Pearl lumbers back to her office. Her shabby low-heeled pumps thump on the carpet. The stretched out jacket of her knitted suit drifts in folds around her widening behind. Gaby stands at her door and watches. Pearl seems so annoyed. Gaby knows she hates issues that challenge her expertise as a supervisor. Everybody knows that Pearl likes to be a supervisor without having to actually *perform* supervisory tasks. Charlene has become a work burden for Pearl, as well as Dr. Alden.

****

Charlene isn't in the parking lot when Gaby trots out to her truck with Martha. She scans the whole area for the red vehicle. Martha, leashed and close, wanders along, enjoying the opportunity to sniff. Gaby's heart beats a little faster when she imagines someone suddenly knocking on the window of her truck or approaching her from behind. She hates feeling this paranoid.

Dusk is imposing itself upon the little town when Gaby parks in her driveway. Every nerve ending jangles as she scans the yard and the porch before she climbs the stairs to unlock the door. She gives another quick look in all directions before she opens the door and goes inside. She secures the lock, turns on the porch light for Joe, and stands on the front mat. She watches Martha for any telltale signs there might be someone in the house. They walk through the living room and dining area, with Martha still on her leash. Gaby switches on lights and lamps as she moves. Once in the kitchen, she turns on more lights, and makes her way to the back door. It seems too quiet. She can feel her heart pounding. The pain in her chest is there almost all the time, a dull ache. Right now, it feels worse than it has all day. *You can't live like this! This is crazy!*

Martha stands and waits for the familiar creak of the door that lets her know they are on their way out to the yard. Gaby hesitates. *Check the lock on the front one more time.* She races back through to the entryway. The door is secure.

Her fenced yard is empty. The gate is locked. Martha is happy to trudge around, do her business, and wiggle her way back to expected pats and praise followed by the rattle of the food dish. Although her house is as she left it, Gaby is so jumpy she doesn't know what to do with herself. *How late will Joe be? Would a glass of wine help?*

Once Martha is fed, they curl up together on the sofa, positioned in the vantage point that permits a clear visual down the street. There is little traffic. She hears Joe's truck before she sees it. All of a sudden, she's famished. She jumps up to answer the door before he has a chance to knock.

"Hi. My God, Gaby, you look like a scared rabbit! What's going on?"

"Come on in. It's great to see you." Her shoulders heave with a sigh. Her anxieties fall out of her mouth in a jumble. "I don't know what I can tell you and what I can't, Joe. You've met Charlene and she told you she's a client. She has given me reason to be scared, but I can't tell you the details." The conversation takes place as Gaby unloads take-out containers from the diner on to the kitchen table. It smells like pork roast. Joe is rolling around on the floor boards with Martha, who growls and tugs at his shirt tail.

"Has she been hanging around again, Gaby? Why can't you call the police? I know she's a client, but you're not breaking confidentiality if you tell the police that she's harassing you—are you?" He looks up from the floor, concern and puzzlement reflected in his expression.

"According to Pearl and Dr. Alden, I shouldn't contact authorities because all she's done is torment me on some level that's hard to explain. Let's use a hypothetical example: a customer you haven't had a great relationship with, keeps turning up at other job sites. They always have an excuse of some sort; they're not *doing* anything; but you can't help feeling you shouldn't let your guard down or a horrible event will happen—like their very existence is some sort of veiled threat. That's how I feel. That's the situation. I'm glad you're here. I appreciate the company tonight, Joe."

"I want to help. You need me to stay over?" He responds to her look by holding both hands up in the air like stop signs. "No strings attached, Gaby. I can stay on the couch and head back to The Station in the morning to get ready for work. Think about it." He lifts himself up off the floor as he gives Martha's tail one final pull. "You think about it. Let's eat. I'll go get washed up."

As usual, the meal is fabulous. They drink wine. They talk. They play some more with Martha and take her for an uninterrupted walk around the block. They watch the news. It's a peaceful and stress-free evening.

"I think I can manage, Joe. There's no need for you to sleep here on my couch, comfortable as it may be. I'll be fine. I think Mimi is dropping by after work tomorrow, so I'll have some company."

"Whatever you need to get through this, my friend. Now, you're sure you'll be okay?"

Gaby nods and pats his arm. "You helped me a lot tonight, Joe. I was a wreck, but I'm good now."

He goes with her out to the backyard one more time with Martha, and checks the lock on the gate. She sits on the couch and listens until the sound of his truck disappears around the corner at the end of the street. The pressure in her chest returns to prominence.

Sleep eludes her. She tries to recall fun thoughts, like her sister's children. She tries self-hypnosis and focuses on the black behind her eyes, zoning in on one speck above all others. Martha, who is supposed to be asleep on her dog pillow beside the bed, plops her front feet firmly on the side of the mattress in front of Gaby's face. "Okay. Just for tonight. You are going to be far too big to sleep in the bed."

Martha settles down and Gaby drifts off, awakened by the weight of Martha's torso stretched across her chest, and the sound of a soft growl coming from deep inside the pup. Gaby smiles through her exhaustion and puts her arm around her dog. This serves to settle them both, and they go back to sleep.

The next morning, as she locks the front door, and they start to go down the steps to the truck, Martha pulls back on her leash. It appears essential she sniff an unfamiliar item she's spied on the porch—a piece of brown suede fringe.

Chapter 19

Shall we give it a go?

Gaby shakes from the inside out as she reaches the office parking lot. The weather is colder today than she expected and she should have worn a warmer coat. She'll be frozen if she indulges Martha in her normal wander and sniff approach to the door. She scoops up her dog and tears into the foyer of the Hexagon. Although only the crack of dawn for most, Mimi is already at her desk, sipping coffee as she peers out over her thick-rimmed glasses when Gaby races through the door.

"Are you alright? You look like you've seen a ghost?"

"Hi. I'm freezing! I ran from the truck—and Miss Martha here is getting to be a heavy-weight. Either she's going to be a very big dog, or we might have to cut back on the kibbles. She seems to grow more every day!" She giggles as she sets a wiggling dog down on the floor. "Do you still intend to drop by after work? I need the company, Mimi. I'll even make you supper."

Mimi looks concerned but doesn't ask any questions. Gaby is fully aware she's read the file. There are no secrets. "I'll be there. Don't worry. All's quiet at home. Not so much outside work to do now that the temperature has dropped. I told Tim I might stay over. I'll do Thanksgiving grocery shopping tomorrow after work. That should be fun, eh? Friday night at the supermarket—fate worse than death!"

"You're more than welcome to the couch, Mimi. Your company would be great. What time is Rachel supposed to be here? I hope she likes dogs."

"I told Dr. Wilkerson any time after 8:30 AM. I know that's early, but she wanted to see you early, and you said it was okay." Mimi sounds worried.

"No. No. That's fine. I couldn't remember. I'm a little nervy." Mimi gives a knowing nod.

Shortly after she's settled Martha and found herself a cup of coffee, Mimi calls to tell her Rachel is in reception. "Send her down, Mimi. She knows the way."

Gaby stands at her door to watch for the psychiatrist. As usual, Dr. Rachel Wilkerson looks and moves like a model on a New York City fashion runway. Tall and angular, with long dark hair falling loosely to her shoulders, she's dressed in her standard straight skirt with a kick-pleat. The fabric is a brown tweed of some sort and works in perfect harmony with a yellow, frothy blouse—open-necked and supporting a heavy gold chain necklace. She has paid attention to the temperature, as she carries the most beautiful sheepskin coat that Gaby has ever seen. Rachel waves her hello and glides into the office.

She looks down at Martha who has approached her for a pat. "What have we here? Do they let you bring a pet to work? This is new."

"An exception for a couple of days, Rachel. Her name is Martha. Have a seat. Let me hang up your gorgeous coat."

"Oh, thanks. Quite heavy, but I love it. Had it made for me in Montreal last year."

"Do you want coffee or tea?"

"No, thanks. I had coffee at the hotel before I came over here. I'm anxious to chat because I am scheduled to leave later today to go back to Edmonton. I wanted to get some details cleared up. I may have to stay, though. It depends a great deal on what you have to say."

Gaby sits down and takes a sip of her now cool coffee. "Tell me what exactly you want to talk about, Rachel. You have piqued my curiosity, that's for sure."

Rachel leans over toward Gaby. I know you can't discuss Charlene Quinn with me, but I have consent to discuss Patrick Hollinger with you. I don't want to put you in a compromising position, so I think I've come up with a way to get my questions answered without you having to respond in any way that could be considered unethical. Shall we give it a go?" She looks pleased as she leans back in the chair.

"Okay, Rachel. You talk. I'll listen, for now." Gaby is nervous. She likes

Rachel, but every little nuance about this case makes her fearful, somehow. She has enough on her mind without worrying that she'll give information to Rachel that should be held in confidence.

"Patrick Hollinger has been my patient for more than six months. He is a paranoid schizophrenic who has managed quite remarkably on basic medications. His mother was not managed well, and killed herself some years ago. Patrick has successfully kept his demons at bay. He has told me the details about his unfortunate relationship with a girl named Charlene Quinn. He also told me that she is a client of yours and I will assume, throughout this conversation, that this information is correct."

Gaby continues to sip her coffee, remaining silent.

"Although still not hearing voices again, about a month ago Patrick started showing signs of paranoia regarding Charlene. He told me he didn't want to see her anymore, but that she wouldn't leave him alone. He said she will often go to the diner and sit in a booth during his whole shift. He requested that he not work out front and is back in the kitchen doing dishes. Apparently, the owner is doing many of his shifts. I question his ability to be able to work with the public again. He also said Charlene is bound and determined to attend a group Thanksgiving dinner at his apartment building and that she told him you and Joe Dodd—another resident, and a carpenter, I think—plan on inviting her. He says she parks in front of The Station and sits there at all hours.

"In addition to all this, he says he is quite sure Charlene has killed someone—perhaps even the missing girl; maybe someone back east. He's not sure, but she showed him a wire affair with dowels on the end. She says it can be used to strangle people.

"Gaby." Rachel pauses and leans closer to the desk. "In your considered opinion, do you think my patient requires a medication adjustment?"

She doesn't hesitate. "No."

"I told him that I would recommend he go to the police, but I didn't want to send a patient with delusions to law enforcement."

Gaby has not changed expression. Her heart bangs. The pain is like drumming. This could be the way out for her, and for the office. If Patrick reports his concerns, a more thorough investigation might proceed. "I concur with your recommendation that he take his concerns to the RCMP."

"Okay!" Rachel sits up straighter in her chair after she pats Gaby on the hand. "You have been a great help. Now...let's talk about Laura Creighton. I read your referral. I don't think she has Parkinson's disease. I think she has a form of dementia that has Parkinsonian-like symptoms as well. I intend to speak to her doctor after I meet with her. She will need to find supportive housing of some sort. Is that available around here?"

"There are a couple of boarding homes that focus on the elderly. She will need the nursing home soon enough, but one of the boarding homes will work for now. I can help her with that."

"Good. Well, I think that's it." She looks down at the biggest wrist watch Gaby has ever seen. "I think I've taken up enough of your time. Based on our chat, I intend to stay over again tonight, so I can be nearby for Patrick after he goes to the police. I have to call Edmonton, so my secretary can clear my calendar for tomorrow."

In a spontaneous move precipitated by a measure of relief, Gaby asks Rachel if she would like to have dinner at her house that evening. "It won't be fancy—a stir fry or whatever—but you're more than welcome. Mimi will be there, too."

"Why, Gaby! That would be fabulous! I'm always stuck at the hotel. Let me bring a treat! What can I bring?"

"Well, let's go hog wild. You could pop in to the diner for a pie—whatever they can scare up. I'm at 15 Poplar Street. Let's say 6:00 PM?"

"I'll be there!" Rachel and Gaby stand at the same time as Martha wanders out from under the desk. She leans down to the pup. "We will get better acquainted tonight, Martha." She sweeps her coat from the hanger and exits the office in a swish of high heels and long hair.

Gaby is left to wonder what will happen next. She must document her session with Rachel, in case a reference to it comes back to haunt her later on. It'll be fortuitous if Patrick can convince the RCMP to take a closer look at Charlene and her background.

****

Dr. Alden appears reluctant, as he ushers Gaby into his office. "Where's your dog? Everyone says you're bringing your dog to work." His tone is accusatory. This may not go well.

"Martha's back in my office with the door closed, sir. I'll take her home at lunchtime. I have been uncomfortable leaving her there since Charlene appeared *in* my house a couple of days ago. Every detail is in my report. Did you get the additional notes I asked Mimi to add after my meeting with Dr. Wilkerson?"

"Yes. Yes. If that fellow isn't having a psychotic break, maybe he'll tell the police she killed somebody and that will be the end of this mess. We can only hope." He sighs and shakes his head, like he's clearing cobwebs. "So...you feel okay about leaving your dog at home because Charlene will be here?" He's managed to connect the dots.

Gaby shrugs. "More or less. I don't intend to bring her to work every day, Dr. Alden. I've been rattled lately. To top it all off, I found a fringe from her purse on the veranda this morning. Martha was growling in the middle of the night and I can't help but wonder if Charlene spent the night on my porch." She shrugs again. "Of course, I have no way of knowing if the fringe was there before and I hadn't noticed it. Now, do we need to do a review before our session? I'm happy to answer whatever questions I can." She silently notes that Dr. Alden isn't remotely interested in who might have slept on her veranda.

They discuss Rachel Wilkerson's visit and the information she provided. Clark Alden is nervous; agitated, almost. Gaby's afraid he might be out of his depth. Charlene is so manipulative. Gaby's only role is to sit in the session and observe, so that's what she'll do.

At noon, she takes Martha home. There is no sign of Charlene's vehicle anywhere. Gaby and Martha both have some lunch. Gaby roots out her winter down-filled car coat; the temperature is dropping as the day wears on. God! It looks like it could snow before Thanksgiving! Bad enough that there's always snow on the ground by Halloween! She settles Martha, checks the locks on the back gate and then the back door, secures the front, and returns to the Hexagon.

With much relief, she sees the red Land Cruiser in the provincial building parking lot. Charlene must be waiting inside. Mimi will be thrilled!

There she is, sitting in reception, dressed to the nines in a black leather mini-skirt and a sleeveless white blouse sporting a plunging V-neck. She's wearing a red lace bra underneath—as bold as you please. Her motives are as transparent as her blouse. She expects to influence Dr. Alden in ways Gaby suspects he hasn't been influenced in a while. Charlene clutches her fringed purse and smiles with conspiratorial sweetness at her counsellor when Gaby pushes through the door.

"I'll come and get you in a few minutes, Charlene." Gaby nods at Mimi as she exits reception.

Dr. Alden's in his office. She pops her head in. "My office or yours, sir?"

"Bring her here, Gaby—but not for another fifteen minutes. I want to review the documentation one more time."

"No problem. I'll bring her in when the time comes. Don't take any notice of how she's dressed, Dr. Alden. She does that for effect. She thinks men can't focus if her blouse is unbuttoned." Gaby hopes her remark will help keep her boss' supervisor on track.

As planned, Gaby retrieves Charlene, shows her into Dr. Alden's office, and introduces them. Clark has made the mistake of not coming out from behind his desk, so Charlene leans over as far as she can to shake his hand. She can see Dr. Alden trying hard not to look at her cleavage. He's probably lost focus already. Gaby thinks of Elliot and hopes they haven't heard her sigh.

The initial purpose of this session was established as a way to remove Charlene from Gaby's caseload and refer her to a psychiatrist. Rachel Wilkerson, of course, is no longer in the running, but Clark Alden has many colleagues. Charlene seems to see the situation in a somewhat different light. Gaby has difficulty determining who is interviewing whom?

"Have you read the file, Dr. Alden? Has Gaby shared all my intimate little secrets with you?" She glances over at Gaby, sitting away from the desk and to the side. "She hasn't heard them all, you know—at least not yet." Her voice teases and taunts. Dr. Alden is sweaty and flushed. He doesn't seem to know where to look. Gaby's afraid she'll have to intervene. "You can't tell the police information I tell you. I know about confidentiality. Now..." she leans over toward the desk, "if I told you I was *going* to hurt somebody, that's a different story." She looks over at Gaby again. "Poor old Pat Hollinger seems to think I'm going to hurt him. Such a baby! He's mental. He can't help it."

She's enjoying this. Gaby knows, already, this meeting was a mistake.

"Even if I told you I know where Roz is, you can't help the police." Clark Alden's head snaps up and he stares at Charlene through blinking eyes.

"Did you hurt Miss Dover, Charlene?"

"Oh, Dr. Alden. I'm such a tiny person. There are only two *sizable* parts of me, and they certainly couldn't hurt anybody." She wipes an imaginary piece of fluff from the front of her blouse.

"Charlene, if you were involved in Roz Dover's disappearance, it is imperative that you speak with the police. Miss Ridgway would accompany you to the police station. Right, Gaby?" The look on his face is pleading.

Gaby nods, but makes no verbal commitment. She'd rather eat dirt than go to the RCMP station with this woman.

Charlene pulls back. She pushes her chair away from the desk. "I have no intention of going to the cops. The police are stupid. If they can't figure out what happened or find her on their own, I don't intend to volunteer information."

The interview deteriorates from there. Dr. Alden tries, without success, to get an agreement from Charlene to see a psychiatrist. She refuses. She will see no one but Gaby. With a slight nod to Dr. Alden, as a means of communicating her intentions, Gaby stands up and moves into direct eye contact with Charlene.

"I do not intend to see you anymore, Charlene. As I have stated with utmost clarity, I am not able to help you. You need to be seen by a psychiatrist, not a counsellor like myself. Our professional relationship has been jeopardized because you have attempted, on numerous occasions, to insert yourself into my private life. We cannot continue under these circumstances." She craves a glass of water. Her throat is dry, like it's filled with crumbs she can't swallow. Her hands are shaking, the pain in her chest threatens to overtake her, and she's feeling light-headed; trapped. She can't leave until Alden concludes the interview.

"Miss Quinn, I am afraid the services available to you at the Hexagon are not adequate for your needs. I am sorry, but unless you accept my referral, you will have to acquire psychological support someplace else." Thankfully, he stands up.

"Perhaps you could show Charlene out, Dr. Alden. I have issues in my office that require my attention. Charlene, I wish you all the best. I hope you can find someone to help you. And of course, my advice is that you turn yourself in to the police." Gaby nods to Dr. Alden once again and leaves.

Back in her office, with the door firmly closed, Gaby lets the tears roll unchecked down her still-flushed cheeks. Her heart pounds out of her chest. Her head aches mercilessly. She calls Pearl. They will debrief with Clark, once Charlene leaves. "I'm going to run home and get Martha, Pearl. I don't think this is over, yet, and Patrick's mental stability might well not be the only casualty in all this. I know she's capable of doing something horrible to Martha just to be vindictive."

When Gaby locks her front door and sprints toward her truck, Martha in tow, she can see Charlene's red vehicle up the street. She can only hope Patrick has met with the police and made a complaint. Poor Patrick. She doesn't think his self-demotion into the diner's kitchen will help him escape Charlene's influences; and she doesn't think eliminating her from her caseload is going to make a bit of difference regarding her own safety and security. It will likely make the situation worse.

****

Rachel Wilkerson calls Gaby toward the end of the day. She reports that Patrick saw the RCMP and made a statement regarding his concerns. He also gave them Rachel's contact information, for confirmation, and they had followed up with her. Patrick reported to Rachel that he didn't know what was going to happen, but he had given them every detail he could recall about Nova Scotia as well as Hayworth. He figures they will have to deal with the RCMP in Nova Scotia first. She will be over for supper armed with a lemon meringue pie, and they can refrain from talking work. She's excited about her visit.

Gaby and Martha stumble into the house as Gaby tries to manhandle a bag of groceries while Martha makes a beeline for the back door. She needs to romp in the yard. Mimi's car pulls in right behind her. Good. Mimi can do dog duty while Gaby starts to prepare food. It feels nice to be normal for a little while.

The evening goes better than Gaby could have hoped. Rachel, away from work, still looks like a model in her tight blue jeans, cashmere sweater, and gold hoop earrings. She's tied her hair in a ponytail and looks ten years younger. The women talk about relationships, life in Hayworth, travelling back and forth, and whether Rachel could have enough work in Hayworth alone to make a living. For Rachel's benefit, Mimi tells them about her family and life on the farm with her in-laws and husband. Gaby talks a bit about Joe. She doesn't know if it could be serious or not. She takes one day at a time.

Rachel leaves about 10:30 PM. She has to drive back to Edmonton in the morning. Mimi and Gaby both have to work. They anticipate the monthly staff meeting, scheduled tomorrow, with the usual impatience. They are a necessary evil, but sometimes having the flu seems like more fun that one of Pearl's staff meetings. Gaby stands at the top of the veranda steps and waves to Rachel as she pulls her Mercedes away from the curb. As she scoots Martha back inside, she notices the Land Cruiser parked up the street with the lights off. She doesn't tell Mimi.

Chapter 20

Have I hit the high points?

The room is all abuzz when she finally drags her weary behind into the meeting. Leaving Martha at home is adding to her anxiety. Everyone looks up when she appears. Pearl is already at the head of the table. Edith is wedged in close to Pearl. She's dressed in a ratty beige sweater, covered in stains from too many coffee breaks. She emits little gurgling sounds as she chews on a cinnamon bun the size of a saucer. Frank is leaning back in the chair at the end of the oval table. His hands are folded across his ample girth and rest on a wrinkled shirt as well as what looks like a hand-knitted tie. Elliot, as usual, has his head down as he mumbles away to Frank, who keeps his eyes glued on Gaby. It's unusual for her to be the last arrival. She takes her seat halfway down the table.

"Okay, now that everyone's here, we can begin. Dr. Alden is not able to attend this morning, but I have a few words to say to you all about the Quinn case, on his behalf." Pearl shuffles papers while she tries to wipe a scrap of grey hair off her forehead. She turns her attention to Gaby. "First, I would like you to inform your colleagues about this case, Gaby. If you need to fetch your file, please feel free to go get it. Everyone needs to know details now, in the event she turns up unannounced."

Gaby nods, looks around, and without a word leaves the room. She doesn't need her file, but wants the opportunity to compose herself yet again. She suspected Pearl would want her to case conference today, but a little bit of advance warning might have been thoughtful. During coffee break, she will run home to check on Martha. She wonders how long she'll be able to live like this—looking over her shoulder, headaches, nagging chest pain, and scared to go to sleep.

Back in the meeting, Pearl drones on about caseload assignments as Edith sets up her standard plea for someone to take over cases she feels are not "right" for her. Now that Charlene is no longer a client, Gaby makes up her mind she won't argue if transfers are suggested. "Well, with housekeeping issues out of the way, Gaby, you have the floor. Remember, keep it simple. They can all read the file, if they so choose. We are conferencing this so as to minimize risk to co-workers. When you're finished, I will provide Dr. Alden's information."

Gaby takes a sip of her coffee and begins. She describes her original meeting with Charlene and the difficulties she experienced as she attempted to focus the girl on moving forward; on improving her interactions with others. When it became obvious that there were no clear goals and counselling was fruitless, Charlene revealed the murder in Nova Scotia. Gaby makes it clear how Charlene was well-informed about the ethical code and how all of them are obliged to maintain confidentiality. She tells the staff about the police investigation. She shares some of the incidents that have occurred at her home, and her feelings of insecurity, as well as frustration, over the last four months or more. The power of the silence around the table unsettles her. Even Elliot looks up at her all the time she speaks.

"Pearl will tell you Dr. Alden's assessment. All I can say is that Charlene Quinn is no longer my client. I have made it clear that she has issues I am not professionally equipped to handle. She requires a referral to a psychiatrist other than Rachel, who happens to be seeing someone with whom Charlene was involved." She looks over at Pearl. "There. Have I hit the high points?"

"Fine." Before Pearl can continue, Elliot, of all people, interrupts.

"Do you feel your safety is at risk, Gaby? You live alone. Is your fear the reason you adopted a dog?"

"I'll be honest. Yes, I have felt scared many nights. Martha helps. She is proving to be good company. Charlene has been a challenge. She oftentimes sits outside my house—right in front. She also cruises up and down the street. She's 'popped' in, looking to visit. I find it very troubling and unnerving, but my hands are tied, as you know. She's a client—or at least was—and hasn't done anything except trespass. She intimidates me."

"Do you think she's involved in that girl's disappearance?" Edith has somehow managed to locate another cinnamon bun and has no qualms about engaging in the conversation with her mouth full. Both her eyes and her cheeks bulge as she speaks.

"She has hinted at it. I can't tell if her attitude is bravado—a means to keep me involved—or if she tried to confess to a crime. She's a sociopath and very skilled at manipulation of people. The police have asked her questions, but she says they're all stupid." Gaby has not told them about Patrick Hollinger. That information is in the file, but she feels like it is extra material not required for discussion. It has little to do with safety in their workplace.

Pearl interrupts at this point. "Dr. Alden has referred her to another psychiatrist who has a private practice here in town. We don't refer to him very often because he handles police and military clients for the most part. Since Dr. Wilkerson is in conflict, Dr. Goralski has consented to see her. Dr. Alden is not optimistic that she will attend an appointment. To continue, Dr. Alden feels that Charlene Quinn possesses no consideration or empathy for others. He thinks she is dangerous and is convinced she has murdered Roz Dover and hidden her body."

Pearl looks around the room at her staff. "We must all be vigilant. Mimi has been instructed to contact the RCMP if Charlene tries to see Gaby, or makes any kind of scene in the office. We have informed the RCMP that we feel threatened. Under our confidentiality guidelines, we can do little else."

Mimi, who is positioned to Pearl's left, casts a knowing expression at Gaby. She had hinted that the crisis was coming to a head, but Gaby is still shocked, although not unhappy, that her superiors went to the police.

Pearl continues. "The police know there has been an element of harassment but we can only request their assistance due to our concerns about future threats. We cannot reveal information we know about this woman's past, or any suspicions we may have. We have documented, for them, problems experienced by Gaby." She turns to Gaby. "I expect Constable Werbowski will contact you before the day is over."

"I'm a little unclear about what I can and cannot say, Pearl. There's no doubt she's tormented me and therefore made me nervous. She wants to ensure I don't talk, but I can't tell Fiona that."

"Tell the police about the issues at the house. They know they can't ask you to speculate about the reason they happened. We can talk to them because of fear of future issues. Don't worry. Clark spoke to the department lawyer. There's no problem."

The meeting is over. Gaby feels vulnerable again. She hurries home to check on Martha. Charlene's truck is parked in town. She brings Martha back to the office. She doesn't care if someone complains.

****

She bought yeast after work. This morning, in her sun-drenched kitchen, with all the doors locked and Martha stretched out on the floor, close enough to be watchful but not so near as to be a tripping hazard, Gaby makes bread. She hasn't done this since Grant died. He loved it when she made fresh brown bread from her grandmother's recipe. She's out of practise. Her little kitchen radio is tuned to CBC's hour-long Canadian-artists-only program where they play songs by singers like Anne Murray and Ian and Sylvia. She reviews the directions. *Place a packet of yeast into a quarter cup of hot water mixed with a teaspoon of sugar.* Familiar steps. The hot water from the tap will suffice. She mixes in the sugar and sprinkles the yeast over the top. The space fills with that aroma—the one that conjures up images of kitchens from her childhood and warm molasses running down fingers; of warmth; of comfort; of Grant's smile.

She boils the kettle and assembles the ingredients—butter, salt, Quaker oatmeal, molasses, and flour. *Mix one and a half cups of boiling water, one and a half tablespoons of butter, one and a half teaspoons of salt, three-quarters of a cup of oatmeal, and a half cup of molasses in a bowl. Add the yeast mixture.*

She sets the oven to three hundred and fifty degrees. She greases her old loaf pan—pottery with stains and scars from countless loaves so many years ago. She is morose. It doesn't help that the radio serenades her with Andy Kim's "Rock Me Gently", followed by Gordon Lightfoot's "Sundown"— both popular songs the year Grant died. She's tried to put all that behind her. Perhaps making bread wasn't such a good idea.

She begins to add the flour. *Approximately four and one-half cups, added gradually until the dough can be worked without feeling sticky. Knead.* She forms the dough into a ball, presses it into the floured butcher block with her palms, and pulls it back over itself. Her hands think independently, recalling old movements. The rhythm returns. The dough feels warm and pliable.

Cut the dough in half and form two smaller round loaves. Place them side by side in the prepared pan. Cover and let rise in a warm place for an hour, and then bake for about fifty minutes. Gaby follows the directions, places the pan at the back of the stove top, and covers it with a clean dish towel. She looks at the clock—9:45 AM. The bread will be cool by noon. Feeling satisfied with her morning's task, she cleans up her kitchen and makes a pot of coffee. Constable Fiona Werbowski said she would be over sometime today. If she arrives this morning, at least there'll be some coffee made.

Since all of her thoughts have been about home, Gaby decides to call Nina, who will undoubtedly be thrilled she has accomplished a household task more domestic than buying wine and concocting a chicken stir fry. They talk for almost twenty minutes, and Gaby permits herself the gift of ignoring the consequence of the phone bill. She might as well spend her money on long distance as on anything else. There aren't many places to shop here in Hayworth. Nina is Nina. She rambles on about the children, complains a little about her husband—always making it clear that he's the best, regardless— and asks about Gaby's love life.

"Today, for whatever reason, my love life is all memory, Nina. The whole time I was making bread this morning, all I could think about was Grant. Then the damned radio seemed to play every tune that was popular the year he died. Do you remember 'Rock me Gently'? God, all I wanted to do was weep. I've had one of those days, and it isn't even noon here, yet!"

"Is there more trouble with that weird client?"

"Yes and no. She's not my client any more. She should be seeing a doctor—a psychiatrist—but I don't think she will."

They talk a bit about Thanksgiving plans. The kids are anxious to get outside for a while—rolling in the leaves, maybe—so they make their goodbyes.

She returns from the kitchen and enters the living room when the doorbell rings. Martha barks and wags as Gaby peeks through the curtain and sees Elliot and his wife Celina, of all people, standing on her porch. She throws open the door. "Well hi there, you two. Your timing's perfect. I have coffee already made. Come on in. What in the world has brought you to this neck of the woods on a Saturday morning?"

They tumble in the door. Elliot still avoids direct eye contact, but Celina has no trouble taking up his slack. "Elliot, poor darling, has been worried sick about you. Of course, he can't tell me why; just says the situation 'concerns a client'. That's what he always says when work is involved." She throws her jacket over a nearby chair and flops down on the sofa. "I haven't seen your place in ages! What smells so good? Have you been making bread? How very domestic!"

Gaby is no match for Celina. The young woman is overwhelmingly vivacious. She has all the personality for she and Elliot put together. Gaby has never been able to determine the connection. "Yes, brown bread rising on the back of the stove—my grandmother's recipe. I still have to put it in the oven. What do you take in your coffee, Celina?" She knows Elliot will want his black.

"A splash of milk, Gaby. I can't believe you eat bread! I haven't eaten a piece of bread in, heavens! It must be five years. Too fattening, my dear. Too fattening." She crosses her long legs. Regardless of the cold snap, she's wearing a grey tweed mini-skirt and a silky-looking pink blouse. Her jacket, now removed, looks like the remains of a very fluffy white poodle. Martha has been more interested in the jacket than in the people.

After some minor chat about vague generalities, Elliot reveals the reason for their impromptu visit. "I was worried she might show up. We went for a little drive and I looked for her truck. I couldn't find it but thought we'd stop in anyway, and see how you're doing."

"Isn't he the sweetest guy?" Celina gushes as she sips her coffee. The smell of the bread consumes the air in the house, gift-wrapping them in the warmth of molasses, oatmeal, and yeast.

Celina uses her diet discipline as her excuse. "We have to go now, Gaby. If I stay any longer, I'll dig into your bread when it comes out of the oven." She picks up the poodle-skin-looking coat and struggles to get back into it without tangling her necklace in the process.

Elliot leans over toward Gaby. "If you need anything at all, call me, Gaby. We're home all weekend."

"Thanks, my friend. I think I'm okay. Joe has invited me as his plus one for dinner at The Station on Monday. We're also going to the diner for supper tonight, so don't worry, I'm fine. I have some distractions." *Support sometimes comes from the most unexpected places.* She is more grateful than Elliot could ever possibly imagine.

"That bread's so tempting! Come on, Elly. We need to go!" He makes eye contact with Gaby and grins as they go down the steps. There's love there—no doubt about it. Elliot may have his hands full with Celina, but Gaby thinks he's quite happy with his circumstances.

****

Right after lunch, Constable Werbowski turns up. She's a kind and thoughtful young woman, perhaps thirty. Cops seem to socialize with cops, so Gaby hasn't seen her out in public, as a civilian, very often. Today is a surprise, since she arrives in an unmarked car and is dressed in slacks and a sweater. There isn't all that much to her five foot four inch frame without the hat and all the paraphernalia. Her dark hair is not caught up in its customary bun, but pulled back into a pony tail at the nape of her neck.

"Hi, constable. Come on in. Are you off duty today?"

"Hi, Gaby, and call me Fiona, please. We've worked together often enough; I think you can do that. As for the clothes, I waited to come and see you once my shift ended. It causes less attention in the neighbourhood—you don't need a patrol car parked outside. Listen, all I need is for you to tell me the kinds of incidents that have caused you to be fearful of Charlene Quinn. I need times, places, and your reactions. We won't analyze why she behaves in certain ways, only when and where, okay?"

They sit down in the kitchen after Gaby locks the front door and introduces Fiona to Martha, who appreciates all the company by sitting nearby, leaning against a visiting leg, or sleeping with her head resting on a visiting foot. They have tea. Gaby has assembled a document with dates and times when Charlene cruised by the house, parked out front, entered, stopped her while she and Joe were walking, stopped her in the parking lot, and tried to get in through the back gate. The list is extensive. When all together, the number of issues possesses a certain shock value.

Fiona asks basic questions. She never ventures into territory that might put Gaby in the position of feeling as if she has to explain Charlene's actions or behaviour. At no time does she need to say that Charlene was her client. The conversation is all about threatening acts and fear of additional threatening acts.

"You have a sweet little house, Gaby. I've often thought of buying, myself. Interest rates are so high, though. I keep hoping they'll come down."

"I know what you mean. I had a little help because I sold my house down east after my husband died. I was able to take the plunge here, as a result."

"I'm sorry, Gaby. I didn't know."

Gaby hates to reveal details about Grant, but feels Fiona should have some history. "I'm okay. It happened back in '74. He was a nice man. It was very sad at the time, but I came out here to try and start over. This whole issue hasn't helped, and I'd like to put it behind me."

"Right now, all I can tell you is that our investigation is ongoing. We have information from other sources, and we're reviewing evidence with other jurisdictions. You may or may not know what I'm talking about, but hang in there. This will all go away very soon." She stands as she speaks. "Here's my card, and I've written my apartment phone number on the back. Call me if you need help or think of other information, okay? We will take care of this, Gaby."

Relief can be palpable. Gaby feels consumed by relief as she watches Fiona pull away from the curb and drive down Poplar. She has enough time to wash her face and change her clothes, as well as walk and feed Martha, before Joe's arrival. They both like the Saturday night special at the diner.

****

Gaby is still high on relief as she and Joe find a space for his truck in front of the diner. Charlene stomps out, leather jacket in hand. She sees Gaby in the vehicle and marches right up to the window. "Roll down your window, bitch!"

"Hey now. Hold it right there!" Joe starts to get out of the truck.

Charlene continues to scream. "You said you'd get me an invitation to Thanksgiving dinner! You didn't do it! You're going to be sorry!" She rounds the front of the truck and jumps in her own vehicle.

"We need to go back to the house, Joe. Patrick isn't working the front right now. She can't torment him. That's probably why she's mad. Run in and ask for two dinners to go. I have to be home. I can't leave Martha. I have this horrible feeling she's going to try and make my life worse. Let's get home as fast as we can. I'll call Fiona and tell her what's happened." She doesn't even attempt to keep the panic out of her voice.

Chapter 21

Perhaps that ship has sailed

Gaby wakes up early Sunday morning, instantly aware of how poorly she slept. Her eyes are still closed as she listens to the chilly silence that envelopes her little house. Martha's on the bed again. She doesn't care, as she slowly exposes one bare arm to the elements of her bedroom, and rhythmically scratches her puppy's silky ear.

Last night was scary. They went into the diner together. There was no way Joe would let her stay in the truck by herself while he went in to buy two specials to go. There was no telling what Charlene was up to. She was so angry!

Margo Johnson, the owner, provided the specials on paper plates, wrapped in tin foil. They returned to Gaby's. Charlene was nowhere to be seen. She had succeeded in ruining a nice evening, nonetheless. The air was heavy with Joe's unasked questions. It was heartening, though, to know that when she said she was afraid this woman was capable of burning her house down, he acknowledged her. She told him the police were by to see her; that the issue was well in hand. None of this helped to curb her dread.

If circumstances get much worse...she realizes she might need counselling herself if a resolution isn't found soon. A friendship with Rachel Wilkerson might not be such a bad idea.

Joe was sweet. They ate their dinners in the living room in front of the television. They drank beer and relaxed, watching *The Dukes of Hazard*. Joe stayed until well after 2:00 AM. They held hands. They kissed a couple of times. Under other circumstances, she would have signalled she wanted him to stay. She thinks she's ready. *God! You've been alone for seven years!* She frets about the possibility they could ruin a valuable and supportive friendship. Perhaps that ship has sailed.

Martha gets up, crawls off the bed, and turns toward the front door. They never go out the front door when they first get up. "Hold on girl." Gaby runs to the bathroom, adds a housecoat over her flannelette pyjamas, and calls once again. "Come on, Martha. Out the back. Here girl."

Martha hangs her head and drops her tail, but returns to the back of the house and stands by the door as Gaby struggles into her down-filled coat and boots. The cold air slaps her in the face as she waits on the step and watches the pup. Martha stops at the gate and sniffs before she follows Gaby back into the kitchen. Gaby makes coffee. The smell fills the room with cozy warmth. Martha ignores her food and returns to sit on the mat at the front door. She looks at Gaby with her one blue eye and one brown eye, insistent and sorrowful.

"She's not around, Martha. We're okay." Gaby realizes she's whispering to her dog. "Come have your breakfast. I want brown bread toast. The weather is too cold for cereal." She pats Martha on the head and then pats herself on the leg, in an attempt to encourage the dog to follow her back to the kitchen. Martha does as she is told, but her expression makes it obvious she's not happy.

She refuses to eat. This is unusual and troubles Gaby. Martha takes up a post as sentry, now, at the back door.

The radio is tuned to CBC—the Sunday political show. The air in the kitchen is heavy with the scent of warm brown bread mixed with the coffee. Gaby munches away. The texture of the soft, fresh bread slightly toasted, and with thick crusts, is the perfect vehicle for peanut butter this morning.

"Martha, did you not finish when we were outside? Is that the trouble? Do you have to go out again?"

Gaby claws into her big coat and boots once more. "This time I'll go with you. No fooling around. It's too cold outside this morning." She bends over to pat the pup and opens the back door while she braces for the rush of earlier than expected cold air that elbows its way into her warm house.

Martha runs straight to the gate, which remains locked. There's nobody around—then she sees it. The red Toyota Land Cruiser is parked way down the street. If it were not after dawn, or if there were leaves on the trees, she would never have noticed it. But that doesn't explain Martha's behaviour. If Charlene is down there in her truck, this isn't the first time. "Come on, girlie. It has to be more than that truck troubling you. What is it, really?"

Back inside, Martha returns to the mat at the front door. She whispers a whimper and continues to look up at the door knob.

"If I open this door so you can look outside, can we go back to our breakfast?" A quick peek past the curtain reveals empty stairs leading to her entry. She reaches for the door to unlock it, remembering that Joe told her, in no uncertain terms, to lock the storm door as well, which she did faithfully after he left. They removed the screen door and replaced it with a winter outside door about two weeks ago. Martha wags her tail and stands up. "See. Nobody's there. Are you satisfied?" Gaby starts to close the door when she catches movement out of the corner of her eye. She looks to the side. Charlene is sitting in the old rattan rocker Gaby keeps on the porch. She's wrapped in a ratty, patchwork quilt and has a knitted hat pulled down around her ears. Suddenly, she's grateful that the new door is considerably more robust than the screen.

"I thought you would never open the goddamned door!"

Gaby's heart is in her throat. She refuses to unlock the storm door. "What are you doing on my porch? Go home, Charlene!"

"You will pay, you know—for not helping me; for abandoning me; for blabbing to the police when you said you couldn't. You will pay for this!" She's screaming. She stands up, wrapped in the quilt, and stares in through the fogged-over glass that is the only element separating the two women.

Gaby wants to slam the door and call Fiona, but she feels herself rooted to the spot. *Don't engage with her! Don't talk to her!* She remains silent but doesn't close the inside door.

"Like the quilt? It was on Roz's bed. I took it after she didn't come home. Do you think I hurt Roz?" Charlene's smile is crooked. Her bright red lipstick has smeared in the night. Gaby can see the stain from it on the pink patterned quilt.

"I waited in my truck until after that idiot left last night. He was here for hours. I can't believe a classy lady like you would get involved with a broken-down old carpenter like Joe Dodd. He isn't even good looking! What's the matter with you, anyway? You'd better get involved with someone who has a good paycheque though, 'cause you're not going to have a job much longer. I've seen to that!"

Gaby stands there, still quiet as she tries to calm down. *Don't be paranoid. This woman is sick, but she isn't going to hurt you.* She can feel Martha sitting beside her foot and leaning against her leg. Her dog is a comfort.

"You know, Gaby, if you said I could be your client again, I would promise not to hurt anybody else—like Patrick, or like Crystal or Ila. It wouldn't be easy, but I'd promise if you say we can do counselling again." She smiles her troublesome sweet smile.

"Charlene, my obligation is to protect the public from future acts. You have now threatened the well-being of certain people and I am obliged to report that." Gaby shakes as she continues. "Get off my porch, Charlene. This has gone on long enough." She slams the inside door, returns to the kitchen, and picks up the phone.

Charlene stands on the veranda and shouts obscenities at the top of her voice. She says that Gaby will never counsel anybody again. She screams she will kill herself and take others with her. She cries—loud, piercing cries like the animal in a leg-hold trap Gaby saw on a news clip once.

Gaby calls the RCMP station, identifies herself, and asks for Constable Werbowski. "She's out on patrol. Can I tell her to call you?"

"Can you ask her to come to 15 Poplar Street? I have a situation with a woman named Charlene Quinn. Constable Werbowski assured me that if I called, someone would be here."

"A car is on the way right now, Miss Ridgway. Are you in imminent danger?"

"No, but I can't predict what she'll do next. She's on my porch and won't leave."

"You should see a patrol car soon, and Constable Werbowski is on her way as well. You can stay on this line if you like."

"No, I'm okay. I can see the patrol car now. Thanks." She hangs up the phone and stands at the edge of her front window, the curtain pulled back a tiny bit to afford a view. Martha is between her feet. Gaby's hands shake. Her head pounds, like her eyes will soon fly out of her face. The churning in her stomach makes her feel like throwing up.

****

"I came by to bum a cup of coffee and see how you were holding up when I saw the cop cars leaving. Was that Quinn's vehicle being towed?" Joe, like a slightly-delayed knight in shining armour, has managed to rumble up to the front of 15 Poplar just as the dust settles on a situation that is sure to serve as gossip fodder for the neighbours during the many extended winter nights yet to come.

Gaby nods and opens the door. Martha is so happy to see a familiar person, she wiggles in all directions. Joe, of course, is her special friend.

"Can you tell me what went on?" Gaby appreciates the fact that Joe learned, from the beginning, that there is much she cannot share.

"Constable Werbowski—Fiona—came to see me about Charlene's behaviour. She said to call if it happened again. It seems Charlene slept on the porch last night. She waited until after you left and then she rolled up in a quilt on my rocker and stayed put. Martha wanted to go out the front way this morning. When I opened the door to prove to her there was nobody there, guess who was sitting in the rocker?"

"What will they do?"

"The police? I can't tell you much. They will hold her for questioning and, I expect, charge her with trespassing or some other damned offence. I'll put coffee on. You sit down with Martha. The poor little dear needs some attention. If you're not on your way someplace, maybe we can all three go for a walk later."

She can't tell Joe the details, although Fiona has made it clear that Charlene will be held for a while. They intend to send her fingerprints to Halifax. Patrick's information and concerns have led to them cooperating with that jurisdiction in order to determine if she had any involvement with a body found off the 104 Highway near Isle Madame, Cape Breton Island, Nova Scotia some six months ago. Charlene may well be charged with the murder she has already confessed she committed—thanks to dear old Patrick. All Gaby can report to Joe is about the stalking and tormenting.

"Coffee's on. How about breakfast? I have brown bread and peanut butter."

Joe looks up from his romp with Martha and grins from ear to ear. "Whatever you have, kid, is fine with me as long as I can stick around with my two favourite girls. Now don't tell Blanche I said that, Martha. It's hard to live with a diva cat that gets jealous." He nuzzles the dog's ears.

They eat. All of a sudden, Gaby is ravenous. They demolish the brown bread. "I didn't know you could bake. When did that happen?"

She tells him about Grant. She hasn't told the whole story to anyone in Hayworth before. She trusts this man and thinks she wants to have a relationship with him. She tells him many of the details; stories she hasn't shared before. She talks about making bread and knitting while her husband was dying. "I thought about him all morning, yesterday, while I made the bread. It was the first time in seven years that I made it—not since he died. I think I'm trying to finally let go. I felt like I had to make the bread to prove I could do it even though he's gone." She sees the questioning look in Joe's eyes. "Too much self-analysis, Joe?" Her soft laugh is uneasy.

"No, not at all. A lot of elements about you make sense now, though. Do you want to go for a drive—get away for an hour or two? I want to show you a couple of places I'm particularly fond of. Martha can come. We won't leave her here, in case they let crazy lady out of the hoosegow."

****

Gaby, with Martha leashed and trotting ahead of her, climbs into Joe's big blue monster. Martha plunks herself between them on the bench seat, leans against Gaby, and lifts her head to try and see out the front window. She still isn't quite big enough.

Joe navigates toward downtown and pulls the truck into a parking spot in front of a saloon-style storefront on Main Street. The left-hand side is occupied by a nail salon, complete with scruffy pink curtains, and a sign that reads: Olive's Manicures. The right-hand side is being renovated. A sign advertising that Alberta Lighting will soon open a branch at this location is plastered to the window along with newsprint—hung to maintain opening day suspense.

"Want to go in and have a peek at the renovations?"

Gaby is curious. "What? Is this your business, Joe?"

"No, no, Gaby." Joe explains. "I can see why you might think that. No— I'm their landlord. I bought the building back in the summer."

Gaby is sure she must look a little gob-smacked, but Joe's a big boy. She guesses he can buy commercial property if he wants to. "Sure, we can have a look, if you're sure your tenants don't mind."

They leave Martha in the truck. Joe unlocks the door. They're assaulted by gyproc dust and urethane fumes. The lighting company's contractors have been busy. It will be bright and airy when the space is finished.

Joe snoops around. He rambles on to Gaby in the process. "After Ben closed her antique shop, this side of the building was empty. The owner, an investor from Edmonton, wanted to sell, but there were no takers. It was on the market for over a year. I decided, in August, that maybe I should buy it."

"I guess investment here in Hayworth isn't that horrible an option. I bought here." Gaby shakes her head as she responds. No one seems to think the town will grow, so prices are low for Alberta, and Main Street is not, by any one's assessment, considered a hub of activity.

"Well, there's the point." Joe stops by the new counter and looks at the veneers that have been recently installed. "I worked for a woman who told me her brother owns Alberta Lighting and they wanted to open a retail space here in town because there's a new subdivision being approved. It's located out past The Station, at the far end. Her brother figured there would be lots of work. Interest rates are still pretty high, but rent from both sides of this property will pay the mortgage, so I'm okay. My sisters seem to think I need a retail shop, myself. They think I should sell cabinets rather than install sets sold by somebody else. Olive's lease is up in March and she wants to relocate to the mall, anyway. Who knows? What do you think?"

Gaby is pessimistic when it comes to Hayworth. The town always seems to be on the brink of a boom about to occur in the oil and gas business, but Hayworth has never seen much benefit. Interest rates are high. There are service jobs, of course. People could live here and work in the oil patch up north, instead of having to return to Edmonton. Maybe that will be the point of the new development—to get workers to invest closer to their jobs. "I think that you have made a valuable commitment to your community. You will be a fine landlord. Having your own retail shop will certainly help streamline your work, because you're always on the run, chasing leads. At least, this way, people can drop in for a quote and call you at the shop instead of at home at all hours." She looks out from under wispy bangs that are tickling her eyelashes. "You know that's what happens. You'll also need staff."

"That will be my downfall. No time to worry about that, yet—maybe months from now. Come on." He grabs her hand. "I want to show you another property I bought. Went on a little shopping spree—inspired by my sisters, who seem to relish the idea of watching their little brother spend his money!"

She likes the feel of her hand surrounded by the big calloused mitt that is his.

The next stop is a field, beyond the area at the end of town Joe explains is designated as the new subdivision. It slopes a little, away from populated areas. There are trees, but not many.

They stand outside the truck for a minute, and include Martha as they walk toward the ridge with the trees. The ground is frozen and covered in stubble. The hike is not pleasant underfoot due to the uneven ground. "What do you think?"

They've reach the top. Gaby is overwhelmed by the view. Although the land looks flat from the road, the terrain is sloped to the point where she feels she's standing on top of a hill. All of Hayworth is laid out below and in the distance. "You bought this property? How big is it?"

"Five acres. Nobody can build nearby. I could put a house up here protected by the trees at the back, with a nice view and no close neighbours. The location is not that far from town, but it feels like you are. I'll say it again. What do you think?"

"The view is breathtaking, Joe. I've never even noticed this before."

"I bought it from the same guy who sold the development property. He plans to move south. It felt like a good deal. I'm glad you like it. Let's go back to The Station and I'll make us an omelet. You've had a busy day already and Thanksgiving, tomorrow, promises to be crazy."

Gaby looks down at Martha. "Don't worry about the dog, Gaby. She and Blanche have met before. Remember? I took her home at first, in case I hadn't read you right and I would be keeping her. They're fine. Blanche is old. She can manage a pup."

Chapter 22

They have a bond

The house is full to bursting with the sweet, nutmeg scent of freshly baked apple crisp. Gaby feels especially domestic as she admires her creation cooling atop a wire rack on her kitchen counter. Ronny said people could start to arrive anytime after 2:00 PM for late afternoon dinner. Gaby feels a little fluttery with excitement.

She dresses with care. She wants to be casual and comfortable, but with a dressed up edge. She chooses baggy, chocolate brown velveteen pants and pairs them with her favourite pale yellow cotton sweater. If memory serves her, Maggie Woodward is a knitter. That might provide a topic of conversation. She adds gold disk hoop earrings and drags her hair behind her ears. All ready.

Martha has been fed, but she drops a water bowl and a handful of kibble into a small grocery bag so the pup will have a snack when everyone eats. Martha doesn't beg at the table, but this is a big group, so all bets are off. They have been very kind to include her, and she wants Martha to mind her manners.

When she's ready to leave, she calls Joe. "I'm on my way."

"Good. I'll meet you out front. No need for you to appear at the door alone. I heard Cheryl go down already, but you know her, don't you?"

"I think I've met everybody except the managers. What's their name—Wolski? Anyway, them and Maggie's sister, Rose—but meet me at the door anyway."

The drive to the end of town and The Station takes about five minutes. There isn't much traffic. Businesses are closed up tight. The weather is cold. Some showroom windows even have a bit of frost. No one appears too interested in exercising, so there are no walkers about. She pulls her Mazda truck into the front lot, and sees Joe filling the doorway. Her breath catches a tiny bit. His bulky frame standing there, his square face sporting a goofy grin, and his big hand holding a bowl full of what looks like coleslaw, all give her comfort.

It is no easy task to manoeuvre an excited puppy, a purse, and a thirteen by nine inch glass baking dish filled with warm apple crisp out of the cab of a relatively small truck. Joe covers the distance between them in two strides and takes the crisp from her outstretched hand.

"I'll do food. You do dog and door," he says as a means of greeting. Somehow, he manages to lean down and kiss her on the cheek.

She makes a joke. "No time for you to kiss Martha, too. Let's get inside where it's warm." She's flushed a little, but it feels good. Joe laughs at her.

He indicates Number Three with a nod of his head and Gaby knocks on Ronny's door. It's opened immediately by Cheryl Nadler, who looks impeccable, as usual. Cheryl is always so put together. She is tiny, with short dark hair and a gorgeous figure. She wears cute little blouses and straight skirts. Edith, from work, says she's changed a lot in the last year since her friend Ben died, but nobody, even Joe, knows for certain what precipitated the changes.

"Come on in! Welcome, Gaby. Hi, Joe. Can I take those? Did you do all this?"

"Good God, no! Gaby did the dessert. I did the coleslaw. I left a box of beer on the stairs. Be right back." He turns on his heel and disappears from sight for a moment.

"Let me take your coat, Gaby." Cheryl bends down. "This must be Martha. I have heard a lot about you. I will pat you properly once I put this stuff on the counter."

At this point, Ronny appears from the back of the apartment. "Hi, Gaby. Welcome. Joe must be in the vicinity." She looks over Gaby's shoulder as Joe reappears with the beer. Ronny never fails to impress Gaby. She is tall, thin, and her hair is dyed almost white. She has beautiful skin. Today, she's wearing a purple-patterned caftan affair reminiscent of the 1970s. It flutters behind her as she walks. There is the ever-present scarf at her neck.

Everyone shuffles into the living room, as another knock is heard. Ronny attends this time, and greets Amanda and Chester Wolski, who arrive with their little boy, Mason, a big broccoli salad, and a little roasting pan filled with what looks like caramelized carrots. There are introductions all around. Chester is very handsome. Gaby thinks he could be a movie star. His looks are classic and chiselled. His thick black hair keeps falling over one eye. Amanda is chubby in a healthy way, and her hair is coloured a fierce red. She has it tied in a knot on the top of her head with a blue ribbon that matches her long cotton empire-waist dress. Gaby wonders if she might be pregnant.

The centre of attention becomes Mason and Martha. Gaby thinks the two of them are well-able to provide an afternoon's worth of entertainment. Ronny might not be prepared for the bedlam. There's some barking, a little bit of squealing, some running, and lots of whooping. There's some rolling on the floor. Gaby was smart enough to put a tug-toy in her purse, so they manage to entertain one another. Mason isn't quite three, and even though Martha is only a puppy and a gentle one at that, both Amanda and Gaby keep a close eye on the pair.

Chester and Joe have each cracked a beer and stand off to the side out of the fray, probably talking cars. Gaby knows that Chester works for the Ford dealer. Ronny and Cheryl organize in the kitchen. The apartment smells like baked ham and roast turkey. When Gaby turns to Amanda to ask her Mason's birthday, there's a knock on the door followed by the grand entrance of Rose and Maggie Woodward from across the hall. Everyone hears the clatter as Patrick Hollinger descends the two flights from Number Six in the attic. He wiggles his way in and places a pecan pie on the peninsula that stretches across the kitchen.

Rose and Maggie have appetizers and mashed potatoes that Maggie wants Ronny to tuck into the oven once the turkey comes out. Amanda looks at Gaby, and casts her eyes toward the ceiling when she sees Rose setting up cocktail wieners and dipping sauce with little toothpicks sporting coloured plastic ends. She also has bags of potato chips, and onion and garlic dip. "She brings the wieners every time," Amanda whispers in Gaby's ear.

Rose is middle-aged, on the frumpy side, and sports a gathered skirt and sweater-set straight out of the 1950s. She has a plastic hair band tucked into what looks like recently permed hair. Gaby grins as she catches Maggie's eye.

The girl always looks the same in wrinkled slacks and the hand knit sweaters of which she's so proud. She isn't skilled at knitting, yet. This particular project appears to have been torn apart and rebuilt a couple of times, but at least she seems to be determined to keep at it.

"Hi, Gaby! Great to see you. Is that your puppy over there? Glad we left Caesar and Caramel at home, eh Rose?" She turns to her sister, who pats her arm without turning away from her conversation with Cheryl. Food appears out of every corner. It is sure to be quite a spread.

Patrick looks a bit out of place. He nods to Cheryl and crosses the room to stand near Joe, who shakes his hand and wishes him a happy Thanksgiving. He's drinking ice water that Ronny handed to him when he put the pie down on the counter. He must not drink and everyone must already know that. Gaby accepted a glass of white wine earlier, and noticed that Amanda is drinking soda water.

Ronny and Rose start to pass around the chips and wieners, after Maggie delivers a napkin to everyone. Guests perch on various mismatched chairs, some hard and some upholstered. There is no sofa. Cheryl starts to assemble items on the picnic table—plates, cutlery, napkins, the platter of ham, and the salads. She asks Joe if he will carve the turkey and they set about the task of getting that job done.

Ronny, with wieners in one hand and cocktail sauce in the other, asks them all for their attention. "I think everyone has been introduced, but I want to welcome Gaby Ridgway. Maggie, Cheryl, and I know her from work, and Joe knows her from doing projects on her house. I think you've met her at the diner, eh Patrick?"

Patrick nods and looks pleased. "I guess I meet everybody at the diner one way or the other. Hi, Gaby." *At least he's making eye contact.* Both she and Joe noticed, before he stopped waiting tables and went back to working in the kitchen, how he seemed to be avoiding people as much as possible. They suspected it was directly related to Charlene.

"Thanks everyone. You folks have a wonderful little community, here. I now think I might be quite left out way over on Poplar Street." She gazes around at everyone. "Perhaps, for the next potluck, we can have it at my house."

"The next dinner will be for Christmas, Gaby, and I am happy to share the responsibilities with you." Joe stops carving for a moment, looks over at Gaby, and winks.

"I'm in if you guys are!" Gaby wonders if the aroma of a turkey dinner has given her delusions. Fitting this many people in her house for a meal might be a challenge.

"Then we're set," pipes in Maggie. "Christmas at Gaby's. Details to follow."

****

Dinner is fabulous. The food tastes all the better because the meal is shared with a group of people that truly care about one another. Gaby sees that. They have a bond of some sort. She must ask Joe about it. As everyone gets settled with tea and dessert, the conversation automatically shifts to the disappearance of Roz Dover. The case of the missing girl has gripped the community for weeks.

"Did anybody here know her?" Joe asks what seems like a benign question to the group at large and most heads shake no. Patrick points out that Chester must remember her because Charlene Quinn said he worked on Roz's car.

"Did I?" Chester responds with a vague expression on his handsome face. "I work on a lot of cars, Patrick."

"But an olive green Pinto? Come on. You must remember her!"

"Oh, I remember the car, if that's what you mean, but I have no recollection of the girl."

Patrick changes the subject away from the Pinto. "I have some news and I want to tell everyone. I can't keep quiet any longer!"

"Are your sisters coming to visit, Patrick?" Maggie is the first to make a suggestion.

"Are you going back east for Christmas?" Cheryl tries a guess.

"No, you guys! Charlene Quinn was arrested! I went to the police and told them stuff she told me. She said if I told, she would kill me like she did some hitchhiker in Nova Scotia. Dr. Wilkerson said I should tell the police anyway. I did. They're holding her for questioning. They said I made the right choice, but I sure hope she doesn't get out again. I want to work in the front of the diner, but I told Margo that if she gets out of jail, it's back to dishwashing for me!" He looks around the room. Gaby observes that everyone is wide-eyed and open-mouthed except Joe and herself, since they already knew about her being picked up. Chester's attention is focused on Mason.

So now Joe knows what has been going on, Gaby thinks. No one else in the room would be aware that she has any knowledge of the situation. Cheryl might suspect.

Cheryl is the first to speak. "Did the RCMP tell you any other details, Patrick? Everyone here can keep a secret—we already know that." She looks around and nods at all of Ronny's guests.

"They said they contacted the police in Nova Scotia and a body was found after Charlene moved here. They said there was a fingerprint that didn't belong to the guy, on his glasses. They intend to hold Charlene until they determine if the fingerprint might be hers. I hope it is, because if she gets out of jail, I will be in trouble. Can everybody make sure we keep the outside door locked all the time, especially if she gets out? I don't want to find her flopped in front of my door."

The group nods. "That's no problem," says Amanda. "We'll continue to keep the door locked."

Gaby doesn't take part in the conversation. At least she knows for certain that Charlene is still being held, so tonight she might experience a sound sleep.

Patrick continues. "I talked to my dad. He told me that if she gets out of jail, he will send me the money to fly home for a while." He hastens to add, "Only until this whole business gets straightened out. I can't hide in the kitchen at the diner forever. She's dangerous. I know she killed that guy. It had better be her fingerprint on those glasses."

"When will they know, Patrick?" Rose hasn't said much up until now.

"They said by the end of this week. It takes a long time. I don't understand why, but there it is. I think they can keep her for a psychiatric assessment that has to be done in Edmonton, so she'll be there for a few days. I told them about Ila's cat, too, but the cops didn't seem to care much about that."

"What about her cat?" Joe and Maggie ask the question at almost the same time.

"She didn't like Ila's little kitten. She told me she drowned it in the toilet and then threw it away at the dump. I think she figured I'd be impressed. She was surprised that I thought what she did was awful!"

Maggie and Rose gasp. Joe looks over at Gaby again. Martha is sleeping across her feet while Mason has drifted off in Chester's arms. They have worn each other out. She knows Joe has now figured out why she wanted to take Martha to work. Cheryl looks at her, too. She's probably determined, now, that Charlene was a client.

By shortly after 9:00 PM, the group starts to make noises about leaving. Everyone has pitched in so that dishes are washed and Ronny's apartment, sparse as it is, appears none the worse for wear. Joe walks Gaby out to her truck. He carries the clean baking dish while Gaby wiggles Martha into the cab.

She leans on the vehicle's door and looks up at him. He's a lot closer than she thought he would be when she turned around. She reaches out for the dish. "Thanks so much for including me in this, Joe. I felt like part of the family. Everyone is so close; so trusting. I liked it."

Without much of a warning, although she suspected his intentions, Joe leans down and kisses her like he means it. "I like you," he says. "We need to talk about this Charlene-person. You've been under a lot more stress than I thought. Has your boss helped you at all?"

"Maybe, someday, all the grisly details will come out, Joe. I'm glad she's in jail right now—or out in Edmonton, or whatever. She's a great mood spoiler." She grins as she stretches up and gives him a kiss on the cheek. "Call me, okay?"

She pulls out of the lot and returns to Poplar Street. She snuggles her truck into her driveway and looks up at the yellow glow of the porch light, warm and welcoming. It is the first time in simply ages that she hasn't been nervous walking into her own home.

****

The letter from the Canadian Counselling Association arrives on October 21, nine days after Thanksgiving dinner. It includes a copy of a letter of complaint written by Charlene Quinn and dated October 8, the Thursday before she was arrested.

Gaby stands in the post office with the letter in her hand. At first she doesn't know what to do. Charlene has written to the CCA. She says that Gaby has breached her ethical code by revealing topics that were discussed in private therapy sessions. This happened before she was arrested, so what precipitated her letter? Gaby's mind races. She hasn't talked about Charlene outside the office, except for that one conversation with Nina, and that was ages ago. Information Joe knows is because Charlene revealed her relationship with Gaby, herself; and because Patrick held centre stage at Thanksgiving dinner.

Her legs feel like jelly. She continues home for lunch. She sits at her kitchen table. The letter is flipped open in front of her and propped up by the napkin holder. She tries to eat some crackers and cheese. She takes Martha out to the back and stands on the step, freezing. She's forgotten to put her coat on. She goes back inside and makes a cup of tea. She calls Mimi and tells her she'll be a few minutes late. She tries to organize her thoughts.

The letter from the CCA states that an investigator named Edgar Novakovic will be travelling to Hayworth on November 10 to meet with her. She is instructed to obtain a private meeting room and suitable support services for Mr. Novakovic. He wants to interview her early in the morning. He must be travelling to Hayworth the day before. They don't say. She is asked to have her chart copied and available for the investigator; that they have received permission from the complainant and he will have proof of that upon arrival.

Charlene is still in jail. The fingerprint on the hitchhiker's glasses matched hers and now she's been charged in Nova Scotia. She can't get bail and a public defender is going to represent her, once she's transported back to Halifax. *They must be interviewing her in jail, for God's sake! Why would they give any credibility to someone who has been charged with murder and who probably committed another one right here in Hayworth? Maybe the reason they're taking so long to send her back is because of all this?*

Gaby feels sick. She sips her tea. It has taken the last ten days for her to relax again, after months of being on edge and not sleeping. She is propelled back to her previous state of unease within seconds of reading the letter. Her head starts to ache with surprising force. She could lose her licence. She has some money, but not *that* much. She could lose her house!

She looks around at her redesigned kitchen, the soft light, and the big windows. She thinks of the house in the summer, the porch, and the quiet street. She thinks of how cozy she is in the winter. She loves this place.

By the time she returns to the office, she's so worked up she can hardly talk. Mimi wants to know if she's okay. She barely acknowledges the question as she flips through the appointment book to determine if Pearl has any meetings or if her boss is free. "I have no appointments this afternoon and I need to see Pearl right away. Call her, please, and tell her I'll be in her office in ten minutes."

Chapter 23

Who's going to take her caseload?

Gaby, nestled into swirls of powder blue, her chin having disappeared into the over-sized cowl neckline of her latest sweater creation, stares at the wall above her desk. With an annoyance she finds hard to define, she scrapes her wispy hair behind her ears. A week from tomorrow, she will meet with Edgar Novakovic, the Canadian Counselling Association investigator, for a second time. The first interview with him took place on November 10. She has been on pins and needles for the last six days. Gaby contemplates her future, which is about as clear as the visibility outside her window. Everyone is talking blizzard. All of her appointments have cancelled. She hopes the department will determine the office requires closure. Soon the roads won't be safe. She shivers.

Gaby's sense of isolation has deepened since she first received the letter of complaint. She thinks about Pearl's reaction and the initial interview. Pearl was concerned and outspoken, but she has nevertheless distanced herself. Clark Alden hasn't been much better, although he did come into her office to give her a pep talk—something in the order of: "There's a good girl. Chin up. It will be fine." Big help. Her colleagues continue to be more curious than supportive, but what can they say? Mimi has been there through thick and thin. She's been a brick. Cheryl Nadler has made various vague gestures, like a pat on the shoulder or a sympathetic smile. No one knows all the details. Gaby, herself, doesn't know what's going on with the police. Her only information, in that arena, has come from Patrick Hollinger.

Sometimes, it's a mistake to go to a meeting early. When Gaby approached the conference room for the staff meeting a few days ago, she heard Edith's whiny voice. "When she gets suspended, who's going to take her caseload?"

Surprisingly noncommittal, Pearl responded, "I don't know, Edith. Besides, it's not *when*, but *if.* We have to wait and see. Don't be so anxious. Who knows? It all might work out in her favour."

"You don't believe that any more than I do. Be honest, Pearl. We're going to end up with that total caseload again, just like back in 1977 before she first came. What a mess!"

Gaby returned to her office, closed the door, and sat for a moment. She had sensed, for a while, that her colleagues were avoiding both herself and her situation. It's been difficult to nail down their feelings. No one's made a direct comment. Leave it to Edith to express what everyone else is probably thinking.

Now, sitting alone in her office yet again, her anxieties bubble to the surface. What would she do if she was fired? Sell the house? Move back to Ontario? Move in with Nina and her family? *Right...like that would work.* Would she go back to school? Would she ever be able to get her licence back? Her head begins to ache once more. There's a pain in her chest that started emerging when Charlene began badgering her. It torments her, looming as it does, just beyond description. She hasn't seen a doctor. Maybe quitting would be the best option. Get out ahead of it. Find other options. Take a break. The sudden realization of her disillusionment both astonishes her and breaks her heart.

The phone rings and jolts her back from her self-described abyss. "Hi, Mimi. Are we all going home?"

"Not yet." The girl's expulsion of air registers her disgust. "They should have shut the place down at noon. It'll be a treacherous drive out to the farm, if they put off the inevitable much longer."

"You can stay with me." Gaby knows Mimi would rather be home with her kids. She understands. She'd rather be home with Martha.

"I know, Gaby. That might be my only option. Oh! Rachel Wilkerson's on the line. That's why I rang you! She's calling from the city. I thought she was here today, but she didn't make it in. Line two."

"Thanks. I'll come out to see you after I get off the phone." She has to try and keep busy. Her stomach churns and her chest tightens as she presses the button for Line Two.

"Rachel! Sorry to keep you waiting! Smart lady to stay in Edmonton this week. This weather's a bitch!" *Attempt upbeat. Don't let the strain show.*

"Hi, Gaby. I wanted to call to let you know about my telephone interview with your Edgar Novakovic this week." Rachel's voice sounds playful and positive. She usually shows no emotion at all when she's on the phone with Gaby. She's a different person face to face.

"Sorry, Rachel. I must have mentioned Patrick and Charlene in my interview with him on the tenth. I probably said Patrick was a patient of yours and that Charlene gave him a hard time. Did I accidentally reveal information I shouldn't have? I have to be honest. I'm beginning to think I don't know any more." The pain increases—sharp and dull at the same time.

"Don't worry, Gaby! It's a stroke of luck that Mr. Novakovic called and left a message. I called Patrick and obtained his permission to discuss his file with the investigator. He knows you saw Charlene. He knows she committed a crime, and he wanted to help."

"I don't understand, Rachel. How could Patrick help me? Is there a problem because I told you I didn't think the guy was delusional?"

Rachel sighs, as if she's trying her best not to let Gaby's obtuseness get her down. "Not at all. Mr. Novakovic told me he needed to know the nature of Patrick's relationship with Charlene. I told him the truth...and I told him that I had encouraged Patrick to report his information about the Nova Scotia incident, as well as his concerns and suspicions about Roz Dover, to the RCMP. Now he knows that it wasn't you who went to the police to report any previous behaviour. It was Patrick! I think, my friend, you will find yourself vindicated in the very near future! By the way, I called your house before I called the office. I thought they would have locked the doors and sent everyone home by now."

"No such luck, at least not yet. I see my internal line is blinking, so maybe that's Mimi to say I can go home. Tell me more, Rachel. What did old Edgar, the ferret, have to say?"

"Ferret? Why, he was a real charmer on the phone. He said he was investigating an ethical breach and wanted to discuss the relationship between Patrick Hollinger and Charlene Quinn. I told him he could call Patrick, but he said he would prefer to talk to me first. After our discussion, he said there was no need to contact my patient. It is my considered opinion that you are out of the woods. I wish I was there. I'd buy you a drink." Her voice is deep and sultry, like a hot summer day. "Don't call Mr. Novakovic names, Gaby. I think he's on your side!"

Gaby feels the warmth of their conversation reviving her spirits. "So, maybe I won't have to quit after all."

"Quit? I should hope not! Wait and see. I'm certain you're going to be fine. Now, go home!"

They get word to close the office at 3:15 PM. Mimi decides to try and make her way out to the farm. It takes Gaby twenty minutes to do the five minute drive to Poplar Street. She wedges her truck as far off the sidewalk and into her driveway as the snow will allow. The front steps are drifted in. Wet cold pricks her ankles as the snow blows inside her boots. The veranda is a reprieve from the worst of it, but the snow has started to penetrate this oasis as well.

Martha, on the other hand, cannot be contained. After she struggles out of, and back in to, her boots in order to navigate the house and let Martha out the back way, Gaby is reduced to shaking her head and looking for a second towel as Martha returns with snow balls sticking to her legs and face. She trails snow through to the front door and barks for Gaby to open it up. Gaby looks out the window and sees Joe's truck parked on the street. He's digging around her vehicle with a huge shovel.

"Is this what carpenters do in the winter? Shovel out poor counsellors who just got home from work?"

Joe looks delighted when he sees her with the storm door propped open and Martha clutched with one hand. His face is red from the exertion. He's wearing a plaid winter hat with ear lugs that hang down and flap about in the wind. The snow is up to the tops of his boots. "I'll do your walk and up the steps. Time for tea?"

"You might need rum, but yes, I have time for tea." She goes back inside, returns to the kitchen, and fills the kettle. Maybe he'll stay for supper. Perhaps, if she's lucky and he wants a "good" meal, he can *make* supper. She has leftover chicken and lots of vegetables.

Joe appears at the front door and pops his head in. "Give me your keys. I'll pull your truck out and get the driveway cleaned as best I can, or you won't get out in the morning."

Gaby comes around the corner from the kitchen, wiping her hands on a dish towel. "Joe, leave it. I can do that later."

"Not on your life! Hand over the keys, missy. Let me get this done and then we'll have tea. I want to try and make enough room to get that hulk of mine off the road, too, before the plough comes by." His eyelashes have snow stuck to them.

Half an hour later, they are curled up in Gaby's living room, listening to the wind whip around the house. Both vehicles are wedged into the small driveway, even though the back of Joe's truck is across the sidewalk. "Going to stay for supper?"

"I'd love to." He takes another sip of the earthy rooibos tea and looks at her over the rim. The cup camouflages the expression on his face by concealing his mouth, but Gaby's quite sure he's smiling.

"What about Blanche?"

"She's fine." He leans down and gives Martha a little pat. "I'll confess. I went home first and fed the old girl, in case I might score a dinner invitation in exchange for shovelling out the driveway of my favourite counsellor."

"Good. Will you cook? I have cold chicken and veggies. I have rice."

He laughs. Of course he'll cook. It's one of his favourite pastimes.

Later on that evening, filled up on one of his specialties—ginger chicken and white wine—Joe tells Gaby what's on his mind. "I need someone to help me with my books, Gaby. My accountant says that since I'm going to incorporate and have a store front, I have to keep separate books. My sister, Anita, tells me in no uncertain terms that I need someone to help me with this. There isn't anybody else I trust to show all my finances to, so could you help me set it all up?"

"Sure. I guess so." She only hesitates for a second. "My sister, Nina, does the books for their paving company. I'll talk to her and get her to send me some information. We should be able to figure it out. Besides, if I get terminated before Christmas, it might be nice to have a job to fall back on." She shakes her head when a look of horror crosses his face. "Don't worry. You don't have to pay me."

"It isn't that. What do you mean? Are you still worried about losing your job? I thought this whole investigation process was merely a matter of form." His voice elevates. He sounds frustrated and angry all of a sudden. "What has that Charlene done, besides kill somebody down east and your enthusiasm for your work? Honest to God, I can't believe what you went through, and never said a word!"

"No need to get worked up just yet, Joe. Maybe it will turn out okay. I have to wait and see, but I'll help you with your books. It'll be fun! We can figure it all out together." She pats his hand but carefully avoids discussing the investigation. Edgar Novakovic told her to keep quiet, so she will follow instructions.

"We'll have to go down to the lawyer's after the holidays. I am giving you a three percent share in the company. You will be called the company secretary. Don't look like that! It isn't a big deal. There has to be another shareholder, so I named you, that's all. Three percent of next to nothing isn't that much, really."

Before the evening is over, they settle the details and Gaby becomes the minority shareholder in Joe's business, Dodd's Contracting and Interiors. They discuss how she feels about her work right now and how she might need a break. Joe says he will take all the help he can get. She has good ideas. He likes her sense of style. She has all the qualifications he needs—after all, she can balance a chequebook and read a blueprint, can't she? They plan how they'll lay out the show room after Olive's Manicures moves out. They talk about the annual Christmas dinner Gaby will be hosting, with Joe's help, of course.

****

The weather has been beautiful—cold and crisp. Edgar Novakovic would have had no trouble getting here last night. As Gaby prepares for her work day, she knows the investigator will be there, on time, and ready to get down to business. She tries to remind herself of Rachel's comments; that the investigation will turn out fine. She's learned, through the grape vine, that Charlene has been sent back to Nova Scotia. The headaches have improved. If only this were over and the chronic pressure she feels in her chest would go away. That hockey puck remains stuck there night and day, making her tired, resentful, sad, and angry.

She opts for comfortable clothes, choosing a red flannel plaid dress that hangs well below her knees. It has long sleeves and a high waist. She adds knee socks. She will be warm and cozy, at least. Those wool slacks, from the first interview two weeks ago, have been relegated to the back of her closet. She ties her hair loosely at the nape of her neck. The sprigs are uncontrollable.

She doesn't care. Her chest hurts.

As she reaches for her truck keys, the phone rings. It's Joe.

"Good luck, today. I'll think about you...and don't worry about supper. I'll stop at the diner first, if you feel like company."

She sighs. "Of course I want company—at least yours. Come over whenever you like. I'll probably leave early today, anyway. Thanks, Joe."

"You don't have to thank me. We're a team, now. Don't forget that. See you tonight."

She replaces the receiver. She knows they'll soon be a real couple. She thinks she's ready. He's made it known that intimacy is what he wants, but he's a patient man. All this crap has to be behind her. She's made her peace with Grant's memory. Now, she has to resolve her feelings about her work.

Gaby arrives at the meeting room office, coffee in hand. She also has a small notebook and a pen stuffed in the pocket of her dress. She knocks on the door which is slightly ajar, and responds to the command to enter.

"Good morning, Mr. Novakovic. May I get you some coffee before we start?"

"No thanks, Miss Ridgway. We can begin. Please have a seat."

He's more ferret-like than ever, for some reason. He seems shrunken as compared to Gaby's recollection of his stature before—like he's wasting away, or shrivelling inside his clothes. She feels like a lumberjack, by contrast. The red plaid flannel dress enhances this impression.

"I think we could have done all this on the phone, Miss Ridgway. My report is almost complete. I met with Miss Quinn while she was in custody here. I spoke with Dr. Wilkerson over the phone. I have talked with both Miss Markowski and Dr. Alden. I did not see the need to interview Mr. Hollinger, as I felt Dr. Wilkerson was most thorough. I will confirm a few details, if that's all right with you."

"You may ask whatever you like, sir." Gaby remains distant. *Stay calm and answer his questions. So far, so good.*

"My understanding is that Dr. Wilkerson approached you with permission to discuss issues regarding her patient, Patrick Hollinger, correct?"

"Exactly."

"At no time did you discuss Charlene Quinn or make any references related to your ongoing counselling relationship with her?"

"Correct."

"It has been determined that the RCMP received their information from Patrick Hollinger and not from you; information that led them to their follow-up with Nova Scotia law enforcement."

"That is my understanding as well."

"Have you discussed the disappearance of Roz Dover with the police or with anybody outside this office?"

"No, sir. The information in her file is information available to my colleagues and supervisors. There have been no outside discussions."

Gaby sips her coffee. She focuses on the aroma—a smoky, hazelnut blend that one of the staff discovered when they were last in Edmonton. She must find out the name of it. She likes the scent of it near her face. It fills her up with comfort somehow.

"Well, I think we're almost done here." He looks up and across the desk at her. He smiles. He has little teeth. They look like baby teeth. She has never seen his teeth before. "You have been most cooperative. You are meticulous with your files. I wish everyone could maintain a patient chart the way you do. My job would be considerably easier." He stands. Gaby feels obliged to stand as well. "I cannot tell you the result of my investigation, Miss Ridgway. What I will say, although it may be unorthodox, is that you must not worry. Circumstances will work out in the end. Expect my letter in two or three weeks." He smiles again, exposing those tiny teeth. "Before Christmas, for sure."

They shake hands and Gaby, after she expresses her thanks for she knows not what, returns to her office and shuts the door. It is not long after 10:00 AM. She sits at her desk, back to the closed door, with her nose near the rim of her coffee mug. She inhales the aroma like it's some kind of magic elixir. Her ordeal is over.

Not so fast. The investigation may be over. She may well be vindicated and her ethical reputation restored—but her faith in this system she has navigated during her total professional life is in tatters. Her vulnerability has been exposed. Her devotion to her clients has been questioned. Her belief in the system has been undermined, at best, and shaken to its very core, at worst. She's almost forty-two and maybe she doesn't want to do this anymore.

She develops the kernel of a plan. She will contact all her clients early next month, give them her best-of-the-season greetings, and suggest that there may be some caseload re-organizations that will take place after the holiday.

She will talk to Pearl. She thinks she may well need a break. In the end, all of Edith's fears might come true.

Her colleagues are waiting for her when she pulls herself together and returns to the staff room for more of that aromatic special blend of coffee. She nods to each of them and then taps on her mug to ensure their attention. "I know everyone is curious about the situation, since Edgar Novakovic is here today. I had my final interview and he was very nice to me. I should have the investigation results before Christmas. It will be a relief to have all this behind me. Now...who contributed this wonderful coffee? I absolutely must know how and where I can get it. It was my saving grace today!"

Chapter 24

It might be too late

She looks down at bare toes curled over the edge of a ragged precipice. The water below is aquamarine, inviting. She feels unsettled. The sun is hot on her skin but a chill kisses her shoulders, nonetheless. The light hurts her eyes. Now the rock is slippery and the water churns, celadon and angry. She squirms but can't get away. Her chest thumps with the familiar pain that has become her constant companion. The water mutates again. It calms. The colour is deep and rich. She jumps, floating through the air, no holding back. The pain recedes.

She wakes to Martha, stretched out full length against her back. The dog has grown too big for the bed. The duvet is twisted around her legs. She's been restless. The pressure in her chest returns, and she tries to conjure up the feeling of release experienced in her dream. There has been no letter—sixteen days and still no letter.

Today is Friday and the office Christmas party is this afternoon. Last night, the weatherman reported that another huge blizzard would descend on northern Alberta by later today. He expects three feet of snow, high winds, and cold temperatures. She is ready—food shopping done, shovel by the door and another in her truck, candles and flashlights prepared. She even got smart and cooked a chicken and potatoes so she would have cold food for the weekend, if there was no power at all. After her shower this morning, before work, she'll fill the tub with water. Waiting for a blizzard is like expecting relatives to come for a visit—anticipate potential problems and prepare for whatever might happen. The party won't be lengthy today. People will all be anxious to get home.

As she goes about her morning routine, Gaby wonders if this staff party may be her last. Perhaps she should take the bull by the horns and quit—get out before Clark Alden calls her into his office to tell her that her licence has been revoked and she has to resign. The work has lost its power to seduce her. She no longer reads a new referral with excited anticipation; but instead, with wariness that bubbles up from a place of mistrust and anxiety, buried, but close to the surface. She has a house and a mortgage. She has some savings. Can she afford to throw away a reliable government job, benefits, and retirement? Her chest thumps and reminds her of the time.

She looks, with a twinge of regret, at the watercolour depicting her house, still hanging in pride of place by the front door. It would be a lot easier to walk away from all this if she hadn't seen fit to buy a damned house. "Martha, be a good girl. I'll be back at lunchtime and then home early. We will have a cozy weekend watching Mommy go a little crazy." She locks the front door and carefully latches the storm door that covers it. Thank God for the reprieve of the porch.

****

By noon, the storm has started to ramp up. Her down-filled coat is pelted as she slides her way to her truck. The dryness of the snow makes her feel like she's being sprayed with sand. It burns her cheeks.

She returns to work within the hour, orange juice and ginger ale in hand— her contributions for the punch. All six divisions are scheduled to meet mid-afternoon. They no longer exchange gifts, but raise funds for the Salvation Army hamper program. The big news will be when Dr. Alden announces how much money they've raised for 1981.

The first person Gaby sees when she enters the big meeting room is Cheryl Nadler, looking oddly dishevelled. She's busy arranging Christmas cookies on a platter. Mimi, resplendent in a holiday sweater made more festive with appliquéd reindeer, is assembling the coffee and tea.

"Hi, you two. What can I do to help?"

"I think we're good, Gaby." Cheryl looks up from her task. "I've been running behind all day! Three families with new babies to get to know. I've had a fabulous but exhausting day! I'm a wreck. How are you?"

Gaby knows what she means, but avoids the obvious. "Waiting for the storm, like everybody else. I don't imagine people will hang around until 6:00 PM like they did last year. I see you found my stuff to make punch, Mimi." Gaby's gaze has fallen on the huge glass bowl holding centre stage on the credenza.

"I have all the ingredients I need. I think we're set. I have to fill a couple of pitchers with eggnog."

People start to wander in. If everyone shows up, there will be twenty-four counsellors of one stripe or another, two supervisors who each manage three divisions, Dr. Alden, and six secretaries including Mimi. Gaby sticks close to Mimi and Cheryl for the time being, as she tries to be useful. She is on the look-out for Pearl.

"I want to talk to you before the end of the day, Pearl. Can we have a word later?"

Pearl is anxious to get to the eggnog and Christmas cookies. Gaby follows her along the food table and thinks that this is what Martha must feel like as Gaby prepares supper.

"No letter, yet?"

"Nope. I get more worried with every passing day."

"Didn't that investigator tell you not to worry?" Pearl munches shortbread. Crumbs find a place to lodge on her ample bosom.

"Yes, but he might have said that to be nice."

"Didn't Rachel tell you it would all be fine?" More munching.

"Yes, but how would she know?"

"What do you want to talk to me about?"

"My future, Pearl."

The older woman stops mid-chew, and finally tears her eyes away from the array of sweets presented on the meeting room credenza, to look up at Gaby. "Your future is fine! Relax. Wait for the letter."

"It might be too late Pearl. Can we talk?"

"No." Her reply is both no-nonsense and abrupt. "Wait until you get the letter. If there's a problem, we'll try and work it out. It'll be fine. When are you going on vacation?"

"I work next week, and then I'm off until the thirtieth."

"Okay. We can plan to meet next week, sometime. No decisions until you get that letter. Now, where did I set my glass of eggnog down? Have a cookie, Gaby. Enjoy yourself, for heaven's sake! It's Christmas!"

The party doesn't last much more than an hour. Even located in the centre of the Hexagon, and with carols playing on a boom box, they are all aware of the wind howling outside. Dr. Alden confirms what they all already knew—they contributed more money than ever before to their charity.

As the clean-up begins, Frank and Elliot both approach Gaby for a quick word. "Any news?" Frank, as usual, is the one to speak first.

"No, no letter yet."

"We're behind you, Gaby. We know you would never be unethical." Elliot continues to look at the ground, like he always does and like he did years ago, when he brought her that television—the one she still uses.

"Thanks, guys. We have to wait and see, but feeling like I'm in limbo is tough. I'm worn out. See you both Monday."

"I'm off now for three whole weeks!" Edith approaches the group and injects her information without any realization about what's going on. Her hair is frazzled. Her green corduroy dress is too small, and she's wearing the biggest Christmas corsage Gaby has ever seen. "Are you going to call me when you get word from the investigator?"

The men move off as Gaby turns to Edith. "No, Edith. Feel free to call from home, if you can't stand the suspense." She doesn't attempt to keep the sarcasm out of her voice, but doubts if Edith would pick it up anyway.

"I left a couple of files on your desk." She raises her hand in reaction to Gaby's obvious look of shock. "Now, now. Don't worry. You don't have to take them. I'd like your opinions, though. I figured it would be quiet next week and you might have time." She pats Gaby on the arm. "You fret too much, you know. You'll be fine."

To Gaby, her words are hollow.

****

Manoeuvring her vehicle toward the parking lot exit of the Hexagon at 4:00 PM is like trying to get out of the arena parking lot after a big hockey game. Cars and trucks are lined up like dominoes. Gaby wonders how long it will take her to make the drive, considering she can't begin to call it a day before she checks her mail box one last time. The streets are snow filled. Ploughs won't start until the storm has passed. The ass end of her truck seems to have a mind of its own, as she swings into a mercifully available parking space a couple of doors down from the post office.

The old granite stairs are slippery with ice, snow, and water. She makes her way, head down, as she tries to shelter herself inside her hood. The lobby smells like a weird concoction of wet mittens and warm paper. She opens the box and can see the red maple leaf of the Canadian Counselling Association logo before she reaches inside to retrieve her destiny.

She doesn't read the letter right away. She stands in the lobby, by the windows, and stares out at what she can see of the town. This storm is going to be ferocious—not expected to let up before tomorrow night. As the snow falls, it blows sideways. People scurry like mice trying to find a way into the barn. She stuffs the envelope into her pocket, and puts on her gloves before shuffling back down the treacherous stairs and over to her truck. She thinks she's ready to make a decision.

The trip to Poplar Street is no better than the one to the post office. The side roads are snowed in already, and once she makes the turn and grinds her way along to her house, she worries about whether she'll have the traction to make it into the driveway. At this point, since the wind is swirling in the opposite direction, her driveway is clear enough to permit her to spin her tires and get the Mazda all the way in to the backyard fence. It would be wise to leave it closer to the street—less shovelling—but she prefers to have it out of the wind and away from the road and sidewalk. She feels the snow creep over the tops of her boots as she lumbers across the lawn and up the front steps to the veranda. Of course, Martha makes coming home worthwhile.

Once settled, warmed up, and with a cup of tea at her side, she opens the envelope, damp and limp from the cold and wet.

Dear Miss Ridgway:

The Canadian Counselling Association is pleased to inform you that our investigation as to your ethical conduct in the matter regarding Miss Charlene Quinn, has revealed that you have, in no way, compromised the standards of practise as set out in the Code of Ethics of the Canadian Counselling Association. Please accept our congratulations and we thank you for your cooperation. A letter has been sent to your supervisor reflecting our decision.

Sincerely,

Edgar Novakovic

Gaby sits for what seems like an hour, feeling the warmth that is Martha against her hip. The pain in her chest has retreated completely, perhaps for the first time in three months. The wind howls through the rafters of the veranda. The snow is starting to accumulate on the window sills and stick to the screens. Eventually, she won't be able to see outside.

It comes to her in a flash of buried insight. The letter doesn't matter at all! Perhaps it hasn't for a while, now. She intends to leave the Counselling Division; leave the Hexagon. She thinks about Grant. She's missed him for years, but when she needs to talk, she doesn't miss him like she used to. She feels the time has arrived for her to move forward with Joe. He's a good man.

She jumps straight up off the couch when the phone rings. It's Nina.

"What are you doing, calling me in the middle of your day?" Her heart pounds as she tries to compose herself after being startled.

"Don't worry. I'm on the company line. I heard about the big storm you people are about to get, and I also had to find out if you received your letter from the CCA yet."

"Yes, Nina." Gaby sighs. Nina is not going to like what she's about to say. "The storm is fierce, but we're here, safe and sound. My letter arrived. I'm vindicated, like Rachel said I would be, thanks in large measure to the bravery of her client. I was sitting here thinking about writing my letter of resignation."

"What? I thought you said the situation is good, Gaby!"

"It is with the CCA, but not with me, Nina. I seem to have lost my confidence. You know, the father of a child I'm seeing, called and yelled at me last week. He's missed two sessions and seems to think that's my fault, somehow. I was awake all one night worrying about it. I wondered if he'd report me to the CCA, and the whole mess would start all over again. You can't do this job effectively without confidence in yourself." Edith jumps to mind. "I need a break, Nina."

You could drive Joe's truck through the silence at the other end of the phone. Gaby adds, "You know, it costs a lot of money not to talk during a phone call, Nina."

"What are you going to do if you quit your job?"

"Maybe spend more time with Joe. You already know about me becoming his bookkeeper, but he wants me to be involved. I think I might take him up on his offer. See where it goes."

"Exactly how many offers is he making?"

Gaby giggles in spite of herself. "Time to take the plunge, Nina. Grant's been dead for a long time. Joe and I are great friends. We think alike. We enjoy each other's company. I feel safe when he's around."

****

After her conversation with Nina, she wanders into the kitchen. The light behind the range gives a soft glow. The pain in her chest is still gone. She glances out the window into the backyard. "No running out in the back for you, my lovely." She bends over and pats Martha, who stands patiently by her dish. "In another hour, we won't get the door open. Leash on in the front, off the veranda, and out to the street. Will you be able to work with that arrangement?"

Martha cocks her head, and glances down at her dish.

"Okay, okay. Supper it is. Food for you; wine for me."

Settled once more, in front of the television with a fed and piddled Martha, damp paws and all curled up beside her, she barely gets her wine glass to her lips when the phone rings again.

"Hello."

"Hi! How are you and Martha doing? Are you snowed in, yet?"

Gaby tries to peer out her living room window at the snow reflecting through the street light. "It looks bad. We're here safe and sound. What about you?"

"I've been home all day, making stew and thinking about you. Get your letter?"

"Yeh. The letter came. What would you think if I said I was contemplating resigning?"

"Are you serious? Did the investigator think you were unethical? I don't believe it! Can you appeal?"

Gaby's soft laugh stops him in his tracks. She takes a sip of wine. "Relax, Joe. They found in my favour, but I'm serious about packing it in—serious enough that I already told my sister I'm considering it."

"Will you work with me; help me get this new business off the ground? I have a layout of the retail space. Want to see it? I can bring stew."

"Joe, if you plan on driving that monster truck of yours over here tonight, you'd better ask Rose to take care of Blanche tomorrow. I don't think you'll get back home anytime soon. Besides, I think we need to have a chat about us, too. You know—us." All of a sudden, she feels shy, tongue-tied. "If you're here soon, you might still get the truck into the yard. I pulled in all the way back to the fence."

"I'm on my way, Gaby." That's all he says. The phone goes silent.

She sits at the end of her comfy sofa, toes tucked into the crack between the cushions. One hand holds her wine while the other strokes Martha's silky ear. She looks out the window at the snow reflected in the street lamp. It falls heavy and fast, pelted by the wind. The trees seem to be overcome with the force. She hopes that Joe is able to safely get his truck around the corner and then into her yard.

Her thoughts slide back to the many nights she sat in this very spot, in the dark, alone and afraid, her heart thumbing and her chest aching as she waited for Charlene Quinn's vehicle to appear; or waited for her shadowy figure to climb down from the old Land Cruiser parked there.

She hears the rumble. She sees the lights round the corner. The box fishtails for a second, before it straightens up. The snow is deep on the street. There are no tire tracks. The blinker comes on and the headlights flicker twice. He's here.

About the Author

L. P. Suzanne Atkinson was born in New Brunswick, Canada and lived in both Alberta and Quebec before settling in Nova Scotia in 1991. She has a BA in Psychology from Mount Allison University, a Bachelor of Social Work from McGill University, and an MA in Sociology from Acadia University. Suzanne spent her professional career in the fields of mental health and home care as both a therapist and trainer. She also owned and operated, with her husband, both an antique business and a construction business for more than twenty-five years.

Her philosophy of life is based on two qualities for which she continually strives. They are her benchmarks. First: there is no better descriptor than to be called a kind person and good friend. Second: a lesson learned and not shared is information squandered.

Suzanne writes about the challenges inherent in aging and about the unavoidable consequences of relationships. She uses her life and work experiences to weave timeless stories that cross many boundaries. She and her husband, David Weintraub, continue to make Nova Scotia their home.

Email – lpsa.books@eastlink.ca
Website – http://lpsabooks.wix.com/lpsabooks#
Facebook – L. P. Suzanne Atkinson – Author

Watch for:

Segue House Connection: Regarding Hayworth Book III

Coming in the summer of 2017